24-Karat Kids

24-Karat Kids

DR. JUDY GOLDSTEIN

AND SEBASTIAN STUART

St. Martin's Griffin New York

www.stmartins.com

Library of Congress Cataloging-in-Publication Data

Goldstein, Judy.
    24-karat kids / Dr. Judy Goldstein and Sebastian Stuart.
       p. cm.
    ISBN-13: 978-0-312-34328-6
    ISBN-10: 0-312-34328-0
    1. Women pediatricians—Fiction. 2. Upper East Side (New York, N.Y.)—Fiction. 3. Rich people—Fiction. 4. Children of the rich—Fiction. 5. Parent and child—Fiction. 6. High school teachers—Fiction. 7. Satire. I. Title: Twenty-four karat kids. II. Stuart, Sebastian. III. Title.

PS3607.O4846 A14 2006
813'.6—dc22

                                    2006042220

First St. Martin's Griffin Edition: June 2007

10 9 8 7 6 5 4 3 2 1

A Note to the Reader

This book is dedicated to my husband's unfailing
support, to my children's constancy of love and
enthusiasm, to all the children in my practice
who keep me smiling, and to Linda Chester—
my mentor and muse!
—Dr. Judy Goldstein

For Kippy Dewey and Stephen McCauley
—Sebastian Stuart

Acknowledgments

I would like to gratefully acknowledge the key role my partner and friend Sebastian Stuart played in the creation of our labor of love! Sebastian taught me American slang and made this intensive process great fun.

I am also deeply indebted to Diane Reverand's support and belief in us, to Regina Scarpa for tying all loose ends together, and to the energetic and enthusiastic John Murphy, whose contribution in making this happpen was so significant and highly effective.

—Dr. Judy Goldstein

I would like to thank Diane Reverand, Jennifer Weis, Stefanie Lindskog, John Murphy, Regina Scarpa, Linda Chester, Stephen McCauley, Mameve Medwed, David Schmerler, Eileen Ahearn, and Marcia Dworkind, M.D. Most of all, I would like to thank Judy Goldstein, whose warmth, wit, and rigor made her a dream collaborator.

—Sebastian Stuart

1

"WHAT *IS* THAT?" I asked the waiter, looking down at what looked like four giant gumballs floating in tomato soup. The waiter was young and had a nice smile, but I quickly realized that he spoke less English than I did Azerbaijani. Mom piped in before I had a chance to resort to sign language.

"Shelley, be adventurous," she said, looking at me over the top of her glasses-on-a-string. She stabbed a gumball with her fork and popped it in her mouth. I thought I detected an instant of shock before she gamely chewed . . . and chewed . . . and chewed. "Fascinating," she pronounced.

"Mother, if I want fascinating, I'll go see a foreign documentary at the Film Forum. I'm here to eat." Not that I'd had time to go to a movie in seven years, but I had a point to make.

"Eat? Nonsense, we're here to celebrate," my father said, leaning over, grabbing my face, squeezing it all out of shape, and planting a kiss on my smushed-forward cheek.

Which was true. My reward for finally finishing four years of college, four years of medical school, and three years of pediatric residency was this: a family party around an enormous round table at Queens's finest, and no doubt only, Azerbaijani restaurant. Mom had picked Baku Buffet because it sounded "intriguing." *Intriguing, fascinating,* and *remarkable* were Mom's three favorite words, and she was in permanent pursuit of new experiences that would allow her to use them. This had turned her into a Learning Annex junkie, obsessively taking courses on everything from "Folk Art Milking Stools" to "Insects, Eunuchs, and Euripides." I was amazed that one brain could hold the breadth of information that hers did.

This was a pretty typical gathering for my family. All around the table aunts, uncles, and cousins were shouting and laughing, eating off each other's plates, drinking out of each other's glasses, acting like we weren't separate people but a single-bodied behemoth: the Green Family. My brother Ira, a rugged individualist, was huddled in an alcove by the restrooms talking to his bookie on his cell phone. Ira had a little gambling problem—in the same way Orson Welles had a little weight problem. Ira also had a thing for marijuana—with his breakfast coffee. And did I mention the alcoholic binges in seedy motels with ladies you could rent by the hour?

I reclaimed my face from Dad's grip and looked across the table at Arthur, the man I'd been dating for two years. Arthur had been grinning for the past hour, and I wondered why he was in such a good mood. Actually, Arthur had been grinning for the past two years. It was one of his many charming qualities, but sometimes it got on my nerves. How could anyone be so endlessly cheerful, especially when dating me? He gave me a sympathetic look and mouthed, "I love you, pumpkin."

"Have *you* tried the gumballs?" I asked him.

"They're actually sheep testicles," he informed me.

"Well, that makes me feel better," I said, pushing my plate away.

I was hungry and exhausted and anxious and wanted nothing

more than to be at home in my closet-sized Manhattan studio watching some mindless reality show and working my way through a pint of Chunky Monkey. More or less my entire adult life up to this point, all the years of education and training and sleepless nights, had been leading to this moment, and now, instead of kicking up my sensible heels, I just wanted a little peace and quiet to think things over and make some decisions.

Arthur got up and walked around the table to where I was sitting. He kneaded my shoulders with his warm wonderful hands, finding my familiar knots and rubbing them with a gently circular motion, working his two thumbs up the back of my neck. A deep, involuntary sigh poured out of me. The back rubs were one of his charming qualities I never got tired of. Arthur was an English teacher at a public high school in Brooklyn. He was kind, dependable, almost six feet tall with gray-green eyes, and an amazing kisser. But what I loved most about him were those magic hands. He leaned down and kissed the top of my head, "Just relax, munchkin."

"Oh, Arthur," I said, "I'm trying. You don't know the half of it."

I'd been looking for a position in a well-established practice in neighborhoods like the Upper West Side and Park Slope. There was a lot of competition for the few openings that came up, and so far I hadn't had any luck. And I was facing a quarter of a million dollars in student loans. That was the half Arthur *did* know.

The half he *didn't* know was that three days earlier I'd received a call from Dr. Marge Mueller, the head of Madison Pediatrics, one of the best practices on Manhattan's Upper East Side. Dr. Mueller, who had been forwarded my résumé by a doctor at a Park Slope practice, had invited me in for an interview. I'd asked her for a few days to think it over. I wasn't sure I was a good fit for the Upper East Side. And I hadn't told Arthur about Dr. Mueller's call because the job would mean working with the kind of overprivileged families that he disapproved of, and I didn't want him making my decision more difficult by cluttering the process with his guilt-inducing biases.

Biases or not, my relationship with Arthur had been the most serious of my life. He was just the sort of kind, generous, lovable man I'd always been told I would one day meet and marry. Just as I'd always been told I should get good grades, keep my head down, earn gold stars, be polite, do my homework, and finish everything on my plate, even if it meant eating sheep testicles. The problem was, I sometimes felt a little crowded by Arthur, the same way I sometimes felt crowded by the Green Family behemoth and its expectations.

It was as if I'd been living in a hermetically sealed bubble since I was about nine, a bubble marked GOOD STUDIOUS SHELLEY. Inside, secretly, I'd always felt a certain admiration and envy of the more rebellious girls, the ones who blew off their homework, who dressed with flair and flirted with panache, who exuded an easy sensuality and confidence. Nothing came easily to me, especially fun. My only guilty pleasures were food and an obsession with celebrity and pop culture that took the form of E! channel marathons and *InStyle* binges. I dreamed of bursting out of my good-girl bubble, of going to glamorous parties and drinking too many mojitos and dancing with abandon and going skinny-dipping in the moonlight and making love in the dunes—just having some cut-loose bad-girl *fun*. My relationship with Arthur could not be filed under bad-girl fun—under lots of other, probably ultimately more important things, yes, but not guilty pleasure. And I felt I'd earned the right to a little fun before I settled down.

"Shelley, you're a wonderful wonderful doctor, you love kids—you're going to have a job in no time."

Arthur was always so reassuring, but I'd felt like I'd been holding my breath for the past three years, and before I could finally exhale, I needed to be settled and building my own practice.

"Thank you, honey," I said, leaning up and kissing him. The relationship was right on the cusp of seriously serious, but that was on hold for me, too. Before marriage and motherhood, I needed to be earning a good living. Dad was a mailman, a sensational supermensch mailman, who'd had the same Upper East Side route for thirty years and was loved by everyone, but mailmen don't make a lot of money. Mom was a part-time grade school guidance counselor, and they don't make a lot of money, either. "We can't afford it," echoed in my ears all through my childhood. And Arthur's salary was hardly enough for the family we both wanted. Besides all that, I wanted to be able to stand on my own two feet as an independent woman. It was important to me.

"Oh my God, *this* is fabulous. You have to try it, Shelley," Mom said, pointing down to her plate, where a chunk of meat sat under a bright orange sauce. What kind of meat did they eat in Azerbaijan? Goat? Emu? Yak? Think I'll pass.

"I know how to cheer you up," Arthur whispered in my ear.

It was true, Arthur did know how to cheer me up—but I wasn't sure we should hop on top of the big round table and make love in front of God, the Green Family behemoth, the other diners, and the Baku Buffet staff, friendly though they were.

"Do you have something up your sleeve?" I asked.

"Actually, it's in my breast pocket," he said.

Just then my cell phone rang. "Duty calls," I said, and got up from the table. "Hello?"

"Is that you, Shelley?"

I could tell by the thick, cultured accent from somewhere on the overeducated fringe of Europe, that this was Dr. Marjorie Mueller from Madison Pediatrics.

"It's me, Dr. Mueller. Sorry about the noise."

"Where are you, Uzbekistan?"

"Good guess. One minute while I find a quiet corner."

I walked over to the restroom alcove, where Ira was barking orders at his bookie and sweating. As usual he was resplendent in what I called his Atlantic City look—a loose purple shirt made out of some shimmery material, way too much gold jewelry for a man, black slacks, and black leather slip-ons that looked like bedroom slippers. Knowing Ira, they probably *were* bedroom slippers. Ira was the yang to my yin and the fact that he was just so *over-the-top* yang is a big part of the reason I was yinned tighter than a drum.

"Ira, I need this alcove," I said.

"Shelley, I'm so proud of you," he said. "Can you give me something for my bunions? A Vicodin maybe?"

"Ira, I'm a pediatrician, not a podiatrist, now please."

"Love you, Shell," he said, before ducking into the men's room to continue his conversation.

"I apologize for the confusion, Dr. Mueller. It's just . . ."

"Please," she said, cutting me off. "Call me Dr. Marge; everyone does. I'm sorry to call you at this hour, but I was wondering if you'd made a decision about coming in to talk to me. We've become really shorthanded at the practice, and I was hoping that as a fellow alumna of Cornell, I could call upon our school ties to persuade you."

It was certainly flattering to be cajoled by the head of such a prestigious practice.

"You probably think I'm some pretentious Upper East Side doctor who dresses in Chanel suits and Manolo Blahnik heels. Well, I am. Although I'm developing a real taste for Jil Sander. But I'm also a dedicated pediatrician, and I'm not going to bite your head off, I promise. Could you possibly come in tomorrow around lunchtime?"

I knew I should stall, not sound too eager or desperate, make her wait.

"Yes," I said.

"See you at noon, Dr. Green." And with that she hung up.

I stood there in the steamy little alcove surrounded by the smells of sheep testicles and yak steaks and the babble of my boisterous family. I couldn't be sure—what with Chanel and Manolo and Jil—but it seemed like I was being very seriously considered for a position in one of the city's best and fanciest pediatric practices. Me, a schlumpy girl from Jackson Heights who was ten pounds overweight—oh, all right, twenty—and had less fashion sense than your average bag lady and the social skills to match. I was sure that when Dr. Marge de Chanel met me she would think I was a bad match for her patients. Then again, I was, I hoped, a damn good doctor, and I had finished at the top of my class in medical school and excelled during my residency. Maybe I would get the job. But I wasn't sure I wanted it. I didn't know if I'd be comfortable on the Upper East Side. More important, I didn't know what I'd wear tomorrow.

"Suss," Mom called at me from across the restaurant. In case you're wondering what *Suss* stands for, it's "Stand Up Straight, Shelley." Mom invented it so that she could correct my posture privately in public—I'm the only person I know who is admonished with an acronym. But isn't the intention slightly compromised when she yells it in a voice that could be heard in the Bronx?

I reflexively threw my shoulders back and raised my head.

"Much better, dear, now come and try these tiny eels. They were cooked on the way to the table. Isn't that intriguing?" she bellowed.

As I made my way across the restaurant, I noticed Arthur beaming at me like a spotlight on steroids. Then he stood up and clinked his knife against his glass. Unfortunately, Baku Buffet used plastic glasses so no one paid any attention.

"Quiet, please," he said.

No reduction in the decibel level. You've probably figured this out already, but shouting is the normal, accepted means of speech in my family. The only time people *don't* shout is when they have something really important to say, like "Grandma died today." Poor Arthur comes from a family of Ann Arbor academics who speak at a normal decibel level; because of this no one in my family ever listens to him.

"Quiet, please," he said again, a little louder. He looked beseechingly over at Dad—the two of them were crazy about each other.

"Everybody shut up!" Dad screamed.

The whole restaurant went dead silent and turned to our table. Arthur blushed bright red.

"Okay, you've got our attention, say something," Mom said. "The eels are getting cold."

"I just wanted to propose a little toast to Shelley for all that she's accomplished. We're all so proud of you," he said.

The whole restaurant turned and looked at me. From the baffled looks on their faces, I could tell that at least half of them spoke less English than our waiter.

"And there's one other thing I want to propose," he said. Then he blushed and looked down with that awkward shyness of his that I found so touching. The whole restaurant watched and waited. He reached into his breast pocket and pulled out a small velvet box. He opened the box, and there inside, glittering and glinting, was a beautiful antique ring, gold filigree holding four small diamonds. I knew it had been his grandmother's, that she had left it to him, for his bride. "Shelley, will you marry me?" he said.

"What did he say?" one of my aunts shouted.

"Talk louder!" a cousin ordered.

"Shelley, will you marry me?" he said, loud and clear.

It was not what I was expecting. I cast a glance around the table at all those relatives I'd known my whole life and loved dearly, even if I felt overwhelmed and suffocated by them half the time. They were all beaming, grinning, and giggling. A perfect end to the perfect Green

Family meal. They'd accepted Arthur about ten minutes after they met him. They'd been telling me he was *the one,* and now everything they'd said was coming true. I couldn't let Arthur down, not here, in front of his fan club. Maybe even more important, I couldn't let *them* down. And with a sweet, charming guy like Arthur, surely I wasn't letting myself down, either.

"Yes," I said.

The restaurant remained silent for a moment. Then Dad leapt up, made a big coming-together gesture with his arms, and screamed to the whole place:

"They're going to get married!"

Everyone in the restaurant applauded. Ira burst out of the men's room: "I just hit the exacta in the eighth at Aqueduct!!" Then he did one of his impromptu dances—he shimmied, shook, and sang: *"Don't stop thinking about tomorrow. . . ."*

"Remarkable," Mom said, tears streaming down her cheeks.

2

I'VE ALWAYS HAD a love/hate thing with the Upper East Side. I loved the glamour and excitement, the grand old architecture, the luxurious shops and restaurants and salons, the celebrity sightings, the sense of being buffered from so many of life's indignities. But I knew there was another side to the magic. When I was a kid, I would sometimes visit Dad as he walked his mail route, which included a lot of fancy apartment buildings. I remember stepping from the noisy streets into hushed lobbies, the old women who looked like Barbara Bush patting me on the head with benevolent condescension, and the pitying curiosity I got from the rich girls as they bounded home from private school, long hair flying, knapsacks bouncing. Everyone treated Dad and me nicely, but there was no doubt we were *downstairs* people, like the cooks and maids in those English miniseries the upstairs people just love—as long as they don't use the front door or try to marry into the family. As Dad and I walked down the immaculate, flower-bedecked streets of the Upper East Side, I often felt that the world of the rich and successful was another country with its own language and customs and that I was an obvious, envious, bumbling tourist.

So as I made my way up Madison Avenue toward my appointment with Dr. Mueller, I felt particularly dowdy and self-conscious in my sensible navy suit, white blouse, and flats. It was a bright June day, and all around me wealthy women streamed by, tiny shopping bags hanging off their wrists, their lean legs curving gracefully into sleek heels, looking chic, sophisticated, and skeletal. All things I wasn't. I caught a glimpse of myself in a shop window. My determined face and gait made me look like a bulldog on her way to an argument.

I needed a little help. Fast.

I ducked into a boutique. The middle-aged saleslady looked impossibly elegant. Maybe working in a boutique was a new rich-lady fad, like pashmina or Pilates. I headed over to a vast table that displayed exactly three silk scarves. Her saleslady-ship ignored me even though I was the only person in the store. I reached for one of the scarves.

"Ahhh," she cooed gently, gliding over to me. Even though she was cooing and gliding, the message was unmistakable: Don't touch the merchandise. She ran her eyes swiftly down my suit (Macy's, $79.99 marked down from $149.99). Then she lifted up one of the scarves—with a flick and a flourish it billowed out turquoise and pink and orange. "Exquisite," she said with infinite authority, before deftly refolding it. Then she turned and walked away from me, just like that.

Suddenly I saw all those Upper East Side ladies who had swept past my dad in their lobbies as he delivered their mail, pointedly ignoring him even on the days when he had his young daughter with him. Well, I was about to become an Upper East Side doctor.

"I'll take the scarf," I said.

The saleslady turned toward me, eyebrow raised.

"I'll take the scarf," I repeated with as much nonchalance as I could muster.

A look of surprise flashed across her face. She gave a tiny shrug to indicate how insignificant my purchase was and retrieved the scarf. I followed her over to the counter.

"And don't bother wrapping it. I'm going to wear it."

She gave my outfit another quick once-over.

"That will be three hundred and fifty dollars," she said.

I hoped my flinch wasn't too obvious. The saleslady gave me her first smile—of the kind favored by the Marquis de Sade. I pulled out my wallet and scanned my credit cards, looking for one that could handle the charge.

I walked out of the boutique in sticker shock, but tried to stroll with a new confidence as I approached the corner of East Sixty-ninth Street, home of Madison Pediatrics. I stopped to take a couple of deep calming breaths and found myself in front of a pharmacy with a mirrored front. Staring back at me was a plain, tubby young woman with an absurdly garish scarf flopping around her neck. I watched as her face turned red. Then I whipped off the scarf and stuffed it in my purse.

Madison Pediatrics was located on the ground floor of a prewar apartment building, announced by an engraved brass sign screwed into the limestone. Beside it was one for a plastic surgery practice. Maybe facelifts were the newest treatment for postpartum depression.

The first thing that struck me as I walked into the waiting room was the music—opera. *La Boheme,* I was pretty sure. Different, but nice. Then I took in the toys and games and coloring books, the homey clutter and near-chaos that meant only one thing: kids. And there they were, close to a dozen of various ages, in various stages of restlessness, climbing over chairs, stuffing fistfuls of Cheerios into their mouths, reading intently, playing with the games and toys that filled one corner of the waiting room. Then I inhaled the kid smells—crayons and crackers, diapers and soap, all underlaid with a slight medicinal tang. I noticed well-dressed parents and what looked like a couple of nannies. I immediately felt at home—*this* was what it was all about. Kids.

I stifled an urge to greet the children and ask them how they were feeling, and instead approached the enormous, teased-up, fluffed-out tangerine wig that jutted up from behind a computer at the front desk. Was one of the staff dressed up like a Dr. Seuss character? When I got there, the wig turned, and I saw that it framed a kind, open, middle-aged black face.

"I bet I know who you are: Dr. Green," the wig said, standing and holding out her hand. "I'm Candace, but the doctors call me Ass-Saver, because I save theirs on a regular basis. I know—this wig makes me look like a drag queen at Mardi Gras, but I'm coming out of chemo and thought, 'What the hell, I'm going to have a little fun.'"

I shook her hand. "How are you doing?" I asked.

"I'm going to be just fine, Doctor, thank you for asking." Then suddenly she belted along—"*Sole e amore!*"—with the swelling Puccini. Then she beamed at the delighted children. "I have this theory about opera and children, that it calms and focuses them, somehow helps their brain synapses fire better. Don't ask me for any science to back it up, but it sure works around here."

"Well, it sounds wonderful," I said.

"Of course I do have an ulterior motive—I get to listen to the world's most beautiful music all day. I'll let Dr. Marge know you're here."

I took a seat and tried to rein in my curiosity about the children around me. I mean, I hadn't been hired yet; it wasn't my place to start asking questions. A girl sitting two chairs down caught my attention. She looked about eleven or twelve and sat calmly with her hands folded in her lap. She wore a simple gray skirt and white blouse, and had pale skin, curly brown hair, and enormous brown eyes. What I found so touching was the somber, wistful expression on her face, as if she was thinking about something important and sad. There was an older Hispanic woman sitting next to her, reading *Latina* magazine.

"Hi," I said.

"Hello," the girl answered with a polite smile. Her voice carried a hint of a British accent. The Hispanic woman closed the magazine and gave me a sympathetic smile.

"Are you here for a checkup?" I asked the girl.

She nodded. "I don't feel well."

"Oh, I'm sorry to hear that. Where don't you feel well?"

"All over," she said simply.

"Dr. Green!" I looked up and saw a woman coming toward me who looked as if she should have been out shopping on Madison Avenue. Somewhere in her fifties, she had frosted blond hair and expert, subtle makeup, and was wearing high heels and a belted magenta jumpsuit that accentuated her tiny waist, the kind of waist that justifies resentment just as a matter of principle. Definitely the most glamorous doctor I had ever seen. I stood up.

"Dr. Marge?" I said.

"Yes. What a pleasure. Come on in. Let's talk and then I'll show you around." She led me back into the heart of the practice. We walked down a wide winding corridor, surrounded by the comings and goings of a busy pediatric practice—babies, children, parents, nannies, doctors, nurses, and medical assistants, all talking, laughing, crying, explaining, examining, gurgling. The pace and rhythm made my pulse quicken. I peeked into the exam rooms as we passed them. Each was decorated in a different theme: I saw Cinderella, Harry Potter, Captain Nemo, and a generic computer game, sort of Nintendo meets Game Boy at the Matrix.

"We were the first practice to do the themed rooms," Dr. Marge said with a little roll of her eyes. "Now every pediatrician on the Upper East Side has them, and we have to change ours every few years to stay up to date. Here's my office."

It was large and filled with pictures of what I assumed to be Dr. Marge's two grown sons. There was only one picture of the man who must have been her husband—he was posed on a ski slope, looking healthy and almost too handsome. Above the small sitting area was an immense bulletin board filled with pictures of her patients: happy children sailing, scuba diving, touring Tuscany—the usual working-class pursuits.

Dr. Marge perched at one end of a love seat and patted the other end. She had perfect posture and—even sitting—so much energy that she seemed to vibrate slightly. "Sit. I took the liberty of ordering lunch—I hope you like tuna salad sandwiches."

"I love tuna salad sandwiches."

"I had a feeling you might." She handed me a plate with a sandwich, chips, and a pickle, just about my favorite meal, and took one of her own. The sandwich was on thin pumpernickel bread, the pickles tiny; even the golden chips looked haute. "We're a five-doctor practice and one of our doctors had a midlife crisis. Dr. Clark gave us two weeks' notice, left his wife, and moved to Bahia, where he plans to spend the rest of his life making sculpture from found objects. Definite case of Gauguin complex. But so be it, and ergo my call to you."

Dr. Marge was charming and warm, but behind her perfect hair, makeup, and outfit she seemed to be holding herself tightly in check.

"We not only have Cornell in common, Dr. Green, but I also

interned at New York Hospital," she continued. "My sources at both places tell me you are a superb pediatrician."

"Thank you, that's nice to hear. I try my best."

"Apparently your best is very, very good. And your modesty is certainly becoming. May I ask what drew you to pediatrics?"

"Children," I answered without hesitation. "I just love them. It's their vulnerability, their curiosity, their spontaneity. I find children touching, and inspiring. To take care of them, be a part of their lives, well, it's what I've always wanted to do. Not to mention the fact that children are just so much fun."

Dr. Marge smiled at me, then she looked down at her hands for a moment. When she looked up, her jaw was set, her voice resolute. "When it comes to hiring, I've always trusted my instincts. They've rarely failed me. I've shared your recommendations, and your ré-sumé, with the other doctors here. I've interviewed several other candidates, and you're clearly the most qualified. As you know, pedi-atrics is a deeply rewarding profession, and it has been very good to me. I'm at the stage of my career where I want to give back, by men-toring someone young and gifted. I would be honored if you would consider joining our practice."

I could feel her passion. This was a woman who cared. "I'm the one who is honored," I said.

"Just as a further inducement . . . ," she said. She scrawled some numbers on a legal pad, which she then held up in my direction. "You can expect to make something in this range your first year."

I blinked at the figure and my mouth went dry: Shelley, you're not in Kansas anymore.

Of course, money wasn't of paramount importance to me, the work was. And I certainly didn't need that kind of money. How would I possibly spend it all? Arthur would find it obscene, absurd, morally offensive.

"When do you want me to start?" I asked.

"Yesterday. Actually, it will take at least a week to deal with the paperwork, the lawyers, insurance. All the stuff that makes being a doctor so much fun these days."

"And you want me to take over Dr. Clark's patients?"

"Most of them, yes. As I mentioned, we're a five-doctor practice, and we all cover for each other during vacations, emergencies, et cetera. You'll be expected to work every fifth Saturday and to be on call one night a week."

"Sounds very exciting. I'll use the week to familiarize myself with the patients I'll be inheriting." Just talking about *my* patients sent a little shiver up my spine.

"I'm absolutely delighted," Dr. Marge said, holding out her hand. We shook.

Just then Candace's voice came on the intercom: "Angelina Jolie on line one, Dr. Marge."

Angelina Jolie! I adored Angelina Jolie; she was like an old-time movie star—glamorous, sexy, and slightly inhuman—and now she was on the other end of the line, practically right in the room.

"Angelina, how nice to hear from you," Dr. Marge said with cool charm, ". . . I see. Well, why don't I drop over to the hotel at, say, three and examine him myself? . . . You're very welcome. See you then."

Dr. Marge sat back down, the epitome of nonchalance. I wanted to be cool, but I couldn't stop myself: "Was that *the* Angelina Jolie?"

"We have quite a few celebrity patients. You'll get used to it very quickly. I rarely make hotel visits, but in certain cases I'll make an exception. They're at the Carlyle, which is just a few blocks away."

"What's she like?" I asked before I could stop myself.

"Discretion is the better part of success," Dr. Marge said with a meaningful look.

"Point taken."

She leaned in toward me. "There is one other piece of advice I want to give you. I've found that there's an element of performance in our work. It goes beyond the medical management of the child and the education of the parents—into what I call *persona*. The way you present yourself: appearance, speech, body language. At least on the Upper East Side, your persona is as important to your success as the content of what you say, and certainly more important than the diploma on the wall. How's the sandwich?"

"Fabulous," I said, and then wondered if talking with my mouth full was un-persona-like. Maybe my persona could be the overweight woman with no fashion sense and frizzy hair who makes up for it with her intelligence and diligence. Would that work?

"We always order from Amuse Bouche; it's *the* gourmet shop. As you know, we serve a very wealthy clientele. A fair number of them are new money. They're insecure. They come to us not because we're good, but because people above them on the social food chain come to us. My point is . . . well, let me just put it like this: I don't dress like this for my health. I've found this persona very beneficial for business."

I knew she meant well and was probably giving me very good advice, but the net effect was to make me feel hopelessly drab and fumbling. I made an ironclad decision: I would go on a strict diet immediately. I put down my plate. Dr. Marge leaned over and squeezed my hand.

"You're an attractive young woman, Dr. Green, and please understand that persona is no substitute for competence. It's just something you might want to give a bit of thought to."

"I will. Thank you."

"We Upper East Side pediatricians need all the help we can get these days. As you'll soon learn, we live in the age of hyperparenting. It's an epidemic and Madison Pediatrics is ground zero. Parents are so anxious, so filled with information and misinformation, ideas and theories, that they've just about taken all the joy, mystery, and spontaneity out of having a baby and raising a child. Many of our parents are über-A-type personalities who think of their children as narcissistic extensions of themselves rather than individuals in their own right. They're terrified of anything that they can't control—and you simply can't control a child. The Internet is the bane of my existence. Mothers spend hours doing so-called research, come into the office with reams of printouts, and then they get offended if you disagree with them. And every parent, of course, is convinced that their baby is going to grow up to be Mozart or Picasso or Bill Gates. The pressure on the child can be enormous, and detrimental. Dealing with these parents can be frustrating, even maddening. I find keeping my focus on the child helps."

"I saw some of that during my residency. Parents feel like they have to reinvent the wheel."

"Exactly."

"Dr. Marge, there's a girl out in the waiting room, about eleven or twelve, very serious, curly brown hair?"

Dr. Marge's face grew sad. "Yes, that's Alison Young. Poor child. Her mother died suddenly eight months ago. Of a cerebral aneurysm. On the street, on her way to pick up Alison from school."

"Oh, no."

"Heartbreaking, isn't it? I believe Alison is still somewhat in shock. Complicating it is the fact that her mother had been complaining of headaches for several weeks. Her doctor diagnosed migraines and put her on medication. Alison's father, who's English, is very bitter about the misdiagnosis."

"Understandably."

"Yes. But I'm afraid poor Alison has had to bear the brunt of his anger and grief, which may be impeding her own grieving process."

"Is she seeing a therapist?" I asked.

"I don't know. She was Dr. Clark's patient. Would you like to take her?"

"Very much."

"She's yours."

"She told me she isn't feeling well."

"Yes, Candace told me. I'm going to see her today, and then you can take over. Now let me introduce you to the rest of the staff."

We spent the next hour wandering around meeting the nurses, medical assistants, and the rest of the support staff. Dodging children as we went, we checked out exam rooms, the lab, the dispensary, the staff lounge, the recordkeeping and bookkeeping, all the while surrounded by the hive and hum of the practice. We were able to grab a minute or two with each of the other doctors, and in light of Dr. Marge's advice, it was enlightening to see the personas they had cultivated.

Dr. Gordon Healy had a fleshy face, warm brown eyes, and a round body that looked like it had never seen the inside of a gym. He was wearing a wrinkled shirt, a bow tie that was askew, chinos, and scuffed running shoes, and in spite of his disheveled appearance, inspired absolute confidence. I pegged his persona as Teddy Bear. He took one of my hands in both of his.

"Dr. Green, I'm so happy to meet you. Dr. Marge has been giving us daily updates on all the recommendations she has been garnering on you."

"I hope I can live up to my press."

"Just have fun. It's kids!"

And with that he was off.

Next I met Dr. Crissy Watkins, a woman in her midforties who looked like she had just gotten back from a quick kayak around Manhattan. Trim, toned, and exuberant, with graying blond hair, enormous blue eyes, and a wide mouth, she radiated good health and brisk common sense. She gave me a supersized smile, put a hand on each of my shoulders and said, "What a pleasure! How neat is this? Gosh, gosh, gosh!"

She was the kind of superconfident, sporty woman that I usually found intimidating, but her warmth was so sincere and her energy so infectious that they swept me up. Her persona? Sort of L.L.Bean meets Mary Tyler Moore.

Finally there was Dr. Samuel Cheng, who was young and handsome, wore an expensive suit, and looked terribly grave and owlish behind his round glasses. He listened intently as Dr. Marge introduced us.

"It's not easy being Green," he said, and then roared with laughter and delight.

"Dr. Cheng has a fondness for puns," Dr. Marge said in a tone that indicated she had heard more than enough of them for one lifetime.

"Levity is the soul of wit," Dr. Cheng explained with mock seriousness. Then his pager went off. "The call of the child," he said, before exploding into another burst of laughter and disappearing down the hall. I'd say his persona was Brilliant-but-Fun.

"The children love it," Dr. Marge said dryly. "You'll soon realize that there's an element of competition among the doctors here. We all want to snare the wealthy and famous families. We never let it get in the way of our professional duties and standards, but it does exist. Would you like to join me with a patient?"

"I'd love to."

"She's an investment banker, a single mother with a six-month-old boy and a passionate devotion to breast-feeding. They're here for his six-month checkup."

"Is the father part of the picture?"

"No, she bought the sperm through a private pregnancy

consultant—the donor is handsome, in perfect health, and a financial genius. She paid a hundred thousand dollars for his sperm."

"He's definitely a financial genius," I said.

We walked into the Harry Potter room. Sitting in a chair was a sleek young woman in a pinstriped business suit, with her blouse open and her infant son happily feeding. The sight of the baby made my heart go pitter-pat—his downy skull, his eyes hooded in contentment, his pudgy hands on Mom's breast.

"Donna DeMarco, this is Dr. Shelley Green, who is going to be joining our practice. Would you mind if she sat in on our exam?"

"Of course not," she answered, the soul of blissed-out benevolence. "I hope you realize that you're going to be working with an amazing woman, an *important* woman. Dr. Marge was the one who convinced me of the benefits of breast-feeding. It's changed my life, put everything in perspective. Now a billion-dollar IPO is just paperwork—*this* is what matters." She looked down at her baby. "I dash uptown from Wall Street at lunch every day so that Warren can get his regular feeding. He's named after Warren Buffet."

Okay.

"Warren looks like he's doing fine," Dr. Marge said.

"Oh, he's wonderful, a charm, sleeps through the night, poops like a prince. He *is* resisting his math tutor a little bit, but I think that's normal for his age, don't you?"

"Actually, I think he may be a bit young for any sort of tutor," Dr. Marge said.

"Ssshhhh! Don't say that," she said, adding in a whisper: "Subliminal negativity . . . But listen, Warren and I are going down to St. Bart's for a week—I think we both deserve a little vacation after the stress of the last six months. I was wondering, do you think it's safe to drink the water?"

"I'd stick to bottled water," Dr. Marge said. "And keep Warren out of the sun as much as possible, and when he is in the sun always use a block with an SPF of at least 45."

"I'm way ahead of you, Doctor. I've got self-tanners for both of us."

"No self-tanner for Warren, it may trigger an allergic reaction."

"What about pot? Would a few tokes of pot find its way into my breast milk?"

Dr. Marge shot me a glance. "I would strongly advise against it."

"But pot and the Caribbean go so well together."

"Absolutely not," Dr. Marge said.

Donna stroked Warren's head. "Oh well, he's worth it. I'll stick to rum."

After Dr. Marge had finished the exam and gotten the new mother's drug regimen worked out, she walked me out to the waiting room.

"I can't tell you how excited I am," I said. "I'll be in first thing tomorrow morning to begin the paperwork and start reading files."

"You have an emergency call on line one, Dr. Marge," Candace said.

"Who is it?" the doctor asked with concern.

"It's Dakota Pierce's mother. She finally got Dakota on the potty— but now she can't get her off."

Dr. Marge lowered her voice. "We get a lot of these; we call them 'broccoli calls,' as in, 'Dakota won't eat her broccoli.'"

"Why doesn't the mother just lift her off the potty?"

"Because that would unempower Dakota. Welcome to the Upper East Side, Doctor. We'll see you tomorrow, then."

"Thank you."

"Tell Mrs. Pierce I'll be right with her," Dr. Marge said, and disappeared.

"How did it go?" Candace asked.

"I was hired."

Candace let out a little whoop.

"Thanks. Dr. Marge is great," I said.

"I first came here ten years ago as a filing temp, now I run the place," Candace said. "That woman gave me a chance, and I'd do anything in the world for her."

"She seems to handle things pretty well."

Candace made a doubtful face. "Professionally, anyway. I'm not saying anything more, except I'm mighty glad to have you on board."

I walked over to Alison and knelt down. "I just wanted to let you know that I'm going to be your new doctor." She smiled at me, and I brushed a few curls from her forehead. "Do you want to tell me a little bit more about how you're feeling?"

"Tired."

"Does anything hurt?"

Alison thought a moment. "No, not really."

"All right. Dr. Marge is going to see you today, and after that it will be you and me."

Just then the door to the waiting room flew open and a hysterical young blonde raced in. She was followed, in rapid succession, by: a black man in a livery outfit who was carrying a wailing little girl of about three; a thin blond man who looked like a cast member of *Queer Eye*; a stout middle-aged woman with a broad Central American Indian face; and an older woman in a tailored suit who was carrying what looked like the world's largest appointment book.

"Smith, Smith is *paralyzed!!*" the woman cried. I couldn't tell what she was wearing, because she had a beauty-parlor smock on. Oh, yes, most of her head was studded with little tinfoil wraps, making her look sort of like the Bride of Frankenstein's debutante sister.

I moved toward the girl; Candace was around the desk in a flash. "Everybody back up, give the doctor room!" she ordered.

I gently took the girl from the driver, and turned to her mother and her entourage.

"What happened?"

"She step into the street, I grab her arm," the Hispanic woman explained.

Smith was holding her limp left forearm close to her body. "There now, Smith," I said. She stopped crying, and I could tell that her tears were as much from confusion and fear as actual pain. When I set her down, her forearm flopped ominously.

"Oh, my perfect baby, my perfect baby!" the mother wailed.

"Chill, Mrs. Walker!" Candace hissed at her.

The room went quiet—except for Mrs. Walker's hushed hyperventilation.

"There now, Smith, this isn't going to hurt a bit," I said. I gently stretched out her arm, turned her forearm, and relocated the head of her radius bone. She immediately raised her forearm and wiggled her fingers. The whole waiting room relaxed with an audible sigh.

Mrs. Walker scooped her daughter up in her arms. "Oh my baby, you're not paralyzed, you're fine! Oh, my little goddess." Then she looked up at me and froze—serious beyond serious. When she spoke, it was very slowly: "You. Are. A. Genius. Wait until my husband hears what you've done. Nobody but you is *ever* touching Smith again."

"It was really nothing serious at all," I said, beginning to tell her that it was just nursemaid's elbow, slipped socket, Pediatrics 101, you learn it the first week of residency.

"Sssshhh," Mrs. Walker silenced me. "Modesty is for losers. I'm going to break you of that habit." She set her daughter down and smiled at me, showing perfect teeth set in a perfectly gorgeous, tiny-featured face. "Amanda Walker," she said, holding out a perfect little hand.

"Dr. Shelley Green," I said, shaking it.

"I am honored to meet you," she said with what seemed like genuine warmth. "Can I take Smith home? Is she really all right?"

"She's absolutely fine."

"Shall I cancel her riding lesson?"

"There's really no need."

"I feel fine, Mommy," Smith said. She was basically a miniature version of Mom.

"Well, then. Off we go," Amanda said, turning and walking out of the waiting room, with her entourage trailing. As the door closed behind them, I heard: "Phyllis, I want something very special for Dr. Green. . . . Marcus, my scalp is tingling."

I looked at Candace—her face broke into a broad smile.

"Welcome aboard," she said.

"Thank you for your help."

"That's what I'm here for."

"Listen, I have something that might go with that wig," I said, reaching into my bag and pulling out the scarf.

Candace took one look at it and burst out laughing. "That is the most hideous thing I have ever seen in my life. I love it!"

"It was, um, a gift from a friend."

"Could that have been the same friend who bought me this wig?" she asked with a knowing grin, before tossing the scarf around her neck and hitting one of Puccini's glorious high notes.

3

THE AUDIENCE LOVED every second of Roosevelt High's production of *Romeo and Juliet*. And it was pretty irresistible, both for the gorgeous mosaic of its adolescent cast—equal parts Asian, Hispanic, black, and white—and because the kids had rewritten Shakespeare into their own vernacular. You haven't lived until you've heard Juliet cry: "Yo, Romeo, I say Romeo, where you *at,* Romeo?" and her Romeo passionately reply: "Splitting is such sweet whack." There was more than one place where I had to suppress my giggles, but by the end I was swept up by the kids' commitment and the power of the lovers' tragedy. Sitting next to Arthur helped. He was rapt throughout, and for the last fifteen minutes he was a faucet. Of course, he also cried at Kodak commercials.

As we filed out of the auditorium, Arthur called out, "There she is, our resident genius!" He threw his arms around an attractive—if way too thin—Asian woman. "Jennifer Wu, this is my fiancée, Shelley Green. Jennifer directed the show. It was magnificent."

"It was wonderful," I said.

Jennifer was young and hip, in a clingy black slip dress and with three silver studs in her left ear. She and Arthur were beaming at each other in a way that screamed Colleagues Who Flirt. "I had nothing to do with it; it was the kids. But wasn't it a relief to be able to understand the dialogue instead of having to wade through all that Shakespeare?"

I bit my tongue.

The hallway was filled with ebullient kids high from the excitement of seeing their friends perform, and many of them yelled affectionate greetings to Arthur. I was proud that my shy, modest Midwestern man connected with these urban kids. And he didn't high-five them or mimic their slang, he was just genuine and he cared and they could sense that.

It was Friday night, and Arthur and I strolled arm-in-arm over to a neighborhood pan-Caribbean restaurant for a late dinner. I loved walking with Arthur. He had a keen eye for architecture, culture, and people, and was forever pointing out graceful or telling details I never would have noticed on my own.

"I want to show you a couple of my favorite gardens," he said, as we made our way down the Brooklyn streets lined with modest single-family houses, attached row houses, and low apartment buildings. "It's been such a thrill to see this neighborhood change in the last five years. Immigrants buying houses, fixing them up—it's a true melting pot, and everyone gets along. Look at that!"

He pointed to a front garden in full bloom, every inch of the small yard covered with lovingly tended flowers, glowing in the night. A young black man was sitting on the front porch of the house behind it.

"Your garden is magnificent!" Arthur called.

The man's face broke into a wide grin. "Thank you, mon," he said in a Jamaican accent.

We came to a garden densely planted with neat rows of vegetables. "An old Italian couple live here," Arthur said. "They've been in the neighborhood for almost sixty years, and they keep the whole block supplied with fresh vegetables all summer long."

I rested my head on his shoulder a moment.

The restaurant was a homey place run by a Dominican family, with a thatched ceiling and strings of colored lights everywhere. The ample matriarch showed us to our table with a warm smile.

I didn't really need to pick up the menu. I knew the rice and beans were superb. I knew because Arthur had taken me here at least two dozen times in the past three years. Arthur loved habit and continuity and order. This was one of the things that had appealed to me when we first met. After all, I'd grown up in a cramped, chaotic, two-bedroom apartment, which meant—well, the math is easy: Two bedrooms divided by four Greens=Shelley and Ira sharing a bedroom. Yes, I spent my childhood sharing a room with my two-years-younger brother. At age twelve, I demanded—under threat of throwing myself off the roof of our building—that he move onto the living room couch. I was intimate witness to Ira's evolution from moody, sullen child to hyperactive adolescent to cross-addicted quasi-adult. As soon as I moved out at age twenty-two, Ira reclaimed the room and remains there still at twenty-nine. Our house was a regular Zen monastery, what with Dad's fanatic high-volume interactive sports watching, Mom's half-dozen telephone friends getting daily updates on her "fascinating intellectual growth," and Lucille, a yappy, incontinent, miniature poodle who lived to be twenty (although I'm not sure those last two years spent panting under the bathroom sink count as life). All in all, my family had more boundary issues than the Balkans. I think one reason I became an A student was because I loved sitting in quiet, orderly libraries where people spoke in whispers and closed the bathroom door when they peed.

"I'm going to have the pulled chicken," Arthur said. He always had the pulled chicken.

"I think I'll try the snapper," I said.

"But, Shelley, you always get the rice and beans."

I shrugged. "I guess I'm just in the mood for something different."

A puzzled look passed over Arthur's face. He really did have a hard time dealing with change. I found his bewilderment endearing—in our smugly ironic age, his earnestness felt refreshing, even courageous.

"I'm also trying to lose a little weight," I said. For the past week, I'd been on the only diet that worked for me: starvation. My body did fine with it, but I found myself having odd dreams, including a recurring one in which I lived in a house made out of chocolate cake, marzipan, and Twizzlers.

"I thought you'd lost a few pounds. You look great."

"Thanks. Arthur, those kids think the world of you."

"The feeling is mutual. And congratulations on getting through your first week on the job."

Although I sensed Arthur wasn't thrilled that I'd taken the job at Madison Pediatrics, he'd kept his qualms to himself and been nothing but supportive—so far.

"Thanks. It was all file reading, paperwork, and getting to know the lay of the land," I said. "I should start seeing patients by Wednesday."

"That's wonderful, munchkin. Listen, I made an appointment with a realtor in Carroll Gardens to show us some apartments next Saturday."

Arthur and I had talked about moving in together for a while. And even though we were engaged, the reality of it filled me with a vague unease. In many ways I was just beginning my life and the idea of giving up my independence seemed, I don't know, rushed. Couldn't we wait until we were married?

"Maybe we should wait and see. I may have to work on Saturday."

"Is the practice open on Saturdays?" he asked.

"There's always one doctor in on Saturday. I doubt it will be me, but I'm just beginning and I may want to go in and do paperwork, prepare for the week."

"I'll reschedule the appointment for Sunday."

I considered launching another protest but decided against it. What could it hurt to look at a couple of apartments?

A glint lit Arthur's eye and he said, "Let's talk about the wedding." I knew what was coming next, and here it came: "How about May in the Brooklyn Botanical Garden?"

May in the Brooklyn Botanical Garden is to marriage what tiramisu is to dessert: a cliché. It wasn't that I was opposed to it out of hand, but shouldn't we at least consider something a little more original? But I knew I had to tread gently.

"The garden is beautiful in May," I said.

"And you know how I feel about Brooklyn."

Yes, I knew how Arthur felt about Brooklyn. How could I not, having spent every spare minute of the last three years—of which there weren't many and which I might have preferred to spend on the couch in my bathrobe reading *Entertainment Weekly* or watching a probing *Biography* on Bo Derek—traipsing around every nook and cranny of his beloved adopted home. Don't get me wrong, I think Brooklyn is a wonderful place, but somehow Flatbush loses some of its charm during a driving hailstorm, and Fort Greene wilts a bit when it's 101 and hellishly humid.

"I like Brooklyn, too, Arthur, but it might be fun to think about other places to get married, even other places *in* Brooklyn."

Our food arrived. The snapper was smothered in a ginger and lime sauce, and its aroma billowed up and enveloped me. I took a bite and the fish melted in my mouth—*mmmmm*. Food really does taste better when you're hungry.

"You get the most adorable expression on your face when you're eating something delicious," Arthur said in his mock-sexy voice, the one that signaled that the evening would end with lovemaking. Arthur was a good lover—gentle, considerate . . . predictable. I'm ashamed to admit that he was only my third. My first we won't dwell on—suffice it to say it was a one-shot deal brought on by eight shots of tequila and a desperately insecure twenty-two-year-old's need to lose her virginity. It was about as satisfying as a ten-second ride on a mechanical bull at a country-and-western bar. My second was Fred, a narcissistic med-school classmate who I developed a major crush on—oh, all right, it wasn't a crush, it was an obsession, a pathetic, near-stalking, hang-out-in-the-cafeteria-for-three-hours-hoping-to-run-into-him obsession. After all, Fred was good-looking, confident, brilliant, and loved having females fawning over him. I can't say we were ever officially "a couple" or even that we "dated," but he did deign to have me over to his apartment for "study sessions," which was his euphemism for me making dinner, doing the dishes, and quizzing him on human biology. Then, usually about one A.M., when I was emotionally and physically exhausted, he would announce that we could "get down" if *I* felt like it. I always did. For all that, I have to admit that the sex was wildly exciting. Even though it was all about his performance, I found him so sexy that I didn't care, and he *did* perform. When it was over, he would jump up and swagger around the bedroom naked while I lay on the bed desperate for him to hold me. My "relationship" with Fred taught me an important lesson: Stay away from orthopedic surgeons, they've got bionic egos.

I met Arthur at a raucous party thrown by a fellow pediatric resident to celebrate the end of our first grueling year. He looked so sweet and sexy in his corduroy pants and denim shirt, with his unruly hair, long limbs, and easy smile. Plus it had been three years since Fred and I had drunk a half a bottle of a fantastic Zinfandel.

Arthur was sitting at the kitchen table, deep in conversation. I saw him. He looked up at me. I smiled. He smiled back. He stood up. I stood still. He introduced himself. I told him I was in love with him.

He took me home in a cab but declined my invitation to come upstairs. Instead, he made a date—to go on a walking tour of Bensonhurst. The next month was wonderful; we had a natural ease together. He admired my ability to immerse myself in my work for days at a time. I loved that he read Dickens and went windsurfing on the Hudson. I overlooked his somewhat rigid and self-righteous nature; he overlooked my trashy reading and viewing habits. Then there was the early sex—a nirvana sundae! A man actually making love to me, all of me. I'll never forget the first time: those eyes looking into mine, those hands on my body, the sweet thrilling fusion of the physical and emotional.

One reason I'll never forget the first time is because I was reminded of it every time afterward. Arthur, while wonderful and dependable, was not the world's most imaginative lover. The terrible fact, which I hated to admit to myself, was that I was getting a little bored with our sex life. Of course, I shared some of the responsibility. I had a hard time being uninhibited with Arthur in bed. I felt he thought of me as a "good girl." Plus we never really talked about sex. And I worried about hurting his male pride.

"This pulled chicken is fantastic, too," he said.

We watched each other eat, our eyes locking in gustatory foreplay. He put down his fork. I put down my fork. He reached a warm, promising hand across the table and enfolded my hand.

"Shelley, what's that?!" he said, looking down at my wrist.

"Oh this. It's just a little present from Amanda Walker," I said, pulling up my hand and encircling the gold-link bracelet with my other hand.

"But it's so . . . gaudy," Arthur said.

"I think it's sort of pretty," I said. The courier from Tiffany's had interrupted a long day of reading patient files. The note from Amanda Walker was charming, if hyperbolic. She thanked me for my calm, quick brilliance, and said she knew we were destined to become great friends. At first I was taken aback by her generosity, and considered returning the bracelet, but Dr. Marge told me that gifting was quite a common practice, and that it would be considered an insult to return it.

"It's not *you*," he said.

"Really?" I said, twisting my wrist and admiring the way the light glinted off the gold.

"Shelley," he admonished.

"What? I'm not allowed to enjoy a little present?"

"Whoever heard of a parent sending a present like that? It must have cost thousands of dollars."

"Why, that's impossible . . . do you really think so? Thousands?"

"I don't know, but it seems very unprofessional, almost like a bribe," Arthur said.

"It's not a bribe, it's a gift. Doctors get them all the time. Although she has invited me for tea."

"Tea? At her house?"

"No, on the sidewalk out front. Yes, at her house. Arthur, I can't believe we're arguing over this."

"I don't want this job to turn you into one of those Upper East Side types."

"You hate stereotyping, but I guess you make an exception for the rich."

"What does Mr. Walker do?"

"He owns companies."

"Oh, that's a good honest way to make a living. You know as well as I do that no one gets that rich without stepping on other people."

"Isn't that true about success in every profession? You've told me a thousand times how cutthroat academia is, about what your dad had to do to get tenure," I said.

Arthur dug into his pulled chicken. We sat there in one of those awful heartbreaking silences. Under his thin veneer of anger, he looked so miserable and adorable and vulnerable.

I took off the bracelet and slipped it into my bag.

"Maybe we should have this place cater our wedding," I said.

He looked up at me, smiled, and said, "Let's share a flan and discuss it."

4

I LOOKED AT THE WAILING, hissing, howling, biting, kicking, flailing creature being gripped by his nanny, and thought: I've seen the terrible twos before, but this fit belongs in the Temper Tantrum Hall of Fame. I mean all I'd said was, "May I take a little peek in your mouth, Allan?" and this until-then-well-behaved little gentleman had exploded. I quickly stepped back, afraid of losing a finger to those suddenly Jaws-esque baby teeth. Claire, my medical assistant, a Haitian in her midtwenties, stood well back and tried to disguise her own alarm. The nanny, a big-boned Australian girl, seemed utterly unfazed by the Tasmanian devil she was holding.

Since temper tantrums are normal in a two-year-old, usually triggered by fear or frustration, I decided just to let Allan do his thing for a minute. Surely he would wear himself out. A minute turned to two and two to three. I felt helpless and began to worry that if my new colleagues heard this outburst they would question my ability to control my patients.

There was a sudden lull, and I seized it, stepping forward, leaning down, and saying in my gentlest voice, "Allan, it won't hurt, I prom—"

Maybe the H word was a mistake, because I was rewarded with a fat little fist on my cheek—*ouch!*—and renewed gales of enraged howling.

"Does he behave like this at home?" I asked the nanny, my desperation growing.

"At least a dozen a day," she said.

"What do his parents do?"

"They're not about too much. Busy people."

"I see."

Allan was turning a mottled blue, and I was starting to get really worried. I could just see the headline in the *Post:* BABY DOC KILLS RICH KID. My career would be over before it began. I'd lose my license. Humiliate my family. Arthur would leave me. Oh well, I could always move to Uganda and open a clinic in the bush.

Shelley, snap out of it!

"Allan, snap out of it!" I said sharply, puffing myself up to what I hoped was an authoritative posture.

It worked—for about a quarter of a nanosecond. Allan stopped cold, looked at me in surprise—and then lunged his head forward, teeth bared, hissing like a snake about to strike. I recoiled. The howling seemed to redouble.

Then Candace appeared, carrying a portable CD player. She turned it on and opera began to play. Within a couple of seconds Allan stopped crying and cocked his head, listening intently.

I stood there in shock for a moment—Allan was still, a little smile played at the corners of his mouth, his eyes grew heavy-lidded. I've never believed in miracles, but this came close. "What's *on* that CD?"

"It's Sarastro's aria from *The Magic Flute*. It's the combination of Mozart's music and that big calming fatherly bass voice. Works on boys most of the time," Candace said. "Dr. Green, you look wrung out."

"I've never seen a tantrum that violent before. It's way beyond the terrible twos."

"Around here we call it the trust-fund twos. Its severity rises in direct proportion to net worth. You'll see it again, don't worry."

"I can hardly wait."

My next patient was Lisa Morris, a six-year-old girl whose mother had just called that morning, saying that her daughter had a fever and a sore throat.

Lisa was an adorable, slightly chubby brunette, who sat on the exam table looking miserable and lethargic, with pale skin and red-rimmed eyes. Jane Morris was in her early thirties, well-dressed, and obviously concerned about her daughter's health.

After greeting them both, I reviewed Lisa's medical history with her mom, going over her general health, diet, and development. Then I turned to Lisa.

"You're not feeling very well, are you?" I asked.

Lisa shook her head glumly. "I can't be sick now," she said.

I palpated her neck and found that her nodes were swollen. Then I looked in her mouth and found, as I expected, that her tonsils were red and swollen.

"Lisa, I want to take a culture from the back of your throat. Would that be all right?"

Lisa nodded and opened her mouth. I ran a swab gently over the tonsil area. Claire took it to our lab and ran a rapid strep test. Two minutes later she was back with a positive result.

"Lisa, you have strep throat. I'm going to place you on antibiotics. Make sure to eat something when you take them, otherwise you might get an upset tummy." I turned to her mother. "Strep throat is highly contagious. Lisa shouldn't be exposed to any other children for a minimum of twenty-four hours, preferably thirty-six to forty-eight. That means no school, no play dates. Basically she should stay at home, fairly isolated. Adults are susceptible, too."

Lisa listened to all this intently, and then said in a plaintive voice, "But, Mommy, what about my manicure? I can't miss my manicure. It's at Bergdorf's."

Jane Morris and I looked at each other and burst out laughing. Lisa didn't care about missing school, or not seeing her friends, but the idea that she might have to cancel her Bergdorf's manicure made her disconsolate.

"I'm sorry, Lisa, but I'm afraid you're going to have to reschedule your manicure," I said.

That's when the tears started.

"Darling, I'll do your nails myself at home," Mom said, stroking her daughter's head.

"But, Mommy, you promised," Lisa said through her tears.

"I'll tell you what, sweetheart, to make up for it, when I reschedule I'll add on a pedicure," Mom said.

This had the desired effect, and Lisa sniffled back her tears.

The rest of my first morning seeing patients was a routine parade of shots, skin rashes, and sore throats. The kids were more confident than the ones I'd seen during my residency. They looked at me not with the mixture of respect and trepidation I was used to, but with a casual self-importance that told me I was just one more in the endless parade of people who appeared to serve their wants and needs— the housekeeper, the nanny, the driver, the doctor.

I was putting on my coat to duck out for a short lunch break when I heard a familiar voice echoing down from the waiting room.

"I've just been to a lecture at the Met on Etruscan tomb paintings—fascinating—and thought I'd pop in to say hello to my daughter, the doctor, on her first official day at work."

I felt annoyance and embarrassment bubble up inside me. Couldn't Mom at least have waited a week or, better yet, until she was invited? I sighed, hung up my coat, and headed out to greet her.

"Shelley, darling, congratulations! . . . *Suss.*"

I instinctively threw back my shoulders. "Hi, Mom."

Mom was in her I'm-going-to-a-lecture-at-the-Met mode: her graying auburn hair cut and combed, lipstick, a tasteful beige outfit. Unfortunately her efforts were undermined by glittery cascading earrings that looked like Barbie chandeliers.

"I'm just dropping in for five minutes. I was in the neighborhood, at the Met." Whenever Mom said "the Met" she affected an upperclass accent—suddenly Brooke Astor would pop out for two words. "I did bring along a little something for your staff—Candace and I are already great friends." Candace shot me a bemused glance as Mom reached into a shopping bag and pulled out an enormous cellophane-wrapped platter of brownies. "I baked these myself—the recipe was Eleanor Roosevelt's favorite. Isn't that interesting?" She unwrapped the platter and set it on the counter.

The brownies did look delicious, and I fought the urge to grab one. "Would you like a quick tour?" I asked instead.

"Only if it's no trouble," Mom answered, sweeping past me and down the hallway. I turned and rolled my eyes at Candace, who was just biting into a brownie. She gave me a big smile.

"This place is remarkable, Shelley. I'm so proud of you," Mom said five minutes later, as she plopped down in a chair in my office. I remained standing. "It's so grandiose and yet so childlike. Intriguing juxtaposition."

"Listen, Mom, I just have a short break here, and I need to grab something to eat."

She ignored this. "Shelley, I learned so much this morning. Did you know that to the Etruscans, tomb paintings were like what movies are to us? They used them to tell stories. And myths." Suddenly tears welled up in her eyes, but she just kept talking as if nothing unusual was happening. "The paintings show us that women were equals in Etruscan society, which certainly wasn't true for the Greeks and Romans." The tears rolled down her cheeks.

"Mom?"

"The workmanship itself was magnificent. Why, the dyes are still vivid over two thousand years later." Now the tears were flowing in a steady stream.

"*Mom?*"

"To this day archeologists are uncovering new tombs and learning more about the beliefs and rituals and . . . *Ira is missing.*"

Bingo!

"For how long?"

"He hasn't been home since Tuesday morning." The tears stopped, and she looked at me with real anxiety in her eyes. Ira was Mom's cross to bear, the wayward child she deeply loved, a bottomless pit of guilt, regret, and neurotic need. "Oh, Shelley, what am I going to do?"

"You're going to do nothing. This is the twelfth time in the last five years that he's pulled this. You know as well as I do that he's probably holed up in some motel in Hackensack with a quart of Scotch, two grams of cocaine, and three unlicensed masseuses."

"Oh, Shelley, how can you say that? He could be dead, lying on the street somewhere bleeding and calling my name."

"I doubt he's calling your name if he's dead."

"You're always so practical."

"Someone has to be." I took a deep breath and moved close to Mom, smoothed her hair and lowered my voice. "Mom, you know how much I love you, and Ira loves you. Dad loves you. This should be a happy time for all of us. Look at where I am, Mom."

She took my hand and held it to her cheek. "Oh, Shelley, I really am so proud of you."

"Well, I never could have gotten here without you."

"Really?"

"Of course not. Now let's look at this thing rationally. Did Ira watch a ball game with Dad on Monday night?"

"Yes."

"Did he seem happy with the outcome?"

Mom hesitated, knew she was caught, then nodded her head in reluctant admission.

"Okay, Mom, we both know that Ira will be dragging himself home sometime in the next twenty-four hours, when he's burned through all his winnings. You'll run him a hot bath and make him scrambled eggs and everything will be right in the world."

"Shelley, don't be too hard on your brother."

"Mom, I have about fifteen minutes left on my lunch, I haven't eaten since seven, and I'm going to be here until late this evening."

Mom shifted gears, sat up straight, smoothed her skirt. "I just wanted to bring over some brownies and say congratulations."

"I'm going to be working very hard for the next few months. If you want to come by, please call first."

"Oh, excuse me, I'm so sorry. Next you're going to be ashamed of your family. Well, don't worry, Dr. La-De-Da, I won't be darkening your door!"

Dr. Marge appeared in the doorway. "I hope I'm not interrupting."

"Not at all. This is my mother, Miriam Green. Mom, this is Dr. Mueller."

"Your brownies precede you," Dr. Marge said. "They're sensational."

Mom stood up, erect. "We have Eleanor Roosevelt to thank for that. It's lovely to meet you, Doctor. I just popped in for a second;

I was at a lecture at the Met. I'd love to stay and chat, but I have to get home and finish *Beloved* for my book group." And then she was gone—tears, guilt, chandeliers, and all.

"Well, how did your first morning go?" Dr. Marge asked.

"Aside from one world-class temper tantrum, pretty well, I think. I looked for the results of Alison Young's lab work—I guess they haven't come back yet."

"Actually, they just came in. I have them right here."

She handed me the pages, and I quickly read them. "Sedimentation rate isn't elevated, negative rheumatoid factor and ANA, Lyme titer negative, WBC normal, nothing in the urinalysis. These all look fine."

"Yes."

"I think she needs someone to talk to," I said. "Do you know any child psychologists we can refer her to?"

"Several."

"Has anyone spoken to her father?"

"Not that I know of."

"I'll ask her to come in, try to get her to open up a little bit, and also run a more comprehensive set of tests to rule out anything insidious. We'll get to the bottom of this. She's such a lovely little girl, I find myself thinking about her."

"Funny how certain children touch us like that." There was a pause, and I sensed that Dr. Marge wanted to ask me something, or at least to stay and talk for a moment. "Is there anything at all that you need?"

"No, you've made me feel welcome and supported."

She smiled, and I thought I saw a hint of sadness in her eyes. "It's a pleasure having you on board. Now go and get yourself some lunch." She turned to leave and then stopped. She turned back, as if she'd just remembered something. "Do you like the dance?"

"Um, sure, yes."

"Because I have an extra ticket for Alvin Ailey tonight. My

husband called—he's in Chicago on business and has to stay another day. Would you like to join me?"

"I'm sorry, Arthur has booked us on a sunset stroll through Red Hook. . . . May I ask what your husband does?"

"My husband is a business consultant. He specializes in forecasting consumer trends. Which means that he flies all over the world and . . . is often away from home." Her voice grew wistful for a moment.

"Would you like to join us on the walking tour?"

"That's very kind of you, but I have absolutely no interest in Red Hook, wherever it may be. Of course, after fifteen years as a subscriber I have no interest in Alvin Ailey either. So much of what we do in life is rote, isn't it? Just going through the motions." Then she dropped her voice and said, half to herself, "Oh dear, I'm becoming one of those maudlin middle-aged women." She raised her chin, and when she spoke, her voice was crisp and confident, "I'll find a friend to use the ticket. Now go, go—eat, eat."

My first afternoon patient was, according to his chart, a healthy fifteen-month-old named Max Goldman, of Central Park West, East Hampton, Aspen, and Beverly Hills. I hoped Max didn't suffer from motion sickness, because he must have spent a lot of time in transit.

I was somewhat surprised to find both Mr. and Mrs. Goldman waiting for me in the Captain Nemo room. They were standing side by side in front of the exam table. Behind them I could just catch a glimpse of little diapered Max being held by his nanny, an older woman with pale skin and gray hair. Mr. Goldman had thick black hair that was slicked back, except for the hank that fell artfully over his forehead. He was wearing a beautiful black suit that shimmered a little, and a blue oxford shirt with a burgundy ascot. He had an incongruous paunch and looked about fifty, although it was hard to tell because his skin was so tight and bright—definite face-lift and rejuvenation. Mrs. Goldman was deeply tanned, blond, and voluptuous.

Her hair was in long cornrows that had to be a weave. She was wearing a lot of jewelry and a Chanel suit—about as appropriate on her as it would be on Britney Spears—and she looked about half hubby's age, tops. They both seemed anxious, restless, and desperately insecure.

"Hello, I'm Dr. Green."

"Hi, I'm Fred Goldman, this is my wife Lauren."

"Hi," Lauren said with a somewhat scary smile—she'd gone several shades overboard on the tooth-whitening chart.

We went over Max's medical history. Then Fred asked, "Can we call you Shelley, Shelley?"

I was a bit taken aback. I loved the sound of "Dr. Green" and had worked hard to earn it. But you have to pick your battles, so I said, "Why not?"

"You should probably know that Max is worth twenty-five million dollars," he said.

"As his pediatrician I'm more concerned with his weight than his worth," I said.

Fred Goldman nodded his head solemnly. "That's beautiful, Shelley, you won me over. I love you."

"We love you," Lauren said.

"May I meet Max?"

"In a minute. There's something important we have to talk to you about."

"It's *very* important," Lauren added. She hardly seemed old enough—make that mature enough—to have a baby. "We love him so much, that's why we're so worried."

"Yeah, okay, we're worried, no one's denying it," Fred said.

"Is he all right?" I asked, peeking over their shoulders. The nanny was keeping him occupied with a small toy. He was wide-eyed and smiling, had excellent coloring, and looked just fine.

"Oh, Christ, yeah, the kid's a horse."

"What is it, then?"

They exchanged an angst-ridden glance.

"Episcopal," Fred said with enormous gravity. Lauren gave a little awe-filled sigh.

"Episcopal?" I asked.

They both looked at me incredulously.

"Episcopal, Shelley, *Episcopal*," Fred said.

"I honestly have no idea what you're talking about," I said. Were they planning to convert?

"Episcopal Nursery School, it's only *the* best nursery school in New York City, if not the nation, if not the world," Fred said.

"Gwyneth Paltrow went there," Lauren said, enunciating every syllable of the revered name.

"Ninety-two percent of Episcopal graduates get into Ivy League colleges."

"We only want what's best for Max."

"Listen, Shelley, me and Lauren don't give a shit about stuff like this, but I'm segueing from real estate—I own office parks all over Westchester and Rockland—into show business. You know, producing movies—it's Lauren's thing."

"It's *your* thing, too, honey."

"Okay, it's *our* thing, but the point is the movie business is very class-conscious."

"Everything in the movie business is class, like Meryl Streep," Lauren added.

"If Max gets into Episcopal, it'll be a huge boost for my career. Not to mention his own."

"So we need a letter from you," Lauren said.

"A letter?"

"Yeah, a letter of recommendation," Fred said. "They carry a lot of weight. You know, if you say Max is intelligent, well-behaved, developing normally."

"Plays well with others," Lauren added.

A letter of recommendation for a fifteen-month-old? That had never come up during my residency.

"Don't you think I should get to know Max first? If I'm going to be his pediatrician, I'd like to begin developing a relationship with him. At that point, I would feel more comfortable writing a letter."

"Oh yeah, sure, of course," Fred said.

They relaxed instantly and—nodding their heads in perfect unison—stepped apart, revealing little Max. He looked over and smiled right at me—a natural charmer.

"Fred, why don't we let Max and Shelley have some quality time together?" Lauren suggested. "We can go out for a cappuccino."

"Good idea, hon. You're going to love this kid, Shelley."

"Bye-bye, handsome," Lauren said as they left.

"Say hi to the nice doctor, Max," the nanny said with an Irish lilt.

I approached Max. This was my favorite moment—when it was just me and my wondrous little patient.

"Hello there, little friend," I said.

He giggled with delight and grabbed my finger. This was a trusting, happy child who got a lot of love. And his examination revealed that he was indeed as healthy as a horse, or at least a pony. Moreover, his development was normal, he had reached all the expected milestones for his age, and he had a vocabulary that was an impressive six to ten words.

I stroked his head. "Well, Max, it's been wonderful meeting you, and I think I'll be able, in good conscience, to write a very nice letter for you."

He looked up at me with blissful eyes: "Mama . . . dada . . . *moo*-veez," he said.

And then we shared a laugh.

It was almost eight o'clock by the time I'd seen my last patient and finished my notes. I was the last one left in the office, and I felt an exhausted exhilaration in the marked calm.

It lasted all of five seconds.

"Hello there."

I looked up and saw a woman about my age standing in the doorway. She was tall, thin, striking, with shiny shoulder-length black hair and gorgeous blue eyes.

"Hi."

"I'm Dr. Christina Allen . . . from across the hall?"

Oh—one of the plastic surgeons. I imagined how I looked to her—my eyes sporting their end-of-the-day bags, my furrowed forehead, my so-called chin threatening to disappear into my chubby neck. Dr. Allen, on the other hand, looked like she'd gotten back from a spa vacation ten minutes ago.

"Hi, I'm—"

"Oh, I know who you are—Dr. Shelley Green. May I come in for a minute?"

"Of course."

She was wearing black thin-wale corduroy slacks and a black cashmere sweater with the sleeves pushed up. She sat down and crossed her long legs, the picture of insouciance. I tried not to hate her.

"I'm thrilled to meet you. Amanda Walker has not stopped raving about what an amazing doctor you are. She has big plans for you."

"Oh, you know Amanda Walker?"

"We were classmates at Sarah Lawrence. She's a terrific girl and—wow!—has she married well. She always swore she would. My little Mandy is determined to climb to the very heights of New York society and believe me, Shelley, that is one greasy pole. But like I always tell her: What has Blaine Trump got that you haven't? So, how did your first day go?"

I was a bit stunned but managed to get out, "Well, thank you, it's an exciting practice."

"I always tell Dr. Marge she should change the name to Power Elite Pediatrics. God, I'm horny. I did two brow-lifts today—brow-lifts always make me horny. What's *that* about? I wish it was Friday—I'd go out and pick up some inappropriate man. But never on a Wednesday. I am one kick-ass surgeon, and I would never do anything that might interfere with my ability to cut. Weeknights I'm in bed— alone—by ten. How's *your* love life?"

"Um, I'm engaged."

"Oh God, that's a pity. You're about to enter a whole new world, Shelley, why drag old baggage with you? But listen, I'm here to offer you a deal."

"A deal?"

"Yes, a deal. You see, I'm going to get a baby."

"*Get* a baby?"

"From China. I'm flying over at the end of the summer to bring her home. I know I seem about as maternal as Eva Braun, but the truth is I love kids. And I'm lonely, and I sure as hell don't want a man right now. I make over two million dollars a year, and I want to share it. She's six months old and her name is Ingrid and I love her. Wait until you meet her. Bright as hell. And exquisite. Thank God the whole world isn't Asian; I'd be out of business in a New York minute. Anyway, Ingrid is going to need a pediatrician and I want Y-O-U. So, how about we do a little barter? You take care of my daughter in return for two procedures."

Alice was lucky she landed in Wonderland—it's a lot less confusing than the Upper East Side.

"Wait, let me get this straight. You're saying that in return for being your daughter's pediatrician you'll perform two plastic surgeries on me?"

"You got it, and I'd recommend . . . ," she scrutinized my face, ". . . mmm . . . You're actually pretty great-looking under that disastrous haircut—nice strong features, fabulous skin, good teeth. And your tits sure don't need any help—that is one helluva rack you've got there, Shelley. I could add a little to your chin, and, let me see . . . plump up the lips. My first thought was the nose, but it's distinctive. I'd leave it."

I just sat there, stunned.

"Close your mouth, kiddo, it's not becoming. And you don't have to decide right now. Think about it. But why not take the whole package to the next level? I only want to help—and make sure Ingrid has the best doctor I can find. And save myself some whopping fees, of course." She stood up. "Christ, I would kill for a martini. I think one reason I decided to adopt was because I couldn't face nine months without a drink. Drink and unsuitable men—my two vices. Aren't I lucky they go so well together? It was sensational meeting you, Shelley, I hope we can become great pals."

And with that she blew out of my office, leaving a trail of sharp citrus perfume in her wake.

Once my breathing had returned to normal, my first thought was how unprofessional she'd been. Medicine was serious, important work. Not something to be bantered and bartered over. I picked up the phone to call Arthur and vent.

. . . *You're actually pretty great-looking under that disastrous haircut—nice strong features, fabulous skin, good teeth. And your tits sure don't need any help.* . . .

I listened to one ring, then hung up and sat there for a long moment in the quiet. Then I stood up and closed my office door—because I knew there was a full-length mirror on the back.

5

THE APARTMENT WAS NICE, I couldn't deny that: the top floor of a brownstone, with old wood floors, a working fireplace in the living room, and charming views of Brooklyn treetops. The building was in the process of being renovated, and the apartment was awaiting fresh paint and finishing touches.

I was in the kitchen, which had granite countertops and glass-fronted cabinets. It was a real cook's kitchen, and Arthur loved to cook. As for me, well, let's just say I could do amazing things with takeout.

"Nice, isn't it?" the rental agent said. She was a tiny woman with a nervous smile. "Garbage disposal, dishwasher, built-in wine rack."

"It's a nice apartment," I said.

"It will be all ready by July fifteenth. I know the owners would love to get a doctor in here. I could probably get you the first month's rent free."

In spite of HMOs, malpractice, and surgical horror stories, I had already noticed that being a full-fledged doctor often elicited a degree of respect, even admiration. This always triggered a complicated response in me. On the one hand, it filled me with pride in my profession and made me feel important. And who doesn't love perks? But it also triggered my nagging insecurity, the little voice inside of me that said: *Sure you've got your degrees and enough medical knowledge to fill a library, but medicine is also intuition and instinct, gut feelings and guesswork, and you're dealing with children's lives. Do you really have what it takes?* While most of pediatrics was relatively straightforward, more complex cases such as Alison Young sparked these doubts. It was important that I handle her case with the best judgment.

"And you could pick your own paint colors," the agent added hopefully.

"Oh God, more choices," I said. Picking paint colors for an apartment I wasn't sure I wanted was one complication my life didn't need.

"Ah, a modest doctor. Now that's refreshing."

"Honey, come look," Arthur called to me excitedly from the bedroom.

I found him standing at the entrance to what at first glance I'd assumed was a walk-in closet. I walked over and saw that it was, in fact, a small extra room.

"Isn't it perfect, pumpkin?" Arthur said. Then he snaked his arm around my waist and patted my stomach. Yes, we both wanted children. But I didn't want a baby for at least a couple of years. I wanted to enjoy my budding adulthood for a little while. Arthur seemed determined to lay it all out for me: apartment, wedding, baby. I guess picking our burial plot came next.

"It's nice," I said.

"You seem a little distracted today, Shelley."

"I'm sorry, Arthur, it's just that I have my first prenatal conference tomorrow, and they're very important. It's how you get new patients. Although Dr. Marge hasn't said so explicitly, I know I'm expected to bring new business into the practice."

"Oh, honey, any parents who didn't hire you would be crazy."

"Thanks, but that doesn't mean I don't have to be prepared."

Arthur pulled me closer, leaned down, and kissed me on the forehead.

"I understand. But what do you think of the apartment? Isn't it wonderful?"

"It's charming, but the four flights up concern me a little."

"Oh, they're good for us, keep us in shape. By the way, Shelley, how much weight have you lost? Is everything all right?"

"Everything is fine. I'm just trying to tone up . . . my persona, you know."

"I think your Shelley Green persona is perfect," Arthur said, kissing me again.

I could imagine us living here together. The neighborhood was lively and pretty and safe. The apartment would be comfortable to come home to after a long day with patients. Arthur would be in the kitchen, humming as he cooked up something yummy. After dinner we would settle in to read (Arthur) or watch television (me). Why was I resisting it, then? Why did my mind keep racing back to the Upper East Side, to Dr. Marge and Amanda Walker and Christina Allen, to a world filled with wealth, excitement, and glamour?

"And I think your Arthur Lipman persona is perfect," I said, snuggling into him, feeling a little pang of guilt. "But I'm not sure this apartment is."

"Shelley, this is the fifth apartment we've looked at today. You find something wrong with all of them. This is by far the most charming, the rent is right, and we both love this neighborhood."

I was trying to decide how to respond when my cell phone rang.

"Hi, Shelley."

"Ira, what's up?"

"God, can't I call and say hello to my own big sister?"

"I'm still not over that last disappearance you pulled."

"Shelley, it will *never* happen again. Did you get the flowers I sent?"

A massive fan-shaped arrangement—Candace dubbed it "Mafia funeral flowers"—had arrived for me at work. It was Ira's standard ploy—usually charged to Dad's credit card—when he came off one of his binges.

"Yes, I did," I said.

"No *thank you*?"

"Thank you."

"Boy, that sounds sincere."

"So, what's up?"

"I am. I've turned a new leaf, it's a whole new *moi*. I'm not kidding, Shelley, I've hooked into something big. Can we meet tomorrow? I'll buy you a drink after work."

"A *drink*?"

"All right, a cup of coffee, dinner, whatever you want. I don't want to borrow money, I don't want to bug you, but we have to talk. Please, Shelley-belly, please."

For obvious reasons, Shelley-belly was my least favorite nickname, but I loved my ne'er-do-well kid brother. When he wasn't in a crisis or on a binge, I got a vicarious thrill from his impulse-driven, adrenaline-filled exploits. He was funny, spontaneous, and, oh yes, adorable—thick black hair, a hunky body, and the good looks of a young Al Pacino's Jewish cousin. It's so unfair when your brother is prettier than you are.

"All right, meet me at the coffee shop on Madison and Seventy-fourth at eight thirty. I have a prenatal conference and probably will have eaten."

"Love ya, Shell."

Arthur turned to me, full of resolve. "Listen, Shelly, I'm making an executive decision. We're going to take this apartment."

Although Arthur was soft-spoken and reasonable, he could be decisive, even forceful when he felt he had to be. I stood there, torn and tugged. Arthur tilted my face up to his, pushed my hair back, and looked me right in the eye. "We're taking the apartment."

I had too much on my plate. The practice, my patients, my needy, fascinating mother, my needy, adorable brother. I couldn't handle making one more decision. I just couldn't. It was easiest simply to agree.

"Okay," I said.

Arthur took me in his arms and started to waltz me around the empty bedroom, singing "You're the Top" in his lovely crooner voice.

Afternoon light was pouring in the window, golden and glowing—and as we danced I felt suffused with trepidation.

6

DR. MARGE HELPED ME lay out the stylish snack from Amuse Bouche: smoked bluefish on triangles of thin rye bread, curried-chicken salad, olives, vegetable chips, Italian lemonade in a tall glass bottle, Florentines. It looked incredible, but I was so into my diet that I wasn't tempted.

"Dr. Marge, please go home, it's almost seven o'clock," I pleaded, arranging the plates and silverware on the coffee table in my office.

"Don't be silly, Dr. Green. This is your first prenatal conference, and I want to offer you my support," she answered.

Dr. Marge had been doing nothing but offering me support. While I appreciated it, I wanted to stand on my own two feet. The truth was, I was beginning to wonder if Dr. Marge might need some support herself. She sometimes looked a little haggard in the morning, as if she'd had one too many glasses of wine the night before.

"I never asked you how Alvin Ailey was," I said.

"Oh, I didn't go. I just didn't feel up to it." A distant look came into her eyes. Feeling awkward, I decided to change the subject.

"I'd love it if you would talk me through this process," I said. I sat on the love seat and patted the place next to me.

"Choosing a pediatrician has become an important ritual on the Upper East Side, as much a social occasion as a medical one," she began.

"Ergo the chic spread," I said.

"Exactly. Now, the Logans. Incidentally, what do you know about them?"

"Both lawyers, separate firms, first child, a boy."

"Lawyers," Dr. Marge said with a roll of her eyes. "Be prepared for a lengthy cross-examination. For most of our patients, picking a pediatrician isn't all that different from buying a new car—they want a doctor who fits their lifestyle and self-image, is efficient, attractive, holds up well in emergencies. And, of course, confers status. I like to think of our practice as a Mercedes-Benz. And we come with a free test drive."

"The prenatal conference."

"Yes. In just about every other profession you can charge for a consultation, but not ours."

"Why do we do it for free?"

"First, because we are kind, saintly people who exist only to care for children. And second, because we're in a brutally competitive field and we have to. By the way, Shelley, you look fantastic."

"Thank you. Do you think my persona is developing?" I asked. The practice had advanced me my first month's salary, and I had gone to Macy's and bought myself what I thought was a simple, classic gray suit with off-white piping. The pounds were melting off. I was getting up at 6:30 every morning to do a half hour of stretching. I had also splurged on some expensive makeup and was wearing lipstick and a hint of eye shadow.

"It certainly is. I heard Christina Allen paid you a visit."

"She's quite something."

"Isn't she? I've had a couple of little things done myself."

"Really?" I asked, searching her face for signs of surgery.

"Yes," Dr. Marge said, and that rueful edge crept into her voice again.

"Oh, you're not happy with the results?"

"Professionally, it was the right thing to do."

There was a silence, and she looked down at her hands. That look of vulnerability that I had seen before passed over her face. Just then a phone rang from down the hall.

"Oh, that's me," Dr. Marge said, getting up and going to answer it. Although she was older than me by twenty years, I felt oddly maternal stirrings toward her.

"Looks like you're getting ready for your first pediatric mating ritual," Dr. Healy said as he appeared in my doorway, looking his usual rumpled, lovable self. He was clutching his briefcase, obviously on his way home.

"Any advice?"

"I don't think you need any advice from me," he said. Then, with some effort, he smiled.

"Are you kidding? You're so popular."

"Not as popular as I used to be. But I think it's wonderful that Amanda Walker loves you so much."

Candace had told me that the Walker children used to see Dr. Healy, but she assured me that he was the least competitive doctor in the practice.

"I'd be happy to tell Amanda that I'd rather she stay with you," I said.

"Dr. Green, you don't *tell* Amanda Walker anything. I just think it's so great that you and she clicked, and what a feat, to snare her on your very first day. It's like hitting a grand slam homer at your first at-bat."

"It was an instinctive reaction. A child was in pain."

"I'm so happy for you." He gave me another pained smile, and left.

Dr. Healy was a kind man, and his ego had clearly taken a hit. I made a note to buy him a box of fancy chocolates as a peace offering and a gesture of friendship. As for my hitting a grand slam, well, I'd spent a long time practicing my swing.

"Now that looks delicious."

I looked up to see Candace standing in the doorway, eyeing the food.

"What are you still doing here?"

"Oh, just tidying up records," she said with an exhausted smile.

"You're a workhorse, Candace."

"I love this job."

"Cookie?" I said, holding up the plate of Florentines.

"I couldn't, I shouldn't, gimme one."

"Sit a minute," I said.

She sat next to me and bit into a cookie. "Mmmmm—chocolate is God. I have a confession to make. My late evenings have a way of happening on prenatal conference nights. I hate to see good food go to waste. Of course, that's exactly where it ends up." She patted her midsection.

"Does Dr. Marge stay late a lot?"

"Well, a lot more over the past couple of years," Candace said, giving me a meaningful look.

"Her marriage?"

"Yes."

"What's Mr. Mueller like?"

"Very handsome, very charming. Wouldn't trust him with a wooden nickel."

I could faintly hear Dr. Marge's voice from down the hall.

"And her sons?"

"Great kids, but they're both in college now. She's all alone most nights in this fancy new apartment they bought last year."

"But she must have a full social life."

"Her steadiest companion these days seems to be a certain Mr. Chardonnay. I'm telling you all this because I'm worried about Dr. Marge. That woman has been very good to me."

"And you've been good to her. You're indispensable. By the way, when did you first notice that kids respond to opera?"

"My dad just adored opera, and I remembered how it soothed me as a little girl. So when I got hired here, I suggested we give it a try. And it works. Now parents are always asking me for recommendations on which operas to play at home."

"Have you thought about putting together a CD yourself, sort of an Opera for Kids thing?"

"Now that idea deserves another cookie." She took a big bite. "My nephew is in the music business. I'll ask his advice."

A buzzer sounded—someone had come into the waiting room.

"Let's keep talking, about everything," I said, with a little nod toward Dr. Marge's office. I got up and headed out to greet the Logans.

They were both in their midthirties, rigidly groomed, wearing conservative suits, carrying leather briefcases—and tenser than Tom DeLay in a gay bar. This wasn't going to be easy.

"Hello, I'm Dr. Green," I said, with what I hoped was a warm, professional smile.

"Connie Logan."

"Phil Logan."

No smiles on their end. Just a fixed determination.

"Let me show you around," I said, desperate to keep things casual even as my own anxiety level was rising. Why couldn't my first prenatal have been with a couple of nice, mellow, happily trust-funded, second-generation hippies?

The Logans peeked into the theme rooms with expressions that said, *Don't think you can win us over with cute exam rooms.* They were probably both great lawyers. As parents I wasn't sure they'd be so successful. I thought of that tiny life growing inside Connie Logan's belly, blissfully floating around in his amniotic fluid, little suspecting the regimented reality that awaited him out here in the big world.

"Well, here we are," I said, showing them into my office. "Please have a little snack."

"What kind of fish is that?"

"Bluefish."

Connie Logan pulled out her BlackBerry, punched at it with fierce concentration, and then announced, "Bluefish isn't on my obstetrician's list of Foods that Pregnant Women Should Avoid or Limit."

"Well, that's good to know," I said.

They sat, ramrod-straight, on the small sofa and ignored the food. Phil Logan took a sheaf of papers out of his briefcase.

"Well, it looks as if you've come prepared with questions," I said.

"It's our professional training as attorneys," Connie Logan said. She looked at me with her bright green eyes, and I thought I caught a glimmer of humanity and even humor struggling to survive inside her corporate façade.

"Litigation attorneys," Phil Logan added. I was officially put on notice.

"Well, I'll do my best to answer your questions."

"Having a child is a major event in one's life," Phil Logan announced with stunning insight.

"Doctor, could you tell us at what age you recommend introducing solid foods?" Connie Logan asked.

"At around six months," I began, determined to show them that

I knew my stuff. "Starting solids too early may cause allergies or an overweight baby. Introduce one new food at a time. Rice is a good starter—it's bland, easily digestible, and nonallergenic. Feed from a spoon to help develop eating skills. Then add a new food every four or five days and watch for any allergic reactions. I recommend vegetables first, then fruits. Next, you can add meats. Avoid beef or pork; they can be hard to digest and may contain hormones or antibiotics. Stick with organic food if possible. Finally, you can introduce egg yolks. Egg whites may produce an allergic reaction, so hold off on those until baby's first birthday."

The Logans exchanged a glance, and I could tell I'd cleared the first hurdle. But I had little time to enjoy my minor triumph before they began a rapid-fire barrage of questions:

"What do you think of pacifiers?"

"When should toilet training begin?"

"Cloth or disposable diapers?"

"Are playdates psychologically sound?"

"Will a breast pump cause sagging?"

"Will my hospital phone have call forwarding?"

"Can I have a professional film crew videotape the delivery?"

I answered each question as calmly and methodically as I could, but I could feel my patience wearing thin, especially because it was obvious the Logans had all the answers in front of them and were basically testing me to make sure my knowledge squared with their voluminous research. Then Mr. Logan asked the question that broke the camel's back:

"What is your philosophy of child rearing?"

I took a deep breath and wondered if I should censor myself—but my little voice told me that I was at an important crossroads and that the path I took would determine what kind of doctor I became. I screwed my courage to the sticking place and let it rip:

"My philosophy of child rearing? My philosophy is that parents should relax and let it happen naturally. You're not studying for the bar exam here, you don't need to be a pediatrician, and I don't care how much control you exert in other areas of your life, having a baby is an uncontrollable experience. Let the life you're bringing into the world unfold at its *own* pace, not yours—it's not all about *you,* and a baby isn't the latest must-have accessory. So let go a little bit, be surprised and spontaneous, surrender to the mess. Stop *over*parenting and trust your instincts. *That's* my philosophy."

The Logans sat there stock-still, their lips slightly parted. The room felt suspended for a moment—then they both grabbed plates.

"I'm famished," Connie Logan announced.

"Me too. God, this food looks good."

They eagerly loaded up their plates, popping olives and chips into their mouths. I sat there, a bit stunned.

Connie Logan leaned back in the sofa, took a big bite of bluefish, and asked—with her mouth full—"So, when's my first appointment?"

7

BY THE TIME the Logans left, I was exhausted but exhilarated—I felt I had taken a major step toward finding my voice as a pediatrician. Upper East Side or not, I wasn't going to let myself be intimidated into becoming a doctor who did things by rote. Having a baby was a challenge and a responsibility—at times a mess and a muddle—but it was also a hell of a lot of fun. And it was not rocket science. That was what I wanted to communicate to my parents.

I slipped out of my shoes, put my feet up on my desk, and wiggled my toes. Mmmm. I couldn't wait to get home and curl up with Indian takeout and Carl Hiaasen. Then I remembered—I was meeting Ira to hear his "amazing" news. If he tried to hit me up for money, I'd strangle him.

Only on Madison Avenue could a greasy spoon have pretension—and the Two Guys Coffee Shop had a heavy dose. With its gilded mirrors, tasseled menu, and bimbo hostess the place looked like Donald Trump had waved his magic wand over it. I found Ira lounging in a booth looking like a Eurotrash wannabe in a violet shirt with a vertical black stripe, a gold stud in his ear, and a face coated with bronzer.

"It's the Shell-ster," he said.

"Hi, Ira," I said, sitting down.

"You know something, Sis, you look great." All my annoyance evaporated. "You lost weight."

"A little."

"I'd say a lot, and you're toned. But it's more than that . . . you just look, I don't know, stronger or something."

"Thanks, Ira."

"You're something else, kid," he said with real affection and pride. I was touched—until I remembered what a wily manipulator my brother was.

A waiter appeared, middle-aged and Middle Eastern.

"I'd like a green salad with tuna," I said.

"Just a Campari and soda for me," Ira said with faux suavity.

"Ira—a drink?"

"It's not a drink, Shell, it's a sophisticated aperitif."

Sometimes it's best to quit while you're behind.

"So how are Mom and Dad?" I asked.

"They're wondering why you didn't call."

"I called yesterday."

"I'm just repeating what I was told."

"So, baby brother, what's the big to-do?"

"Shelley, do you know why I'm sitting here looking like an Italian movie star, like the king of the frigging world?"

"No, but I have a feeling I'm about to find out."

"The first thing I'm going to do with the money is move Mom and Dad out of that cramped apartment and into a house in Forest Hills."

"What money?"

"Forest Hills has always been Mom's great dream. I can just see the look on her face when I hand her the keys to the place. And Dad can quit that mail route once and for all. It breaks my heart to see him leave for work every morning, with those bum knees of his."

"Ira, what money?"

Ira snapped his fingers and began to sing some ridiculous disco song.

"Okay, I'm leaving," I said.

"Close your eyes."

I did.

"Open."

I looked across the table, and Ira was holding up some sort of contraption—about the size of a bread box—that had about a dozen straps, belts, and bands protruding and dangling from it.

"Ta-da!" he crowed.

"Ira, what the hell is that thing?"

"What does it look like?"

"Give me a hint."

"Babies . . ."

"It's some sort of accoutrement for infant S&M."

"Very funny, Shelley. It's the Power Papoose."

"Okay."

"Well, you don't seem very excited."

"Oh, I'm bouncing off the walls."

"You know, Shelley, one reason I occasionally overindulge in certain activities is because I'm acting out the subconscious messages my family sends me. Namely: Ira, you're never going to amount to anything."

"Have you been watching Dr. Phil again?"

Ira looked down at the table, crestfallen. I could feel my guilt bubble to the surface. He was my kid brother.

"Hey, cutiepie, tell me about the papoose," I said.

He looked up at me with a sweet, almost guileless smile—and I could tell from the twinkle in his gorgeous blue eyes that I'd been reeled in, yet again. I didn't care; I just wanted him to be happy.

"First let me backtrack a minute," he began.

Ira's drink and my salad arrived.

"Shelley, you remember my friend Joel Halpert from high school, you know, his dad sold personalized ballpoint pens for all occasions?"

"Yes, Ira, I remember Joel Halpert. I especially remember the night Mom and Dad were away when he came over, chugged a six-pack, and asked me to perform oral sex on him."

"Damn, Shelley, I'm sorry, where was I?"

"Schtuping Cindy Belack on my bed."

Ira smiled. "Cindy was good."

"Anyway . . . Joel?"

"Yeah. So Joel took over the business, and he's been branching out into novelties. He does a lot of baby crap, you know, little whirly things that make noise and keep the kid occupied while the parents screw. So he was in Seoul on a buying trip last month—the frigging Koreans *own* the baby-gadget market—and he sees the Power Papoose. He's intrigued, buys ten gross. Then when I told him you were working at Madison Pediatrics, he frigging flipped, he said Marjorie Mueller is a legend in the field, she's in the celebrity columns, treats all these movie-star kids, I mean she's *big*."

I wasn't sure where this was leading, but I wasn't getting a good feeling. Ira was really getting warmed up, and he signaled the waiter for another sophisticated aperitif.

"Anyway, back to the Power Papoose. I mean look at this thing, Shelley, it's genius. You strap in the kid like this . . ." Ira held up the papoose with one hand and fiddled with a couple of the straps. "Or maybe it goes like this . . ." He flipped it upside down, or right side up, and tried again, with no more success. "Anyway, it's a breeze to get the kid in and out. And once he's in, Mom or Dad strap the Power Papoose onto their back and they can take the kid rock climbing, do yoga together, you can even take the kid bungee jumping—think how an experience like that would enrich a baby. If Dad had taken me bungee jumping I'd probably be a CEO right now."

"Ira—"

"I mean look at this brochure."

He handed me a glossy brochure with *Power Papoose Fabulous Fun!* splashed across the top. It was filled with pictures of smiling Koreans, with dazed-looking babies immobilized on their backs, bicycling, playing baseball, eating at restaurants—and yes, there was a picture of a young mother standing on a bridge about to bungee jump.

"Joel says if we can get Dr. Mueller to endorse the Power Papoose it can be bigger than Baby on Board! I mean, Shelley, Baby on Board has made *billions*!"

Just then Christina Allen breezed into the restaurant, looking ravishing in black silk slacks and a tight red mohair sweater.

"Shelley, how are you? My God, you look *great*. The Upper East Side agrees with you. I just popped in to pick up a cheeseburger deluxe." She noticed Ira. "Speaking of cheeseburgers, *who* is this hunk?"

"Oh, this is my brother, Ira. Ira, this is Dr. Christina Allen."

"May I join you?" Christina said, sliding in next to Ira. "It's been a long day—two face-lifts and eighty pounds of lipo-fat—but suddenly I feel full of piss and vinegar. And what do *you* do, Ira?"

"I'm an entrepreneur."

"I hope that means you come up with get-rich-in-a-New-York-minute schemes, but really spend most of your time partying."

"You got my number."

"Ring-a-ding-ding."

"Why don't you show Christina your latest idea?" I said, feeling redundant.

Ira held up the papoose.

"It's brilliant. What is it?" Christina said.

"It's the Power Papoose. Strap your baby into it, and you can do anything."

"I want one. I can take Ingrid waterskiing. Did your sister tell you I'm going to do some work on her?"

"Well, *maybe*," I interjected. "Christina is a plastic surgeon, and I'm thinking of having a few things done—nothing major."

"Ira, your sister doesn't realize how fabulous she is—she has looks and smarts and charm and drive. Believe me, my friend Amanda and I know talent when we see it, and Shelley is one gifted lady." Christina reached over and took my hand. "I mean that, *amigo*."

No one had ever talked to me like that before. Even though we were sitting in a gilded greasy spoon and Christina Allen was glib and a little vulgar, it felt great to hear.

"Thank you, Christina."

"Didn't I always tell you that, Shelley?" Ira said—but he looked at me differently, like he was seeing me for the first time.

"But enough about Shelley," Christina said, turning to Ira. "I want to hear about *you*."

Ira leaned back in the booth and spread his arms across the back, in his glory. "I'm a pretty mysterious and complex guy. Hey, do you know what Woody Allen said when he was asked if sex is dirty?—'Only when it's good.'"

The two of them roared, then leaned into each other and practically nuzzled noses.

I told them I needed to get home and left them to their bondathon.

8

IT WAS 6:30 in the morning, I was in the shower, Arthur was in "the kitchen"—actually a row of mini-appliances along one end of my studio. We weren't having a good morning. We'd gone to see some ridiculous dance concert in the East Village the night before: Four middle-aged couples in leotards acted out the rites of spring to apocalyptic rap music. The choreographer was the brilliant and flirtatious Jennifer Wu, and so Arthur was reverential to the piece, which left me with nothing more profound than a headache. We argued about it on the bus uptown to my place, in the East Twenties off Second Avenue. When we got here, we both sorta-kinda wanted to be romantic. I know I could have used a little tension relief, but I was exhausted and so was he. It was a Thursday night. The argument had left a bitter aftertaste. We just drifted apart on the bed. Now we were paying the price: a morning in which we felt like separate beings going about separate lives.

I walked out of the bathroom with a towel wrapped around me. Arthur turned and looked at me with a forlorn expression, an expression that was my cue to slip into maternal mode, to be solicitous and nurturing and make everything right. Well, this morning I didn't feel up to it. Alison Young was going to be coming in, and after work I was going to Amanda Walker's for our tea. I felt there was an inexorable forward momentum in my life, that good things were happening, things I had earned. Instead of rejoicing in my good fortune, Arthur seemed to feel threatened by it. And this morning I didn't want to have to deal with all that.

"God, Shelley, you really have lost weight," he said, looking at me in the towel.

"I'm so busy, I barely have time to eat," I fibbed. Why was I fibbing to Arthur about my weight loss?

"Well, you're looking good, pumpkin," he said, coming over and gently pushing my damp hair back from my face.

Sometimes being engaged to the world's nicest guy can be tough.

"Thanks," I said.

We stood there looking at each other. It was one of those tentative moments that could go either way—lead to a kiss and renewed closeness or a pulling back. I chose the middle road, giving Arthur a quick kiss. "We've got to get moving here," I said, walking over to my closet.

I had spent more time than I cared to admit thinking about what I should wear to Amanda's. Pants and a sweater? I always felt like pants made me look squat and accentuated what Mom called my rear porch. So I decided to go with a simple black suit, because everyone knows that black is always in style, and a light green blouse to match my eyes. I put the outfit on and looked at myself in the full-length mirror on the back of the closet door. I looked like a high-school guidance counselor dolled up for parent-teacher night—albeit one with a killer rack. I fluffed my hair with my fingers and shook my head with what I hoped was carefree, shampoo-commercial insouciance. You *are* attractive, Shelley, you *are*.

"Well, I'm off," Arthur said, his well-worn leather briefcase in his hand. I'd always loved that briefcase, its leather as soft and lived-in as an old baseball mitt, but today it only looked dated and shabby.

We looked at each other from across my studio. He was at one end, I was at the other, and our relationship was in the middle.

"Have a wonderful day," I said.

"You, too," he said with a sad smile.

9

DR. MARGE HAD MADE IT very clear to me that Madison Pediatrics was a high-volume operation. Unlike plastic surgeons and dermatologists, for example, who can charge astronomical fees for performing relatively simple procedures, pediatricians' fees are limited by the fact that the vast majority of our patients are basically healthy and haven't yet developed an obsession with their perceived physical flaws. Five-year-olds don't come into the office asking for Botox or a little liposuction. And so we have to see a lot of children a day to keep a practice economically viable. Most parents understand this fact of life, and don't make unreasonable demands on our time. But there are exceptions.

Midmorning, I walked into the exam room to find a well-dressed young family settled in for what looked like the long haul. Penny McNulty had given birth to her second child, Ginger, a week earlier, and this was their first office visit. She was sitting on the exam table happily breast-feeding the baby, who had already been weighed and measured by Claire. Fred McNulty was sitting comfortably in a chair, absorbed in the *Times* crossword puzzle. Three-year-old Jeremy was on the floor playing with building blocks, surrounded by a field of crumbs from the crackers he was evidently both eating and smashing with the blocks.

"Good morning," I said.

"Oh, hi," Mr. McNulty said distractedly, peering up from the puzzle.

"Shhhh," Mom admonished. "Ginger likes quiet when she's feeding."

I had a waiting room full of patients.

"What's a six-letter word for *meddle,* third letter is B?" Mr. McNulty asked.

"Kibitz," I answered. He looked up at me in astonishment. "My fiancé is a *Times* crossword fiend," I explained. "Now, I'd like to get started with Ginger's exam."

Dad slowly put aside the newspaper, reached into the breast pocket of his jacket, and pulled out a sheaf of papers. "Actually, we have a few questions before we move on to the exam."

"Of course," I said, although the thickness of the sheaf, coupled with his lackadaisical manner, filled me with a sense of foreboding. I took a quick glance at the pages. They were typed, single-spaced, and each question was numbered. There were a lot of numbers.

"Let's see here, where should we start?" he said, perusing the papers.

"Maybe at number one?" I suggested.

"Hmmm, that's an idea."

"Ginger is a very sensitive baby," Mom whispered. "Let's start with temperatures."

"Good idea, honey. I think the temperature questions are on page two."

Jeremy smashed a cracker with a loud thwack, and crumbs flew to all corners of the room. Parents were discouraged from bringing their other children into the exam room, but I guess the McNultys didn't want Jeremy to suffer separation anxiety, since they were obviously planning an extended stay.

"Jeremy, you'll disturb your sister," Mom whispered.

"Good," Jeremy answered, thwacking another cracker.

"Okey-dokey, why don't we start with this one: What temperature should Ginger's room be?" Mr. McNulty asked.

"Sixty-eight to seventy-two degrees," I answered.

"Okay. And what temperature should her bathwater be?"

I had an image of them actually measuring the water's temperature, and so I hedged my bets and answered, "Lukewarm."

"And what temperature should the room be *during* the bath?"

These were obviously wealthy, well-educated, sophisticated parents, yet their questions fell under the heading of "Hello, Have You Ever Heard of Common Sense?"

"This is your second child, and since Jeremy is obviously doing fine, I suggest you follow the same routines with Ginger that you did with him," I said.

Penny and Fred McNulty looked at me in surprise.

"Doctor, Jeremy was born over three years ago, and the world has changed a lot since then," Dad said.

"It's sad but true. Jeremy was born in a more innocent time," Mom said, looking down at her suckling one-week-old, who faced a future in a brave new world.

"I'm not aware of any change in a child's room temperature requirements," I said.

"Well, we would have been negligent not to make sure," Dad said.

"Profoundly negligent," Mom said.

"May I proceed with the exam?"

"Are you actually going to take my baby from my breast?"

"Unless you want to wait here while I see a few other patients, there's no alternative."

"I don't see why you need to rush us like this," Dad said.

Jeremy thwacked another cracker, then threw a building block across the room and asked, "When is Ginger going back where she came from?"

Thank God for Jeremy, because the mood in the room instantly lightened. The parents and I exchanged a smile.

"I'm afraid you're going to have to get used to your little sister," Dad said.

Mom got down off the table and handed me her baby. I cradled Ginger in my arms and looked down at her tiny body, her chubby limbs and amazing head of flaxen hair, her bright blue eyes looking up at me with innocence and curiosity. I smelled her sweet, fresh smell. I felt that surge of wonder that always swept over me when I was handling a baby in the first weeks of its life. She was so helpless, so pure, so trusting, such a perfect union of the biological and the divine—it was like holding Life itself in my arms.

"She's a beautiful baby," I said to the parents. The three of us looked at each other, putty in Ginger's presence.

"Take her back anyway!" Jeremy said, punctuating his demand with an ear-splitting thwack.

The McNultys and I shared a laugh, and I was able to complete my exam relatively quickly.

My next patient was Ethan Morrow, an eighteen-year-old I'd inherited from Dr. Clark. Ethan was nearing the upper limit to still be seeing a pediatrician. In fact, I had never seen a patient that old before, so I was a little nervous—Elmo trinkets wouldn't win him over.

I walked into the exam room to find a handsome, strapping six-footer, with short, messy blond hair and a ruddy athletic complexion, sitting on the exam table in his street clothes. What was missing from Ethan was that unmistakable air of confidence and entitlement that most of my patients had. In fact, he looked anxious.

"Hi, Ethan, I'm Dr. Green."

"Nice to meet you, Doctor."

I indicated his clothes. "Don't you want me to examine you?"

"I really have no complaints, Doctor." He paused. "Well, actually, I guess that's not really true. I do have one complaint."

"Shoot."

"Girls."

"Girls?"

"Girls."

"Girls in general? A specific girl? I'm here to listen and help in any way I can."

"See, I just finished my freshman year at Penn, and I made the lacrosse team. I played all during high school, and I guess I'm pretty good. Anyway, there are all these sports groupies at Penn. I mean, I'm not really a party guy. I want to study engineering. I'm kind of a nerd, really, even though I may not look like one."

"I see," I said, having no idea where he was going with this.

"Well, the girls at Penn aren't interested in my inner nerd, they're, um, interested in my lacrosse-playing body. I mean, they're *very* interested, I mean they're unbelievably aggressive, Doctor, they come on to me all the time. And I don't like to disappoint them."

Ethan looked down at his hands, which were entwined and tightly clenched.

"So what you're telling me is that you've been sexually active this year."

"Whoa, have I ever. Doctor, I could have sex every day of the week if I wanted it. Three times a day!"

Now he was starting to sweat.

"So, Ethan, am I right in saying that you're feeling a lot of pressure to have sex?"

"Pressure? How about coercion? They knock on my door at

midnight, try to get me drunk, invite me to parties that turn out to be just the two of us. One girl gave me oral sex under the table at the library while I was studying for a calculus exam. It was distracting."

I'd read about how sexually aggressive girls had become at some elite colleges, but hearing it firsthand certainly brought it to life. What did it say about our culture? About competition among girls? About the aftereffects of feminism? But the question that vexed me most was: What did Ethan want from me?

"Well, Ethan, this certainly sounds like it's interfering with your education. Is there a medical element that you wanted to discuss with me? Something to do with sexually transmitted diseases, maybe?"

Ethan took a deep breath, exhaled, and spit out, "I need a prescription for Viagra!"

"Viagra?"

"I mean they come on so strong, it's intimidating, and sometimes I can't, you know, *perform.* I like a little foreplay, a little affection, it helps me get in the mood . . . but to most of these girls I'm just, well, I'm just a penis. A large penis. That's part of the problem. My penis is large. Very large. And word gets around. It becomes like a competitive thing with the girls. I'm nothing to them but a trophy penis."

Okay.

"None of them want to talk about my feelings, about my dreams for the future, about the world's great bridges and tunnels. It's all just wham-bam, thank-you-Sam. Well, I can't just get an erection on demand. I need to feel some kind of emotional connection. That's why I need the Viagra. If I could just get an erection and get it over with and get back to studying—I just want to study."

Viagra as a study tool—now there's a fresh perspective. Maybe Pfizer could work up some ads on the theme.

"Ethan, I think you should talk to a therapist about developing other ways to deal with this issue. You really have to learn how to say no."

"I'm dreading the summer. I took a job as a counselor at a boys' camp in Maine just to get away from girls—and then I found out there was a sister camp across the lake. I have nightmares of a flotilla of girls paddling across the lake in the middle of the night, surrounding my cabin, and gang-raping me. I'm scared."

"Ethan, I think you should talk to a therapist soon, before you go to camp."

"I feel like I'm a penis with a person attached."

"Ethan, I'm going to call the psychiatrist right now."

I did just that and got him an appointment for the following week. He was very grateful.

In the early afternoon I retreated to my office for a quick salad and paperwork review. As I ate and made notes, I was struck by how much of my job exceeded the parameters of mere pediatrician. Like Ethan, many of the older children in particular needed a confidant, friend, and role model as much as they needed a doctor. Dr. Marge sometimes referred to us as sculptors, saying that we molded lives, families, and futures. I had to agree. It was an enormous privilege and responsibility, one that I vowed to cherish and respect. I polished off my salad and got up, eager to get back to work.

Alison Young sat on the edge of the exam table, her thin legs dangling over the side. She looked pale and wan. I'd asked Candace to schedule her for a full half hour. Her father, who was apparently a world-famous economist, hadn't accompanied her. She was with her housekeeper, Mrs. Figueroa, who had been with her the day we first met.

"Alison, it's so good to see you again."

"It's nice to see you, Dr. Green." She smiled at me, the sweetest smile—sad and a little bit lost. I couldn't help imagining Alison on that day last fall, standing in front of school with her knapsack, waiting for her mom to come around the corner . . .

"So, how are you feeling today?" I asked.

"I feel about the same. Weak and tired."

"Anything else?"

"No, not really. I just feel tired all over."

"All the time?"

"Pretty much."

"How's your appetite?"

"I don't have much of one."

"Can you tell me how long you've been feeling this way?"

She sighed heavily, and a faraway look came into her eyes. I suspected she was remembering that day. I was hoping she'd bring up her mother, but I didn't feel I should be the one to do it.

"I'm not sure," she said finally.

"Okay. Now I want to give you a complete exam. Is that all right?"

She nodded.

I conducted my exam with the gentlest touch, trying to communicate to Alison that she was cared for, safe. I found no swollen lymph nodes, no tenderness over the bones and joints, no liver or spleen enlargement, no heart murmur. Her neurological exam was negative and her lungs were clear. In spite of the fact that there were no obvious signs of systemic disease or inflammation, her pallor and listlessness were troubling. Of course, a psychosomatic response to her mother's death was foremost in my mind, but first I wanted to rule out all possible disease etiologies.

"Alison, I hate to have to put you through it again, but I'd like to take some more blood. Would that be all right?"

"Yes."

"Thank you."

Usually I had Claire take blood, for a couple of reasons. First, it saved time. And second, having blood withdrawn can be frightening, even traumatic, for a child, and I felt it was better not to have the

pediatrician herself associated with those experiences. But I wanted
to show Alison that I was taking a special interest in her. She turned
her head away but otherwise sat stoically through the process.

"You're a very brave young lady, Alison. And I'm going to do everything in my power to help you feel better. There are just a couple of
things I'd like you to do, if you don't mind. The first is to give me a
urine sample. And Claire will give you a kit for a stool sample that you
can take home and then send back to us. Would you do that for me?"

"Yes." Alison was silent for a moment, as if she was thinking, and
then she looked at me and asked, "Do you know about my mother?"

"Yes, Alison, I do."

There was a slight pause, and then she nodded her head and
looked down. She looked so fragile in her short-sleeved white blouse
and gray wool skirt, her arms and legs thin and pale—a little girl in a
big city.

"Thank you for being so nice to me," she said.

"It's my pleasure."

"I know why you're doing it."

"You do?"

"Yes. Because you feel sorry for me. Just like everyone at school."

"That might be part of the reason. But I'm your doctor, Alison,
and you're not feeling well. I want to find out why and help you to
feel better."

"Do you think I have a disease?"

"I honestly don't know yet. What I do know is that something
very hard and very sad happened to you."

"Did you ever meet my mother?"

"No, I'm sorry, I didn't. I wish I had. I'm sure she was a very special person."

Alison looked down at her hands for what seemed like a long
time. Then suddenly she looked at me with flashing, angry eyes.

"Shut up, and don't tell me about my mother, you never even met her!" Her cheeks flushed, her chest rose and fell as she took fast shallow breaths. "She was my mother, not yours, so just shut up!"

Alison looked back down at her hands, which were now balled into fists in her lap. She stayed that way for a long time. Her breathing gradually deepened. Then, without looking up, she said, "That was rude of me, and I apologize."

Every molecule in my being wanted to take her in my arms, to hold her, to smother her with kisses. Instead I said, "I accept your apology."

There was a long silence, and I felt as if Alison was testing me, to see if she could trust me, if I really cared. At one point she looked up at me, and our eyes met. Then she looked back down, and there was more silence. Finally she said, "I wrote a report on the flora and fauna of Central Park."

"That sounds interesting."

"Do you know that there are foxes in Central Park?"

"Really?"

She nodded her head. "Of course, rats *are* the most common mammal in the park, but even they contribute something to the ecosystem—the foxes and the owls love to eat them. Over forty kinds of birds nest in the park." As she spoke her voice grew lively and animated, her eyes brightened.

"I've seen groups of bird-watchers."

"There are over thirty kinds of wildflowers that grow in the park, and seven varieties of mushrooms. There are four major bodies of water, two miles of streams, and at least eight kinds of fish."

"That's amazing, Alison. I'll never look at the park the same way again. Thank you for opening my eyes."

"You're welcome," she said.

Then I couldn't stop myself. I took her face in my hands and kissed her on the forehead.

10

THE WALKERS LIVED in a stately prewar apartment building on Fifth Avenue in the Sixties—one of those buildings that spoke of wealth, security, and tiny dogs in Burberry coats. My father's mail route started a few blocks north, so I knew the type of building and felt a tiny surge of triumph arriving as a guest. A doorman, smart in his uniform, opened the door for me with great aplomb. The lobby was vast and filled with cozy seating arrangements that looked like no one ever sat in them. Another uniformed man approached me.

"Hello, I'm here to visit Amanda Walker."

"Dr. Green?"

"Yes," I said, feeling important.

"Go right up," he said with a little bow, indicating an open elevator. A third uniformed man appeared to whisk me up to the Walker penthouse.

The elevator doors opened onto a private lobby—larger than my apartment—that was done up in a modern minimalist style with sleek wooden benches, frameless mirrors, a stainless-steel umbrella stand, and abstract black-and-white photos in silver frames. The elevator closed behind me, and I stood there, suddenly feeling small and out of place. I took a deep breath and reminded myself that I was a doctor, a proud pediatrician, and that I was here on at least a quasi-professional basis.

I rang the bell—which didn't ring but played several bars of "Girls Just Want to Have Fun." Mmmm. Then the enormous door swung open to reveal not the maid I had been expecting but Amanda herself, looking gorgeous in an offhand, thrown-together way—white linen slacks, a powder blue cashmere V-neck pullover, and just enough gold jewelry to make her sparkle a little. I suddenly felt overdressed— and huge, of course. I always felt like a different species from tiny-boned women—I was Gulliver and they were the Lilliputians.

"Shelley!" Amanda cried, grabbing my hands and giving me a kiss on the cheek. "Come in."

She led me into an enormous round entryway with a vaulted ceiling and an inlaid marble floor. A round table in the center was topped with a towering, cascading bouquet filled with flowers I'd never seen before. I tried to disguise my gawking as mild interest. Opening up from the entry was a wide hall lined with paintings in heavy frames and, through an archway, a living room that stretched off toward some distant horizon. The room had a fireplace at either end and seemed to be divided into three or four smaller living rooms centered around groupings of chairs and couches. Everything glittered and glistened and shone.

"Hi, Amanda."

"It's so wonderful to see you. You look *sensational*," she said. She crossed to a brass door and pushed a button beside it. An elevator door opened. Didn't I just get off an elevator? This one had buttons marked 1, 2, and 3, and Amanda pressed 3.

"It's such a lovely day, I thought we could have tea outside," she said.

We stepped out of the elevator, and she led me down a wide hall that suddenly opened into a dazzling sunroom-conservatory. It was a corner room and two of the walls were entirely glass; the other two were painted with a mural of a tropical garden. All the furniture was white wicker with yellow floral cushions. The effect was dazzling if a bit jarring—Palm Beach in the sky. A young blond man was sprawled on a couch talking on his cell phone. I recognized him as Marcus, Amanda's hair stylist, from the day when she had burst into the waiting room with Smith. He gave us a wave and a smile. The French doors were open and Amanda led me out to the terrace.

Wow!

The balcony seemed to wrap around the entire floor. In the distance to the left of me was an elegant lap pool set in a bosky grotto. To the right, again in the distance, was a slice of perfect suburban lawn with a children's play set. We were standing in the middle, a tiled expanse dotted with chairs and tables, chaise lounges, trellises, potted plants and flowers. Everything was immaculate, lush, and somehow both casual and elegant. Most stunning of all was the view: Central Park stretched below us in the full bloom of spring—a great green magic carpet. Across the park were the stately buildings of Central Park West, and to the south the towers of Midtown. It was the most spectacular sight I'd ever seen in my life.

"Amanda, this is . . ." But I couldn't finish the sentence—it was indescribable.

"The spoils of Wall Street," she said, sitting at a round glass-topped table set for two. I joined her. "Listen, Marcus was here to give me a little trim, and I asked him to stay and give you one. Is that all right?"

"Yes. Thank you."

"*J'arrive,*" Marcus said, clipping a smock around me. "Have scissors, will travel." He stood back and appraised me, narrowing his eyes. "You have no idea how great-looking you are, do you?"

"I told you she was a diamond in the rough," Amanda said, as Marcus began cutting, swift and confident.

A middle-aged maid appeared.

"Angie, this is Dr. Green."

"Hi," I said.

"Hello," Angie said with a warm smile.

"Tea, coffee, wine?" Amanda asked.

"Coffee sounds wonderful."

"Cappuccino, espresso, regular, decaf, we could make you a coffee frappe?"

Being rich means having a lot of choices.

"A cappuccino sounds wonderful."

"I'll have a glass of Sancerre," Amanda said. "I have to go to a benefit tonight at the Frick, which is *the* stuffiest place in the entire city. I try to nurture a little buzz before I go—makes all those old-money types a lot easier to take. They think Jerry and I are so tacky and nouveau, but really they're enraged because he's a hundred times richer than they are. No matter what the old families claim, in this town money trumps everything."

"I'll take your word for it," I said. Marcus tilted my chin to the left, a light deft touch.

"Your innocence is coming to an end. I invited you here to make you an offer. Before we get to that, I did want to thank you again for your quick, calm action with Smith."

"I was just doing my job."

"You were doing it superbly, Shelley, and I admire that."

Amanda seemed so relaxed and considerate and sincere. I really did feel as if I had stepped into another world, a world where nobody shouted across the living room or fought over the last slice of

Entenmann's, where people could afford to be gracious and generous, where life was full of ease and style, sophistication and possibility. Was I being naïve? Probably. But it was all so heady that I didn't care.

"Why, thank you, Amanda."

"I've asked the little monsters to come say hello," she said.

As if on cue, Smith and Jones appeared, followed at a discreet distance by two nannies. Smith was wearing a sundress. Jones had on jeans, a red T-shirt, and a Yankees cap. They looked absolutely adorable, almost like regular children. What gave them away was that unmistakable attitude of entitlement. I reminded myself that they couldn't help it—they *were* entitled. The nannies were nondescript women in their twenties who reminded me of the personal assistants that celebrities like Anna Nicole Smith had in those trashy celebrity reality shows that I adored. (By the way, isn't *celebrity reality* an oxymoron?)

"Smith, you remember Dr. Green, and this is my son, Jones."

"Hi," Smith said.

Jones approached and stuck out his hand. I shook it and he said, "How do you do?"

"It's nice to see you both," I said.

"I hope you'll be seeing a lot more of them," Amanda said. "Kim, Alexa, why don't you take the kids down to the playground."

Without a word, the nannies led their charges down to the lawn, where they began to play. It was a little bit surreal to be in this opulent aerie twenty stories above Manhattan, looking over at two kids playing on a perfect bright green lawn with its state-of-the-pocketbook play set.

"They adore you," Amanda announced, as Angie brought out my cappuccino, Amanda's wine, and several platters of finger sandwiches and tiny, elaborately decorated cookies. The rich also had better cookies.

Marcus popped a cookie in his mouth, announcing, "Five dollars."

"Christina tells me you have a very hunky brother," Amanda said, taking a sip of her wine.

I had thought Ira would be an embarrassment in this world—after all, he was everywhere else—but I guess things were topsy-turvy in the rarefied air.

"Being his sister, *hunk* isn't the first word that comes to my mind, but women have always found him catnip," I said.

"Christina certainly does. And I understand she's going to do a little work on you in return for you caring for Ingrid."

I felt myself blush and took a sip of the cappuccino.

"I'm considering it," I said sheepishly.

"Be very careful, Shelley," Marcus said. "You don't want to end up with the cookie-cutter look. Speaking of cookies . . ." He popped two more into his mouth. "Ten dollars, fifteen dollars."

"Marcus loves to tease. Those cookies do *not* cost five dollars each . . . they cost four eighty-five." Amanda and Marcus exchanged wry smiles. I was dying for one of the cookies but took a tiny sandwich instead, which turned out to have nothing in it but cucumber. "Shelley, can I be honest with you?"

"Of course."

"I can tell that you're trying to get out of somewhere, move up in the world. It's written all over you. The fabulous thing about Manhattan is that you can invent yourself here, and if you have enough talent, energy, drive, beauty, wit, charm, sparkle, *whatever*, you can build an amazing life. One of the great things about having a lot of money is that it puts you in a position to help people, encourage them. I believe, and so does Christina, that you could do well in this world. You could have a very exciting life, a *big* life, as Oprah likes to say."

"All done," Marcus announced, taking off the smock and fluffing my hair.

"Sweet," Amanda said.

Marcus held a hand mirror up in front of me. My hair, which usually sat in a defiant explosion on top of my head, a separate entity from the face below, now actually related to my face, framing it with soft curls, bringing out my eyes, highlighting my cheekbones, making me look, if not pretty, then distinctive, and maybe even attractive.

"It's lovely, Marcus, thank you."

"My pleasure, doll," he said with a warm smile. "You're a very striking lady."

"Take these as your tip," Amanda said, offering him the plate of cookies.

"I couldn't," he said, taking the plate. "I'm off to cut Cruela de Kissinger." And with that, he left.

"His pet name for Nancy Kissinger," Amanda said. "He also cuts Hillary Clinton."

"What does he call her?"

"Cupcake. And speaking of big lives, Marcus grew up in a trailer in the Tennessee woods—his real name is Elmer—and now he owns a townhouse in the Village and is flown all over the world by fawning clients." She took a sip from her glass. "This wine is yummy . . . no, no, it has a certain *insouciance*. I have a wine consultant, she's educating me on the vino lingo, isn't that decadent? The truth—I'd be happy with a cheap Chianti."

Just then the sexiest man I'd ever seen in my life strode out onto the terrace. He was lean, lanky, about forty, handsome in a rugged Robert Redford way, with impossibly thick brown hair that spilled over his forehead and sparkling green eyes. He was wearing faded jeans, a thick brown leather belt with a gold buckle, and a blue oxford shirt with the top two buttons open. I struggled to contain my unfamiliar response: lust.

"It's the pool boy," Amanda said with a sly, seductive smile.

"Very funny, Amanda," he said. Then he looked at me and smiled—it wasn't the blazing movie star smile I expected, but a casual friendly grin. "Hi there, I'm Josh," he said. Then he reached for a sandwich and took three.

"Shelley, this is Josh Potter. Josh, this is Dr. Shelley Green," Amanda said.

"Hello," my dry mouth managed.

"What brings you to town?" Amanda asked him, before turning to me. "Josh lives out in Amagansett."

"I'm here for the Sierra Club fund-raiser," Josh said.

"I love the environment," I said idiotically. And then I grabbed a sandwich. And then I put it back. And then I said: "It's so important. The planet and trees and stuff."

Josh laughed and said, "Especially the stuff."

I laughed back in a charming, self-deprecating way—wait, that's not true. I guffawed like a comic with flop sweat. I wished there was some duct tape handy so I could shut myself up.

"Listen, Mandy, mind if I take a quick swim?"

"You're so considerate to ask," Amanda said as Josh headed down to the pool. "My husband's oldest friend, he uses our place as his personal hotel. Shelley, you're drooling."

"I am?" I reached for a napkin and vigorously wiped my mouth.

"I mean metaphorically. He *is* a world-class hunk, isn't he?"

I glanced down to the pool—Josh was stripping out of his clothes, down to his blue-and-white-striped boxers. The soft afternoon sunlight played on his muscles and sinews. His dark chest hair trailed down to his stomach and then disappeared into his shorts. I pulled my eyes away.

"Josh is bright and fun, a bit immature, but devoted to environmental causes. And, yes, Shelley, he's single."

Just then the middle-aged woman I remembered from Amanda's visit to Madison Pediatrics came out on the terrace.

"Mrs. Walker, we have *a problem*," she said in an English accent.

"Phyllis, you remember Dr. Green."

"Of course. How nice to see you again," Phyllis said.

Phyllis was thin, with short hair, pencil legs, and an erect carriage. She was wearing a sensible navy suit.

"What sort of problem?" Amanda asked her.

"You accepted dinner at Anne Bass's on the same night as the Cooper-Hewitt benefit."

"I'll skip the Cooper-Hewitt," Amanda said breezily, taking a sip of wine.

"But, Mrs. Walker, you're *on the committee* for the Cooper-Hewitt," Phyllis said, as if it was the most important piece of information ever uttered.

"Hmmm."

"I've asked you on numerous occasions not to accept invitations without first checking with me," Phyllis said sternly. She was beginning to remind me of an English version of Mrs. Saperstein, my grim grade-school principal.

Amanda shot me an amused glance. "I've been a bad girl."

"You may find this riotously amusing, Mrs. Walker. *I* do not. I take responsibility seriously."

"All right, let's go get this straightened out. Shelley, I'll be back in two minutes." Amanda picked up her wineglass and followed Phyllis into the apartment.

I looked toward the pool—Josh was doing a yoga posture, holding up one leg behind him and reaching out with the opposite arm. He saw me watching. "Hey, Shelley, why don't you come on in for a swim?"

"No, thanks," I said.

He walked toward me. "Oh come on, it's heated."

"Really, I don't have a bathing suit."

"There's a ton of them in the pool house," he said, pointing to a small modern structure past the pool.

I would have ridden the A train naked at rush hour before I changed into a bathing suit in front of that god.

"Maybe next time," I said.

He grabbed a couple more sandwiches. "I've heard about you. You saved Smith from a lifetime of paralysis."

"I didn't, but I've stopped denying it," I said, feeling marginally more comfortable now that we were discussing pediatrics.

"There you go. In this world people take credit for everything they can. Boy, it's a beautiful day," he said, sitting down, stretching out his legs and turning his face to the sun. "You'd never know on a day like today that the sun has become Mother Nature's lethal weapon. Why don't you come to the benefit with me? I've got an extra ticket."

"Are you serious?" I asked.

He looked at me with his dazzling green eyes. "Of course I am. Why wouldn't I be?"

"I don't know. We just met."

"What better way to get to know you? It's just another dull benefit for a worthy cause."

He wanted to get to know me better? Really? "It's definitely the best offer I've had today, but unfortunately I've got plans." I didn't feel the need to tell him what they were: Arthur had booked us on a Taste of Flatbush tour—we were going to graze our way through six ethnic cuisines. And I wasn't even eating.

"Well, let me jump in. I'll give you my card just in case your plans change." He walked down to the pool and dove in. My breathing returned to some semblance of normal.

Amanda reappeared, holding her empty wineglass, and waved to her children.

"I pay that woman eighty-five thousand dollars a year to be rude to me. And she's worth twice that," she said, refilling the glass. Standing with one hand on her hip, she looked down at Josh, who was doing little dips and dives in the water. "I love watching him swim. By the way, he likes you."

"Right," I said.

"Believe me, Shelley, I can tell. Josh is an interesting guy. His first wife left him for a woman. And he's not into bimbos, even though he is one."

"What does he do for a living?"

"Not much. He has family money, although no one is sure exactly how much. He was an actor in his twenties, but he gave that up and dabbled in documentary filmmaking. Now he's involved in the whole open-land thing out in the Hamptons. I don't think he's had a *job* job in years. He's a little bit adrift, but when you look like he does, the world is forgiving. You'd forgive him a little underemployment, wouldn't you?"

"I already have."

"So have I. Listen, it's time for me to get to my agenda. But first, my butter-up, defenses-down present."

She handed me a black box labeled DOLCE & GABANNA. I opened it and took out a little black dress that screamed sex, money, and Sarah Jessica Parker.

"It's gorgeous."

"Christina told me how much weight you'd lost. And, yes, Shelley, you *can* wear that dress. Now that you're putty in my hands, here's the story. My husband is obsessed with Jones's and Smith's health. Freaks out at the slightest symptom. And Jones has a touch of asthma. We have a place out in East Hampton, and we would like to set aside a room for you for the summer and have you come out as often as you reasonably feel you can. Of course, we'll pay you a fat per diem for every day you come. I've discussed it with Dr. Marge, and she says it can be worked out. So how does all this sound to you?"

I was surprised, flattered, and a little wary. Did I really want to get this involved with the Walker family this quickly? I had barely been in practice a month and the doors to the kingdom were being thrown open, and I was being invited in. Should I discuss it with Arthur? I looked around the terrace, over to the children, down at the sandwiches, and then over to the pool, where Josh was sitting on the edge, gently kicking at the water. Admission: It wasn't just the money, or the kids, or the sandwiches that made up my mind.

"That sounds like a wonderful offer and I accept."

Amanda poured a glass of wine and handed it to me.

"Welcome to my world," she said—and we toasted.

11

I GOT HOME in time to take a quick shower and change into something comfortable for my trip to Flatbush. I thought back to the afternoon on the terrace, the crazy luxury of the sky-high lawn and pool, and the crazier way Josh had looked at me, as if he really approved of what he saw. For most of my life, I'd pretty much avoided making eye contact with my body, afraid of the fleshy horrors I might spot, but as I soaped up under the warm water, I dared myself to look. I really had lost more weight than I realized. I wasn't exactly Renee-Zellweger-in-*Chicago* skinny, thank God, but even I could appreciate a new tautness and definition. I'd spent so much of my life being ashamed of my breasts, trying to disguise them with loose-fitting tops and too-tight bras. But I'd seen that gleam in Josh's eyes and the way his look lingered on my chest. What if they really were . . . beautiful?

As I dried off, I wondered what I should wear. Something plain, of course. The thought of schlepping around sampling ethnic food with Arthur and a group of intelligent, sincere, friendly people . . . *yawn.* I was tired of hiding my light—and my boobs—under a bushel. I opened the Dolce & Gabanna box and took out the little black dress and held it up. Could I really get into it? And even if I did, would it be appropriate for Flatbush?

I got into the dress and looked at myself in the full-length mirror. It had a neckline that was both scooped and V-line, in other words it scooped down—way down—to the V. The dress ended midthigh and my thighs actually looked pretty decent. I slipped into some simple, sling-back black heels. My new haircut was shining, my skin was glowing from the shower. I felt . . . sexy.

I sat on my bed, counted to twenty, took a deep breath, and picked up the phone. Thank God I got Arthur's machine.

"Hi, honey, it's me. Listen, I'm so exhausted and frazzled, I'm really not up to Flatbush tonight. You go and have a great time. Love you."

I hung up and redialed quickly, before I was hit by an avalanche of second guesses and guilt.

"Hello," Josh answered.

"Hi, Josh, it's Shelley."

"Why, hi there."

"Listen, my plans for tonight were canceled. Does your invitation still stand?"

"It most certainly does. I'll meet you outside the Puck Building at eight."

I hung up and stood there in mild shock. This was the most un-me thing I had ever done. For a moment I considered calling Josh back and canceling—but then I reminded myself that it was just another dull fund-raiser for a noble cause. It certainly wasn't a *date*. It was a good place to make professional contacts.

12

IT WAS A GORGEOUS New York evening, warm but dry, with a hint of a breeze—a pale three-quarter moon floated in the indigo sky. As I rode downtown in the cab, I was buzzing with anxious excitement.

The Puck Building was awash in lights, two sleek windmills flanked the entrance, and a banner was stretched across the front reading COOL IT! A small crowd, young and glamorous, was milling out front—and there was Josh. Wanting to look like I arrived at these things all the time and remembering all the pictures I'd seen of movie stars getting out of cars, I opened the cab door and stuck out a leg—and my foot landed on something soggy and gross. I looked down and saw a half-eaten Big Mac. Josh saw me and came over. I got out and smiled at him much too brightly—anything to distract attention from my feet.

"Wow!" he said, and he sounded like he meant it. "You look incredible."

"Thanks, you look pretty good yourself."

Josh was still wearing jeans but had on a dark blazer and an iridescent red tie—the effect was sort of Colorado meets Manhattan.

He took me by the arm and led me into the building. The grand ballroom had been decorated with tall grasses, spiky ferns, and other woodsy plants I couldn't identify, all gorgeously lit—the effect was dreamy, romantic. Then I saw Susan and Tim, Reese and Ryan, Harrison and Calista, Meryl, Viggo *oh-my-God-Viggo!*—my head was spinning so fast I thought I might get whiplash. Another dull fundraiser?

I was sure that everyone was wondering what *I* was doing there. Then I realized that *I* was the only one wondering what I was doing there. Then I remembered that I was a successful young doctor, that I had been invited by Josh Potter, that I had on a beautiful dress, and that I had one of the best sets of boobs in the whole city.

I started to relax and enjoy myself.

Josh kept saying hello to people and introducing me. Everyone was young and charming, and I couldn't help noticing that several men ran their eyes up and down my body. There was music playing, reggae, and everyone glowed. There was a festive excited energy in the room that lifted me up like a wave and tossed my spirits into the air.

We made our way to the bar and Josh handed me a glass of white wine. I sipped it and watched as he chatted and laughed with an old friend, a handsome black man, something about wetlands, but I didn't care because—oh my God, Robert DeNiro *smiled* at me and I smiled *back*, like I did it every day, smiled at Robert DeNiro—and then Josh's friend told me his wife was pregnant and that they would call me and I smiled and said "Wonderful" and I was so close to Josh that I could smell his pine soap.

Pretty soon I was on my second glass of wine. Josh and I started dancing and he danced close to me and all around bodies were undulating and people were laughing and glittery and Josh was looking at me in a way that made me very nervous but I loved it and then he leaned in and whispered in my ear:

"Want to take a little walk?"

I nodded.

We walked out into the night air and headed downtown.

"That's quite a scene in there," Josh said.

"It sure is."

"I'm not really much of a party guy. I prefer small dinner parties where you can really talk. Or one on one."

The crowds and the traffic of the city swirled around us, but I felt cut off from it all, as if Josh and I were on some moonlit country road by ourselves. We kept bumping into each other, and ended up walking along with our shoulders touching. I tried to make a few comments about the Kyoto Protocol, but intelligent conversation was pretty much out of the question.

"Listen, I have the keys to a friend's loft. It's less than two blocks from here. Want to come up and raid his liquor cabinet?"

I felt warning signals go off in my body, along with a panicky kind of excitement. "I think I've had enough to drink."

"He's got coffee, too."

"I have to get up early."

"It's decaf."

"Never touch the stuff."

"I see," he said. We walked on for another block. "So I bet you'll have an excuse for every suggestion I make, won't you, Dr. Green?"

"Oh, God," I said. I stopped and looked into those beautiful eyes. "I certainly hope not."

The loft was in a converted industrial building. Josh unlocked the outer door and we walked to the elevator. We got in and he put in a key and pressed a button and up we went. The elevator doors opened on an immense gleaming space with light pouring in from a wall of windows. Josh rested his hand lightly on my lower back as I stepped out of the elevator.

I looked around but nothing really registered. Josh went over to the kitchen.

"What can I get you—soda, juice, tea?"

"Just a glass of water."

We were talking in whispers, hushed, lit by the glow of the city out the windows.

There were stools by the kitchen island and I sat on one.

"Are you okay?" Josh asked, as he filled a glass with ice. I loved watching him move.

"I guess I feel a little dizzy."

"Water is good for dizzy." He came over and held out the glass. "Can I tell you something?"

I nodded.

"I have a strong urge to kiss you right now."

I took a sip of water, hoping my hand wouldn't shake.

"May I?" he asked.

I nodded again.

He took the glass out of my hand and set it down. Then he leaned in and we kissed.

I sort of fell off the stool, against him, and he wrapped his arms around me. We kept kissing and I reached up and touched his face, ran my hand down his neck.

He took me by the hand and led me over to the sofa and then we were making out like a couple of teenagers and then his jacket was off and his shirt and then he reached behind me and unzipped my dress and it slithered off me and then his pants were off and we were in our underwear sprawled out on the couch and our hands were all over each other and his body was so strong and his kisses so tender and then my bra was off and he was kissing me there and then he leaned over the side of the sofa and reached into his pants for a condom.

"I have to go," I said.

His mouth fell open.

"I'm sorry, I'm engaged," I said, sitting up.

"Oh."

I stood up and began struggling into my clothes. And then it came, an explosion of what I think of as Shelley's verbal vomit, an outpouring of shame and insecurity that went something like this: "Oh, it's not your fault, I mean how could you know, it's my fault, it's all my fault, let's just pretend it never happened, it's not your problem that I'm engaged, it's my problem, you didn't do anything wrong, I did."

Josh remained a gentleman, absorbing my barrage with a look of understated empathy.

"Let me come down and get you a cab."

"Oh, that's okay, I'm a big girl," I said, as hot tears welled up behind my eyes.

13

MY CAB RIDE HOME was the mother of all emotional roller coasters. I sat there in semi-shock as waves of guilt and remorse and anxiety washed over me. I kept thinking of Arthur, seeing his face, hearing his voice. I imagined him somewhere out in the wilds of Flatbush sampling tapas and bragging about "my fiancée, the pediatrician." Meanwhile his fiancée, the pediatrician, was *thisclose* to schtuping some stranger in a loft. I was a terrible person, an amoral slut, a hussy. I had screwed up the one true thing in my life. I curled my legs up under me, burrowed into the corner of the seat, and started to cry.

I wanted to hate Josh, to blame him. Wasn't I the victim of a predatory letch who took advantage of my naïveté and inability to hold my wine? In a word: no. I wanted him at least as badly as he wanted me. In fact, I felt guilty for leading him on. That was a pretty unfair thing to do.

I took some deep breaths, and my tears stopped.

Traffic was heavy and the cab stopped at a light. There was a restaurant on the corner, beautifully lit, twinkly, full of beautiful people talking, laughing. Skyscrapers glowed in the distance and as the cab began to crawl uptown we passed stores, cafés, people—a panorama of Manhattan, all light and luxe and lovely, a city suffused with possibility and a comforting, starry buoyancy.

I flashed back to the party and Josh and our walk down to the loft, and the first kiss and the sofa and everything. It had all happened so quickly, seemed to have a life of its own—it felt like an out-of-body experience.

I laughed. I'm sorry, I couldn't help it, but I did.

The laugh triggered more tears, of guilt and confusion and remorse, but there was something else going on, too. Was it exhilaration? I had done something stupid and wrong, yes, but I had also broken out of my good-girl bubble, been spontaneous and wild for the first time in my life.

Fine, Shelley, so you burst out of your bubble, but at what cost? Only your integrity. And there was Arthur again in my heart's eye—kind, charming, loving Arthur. Being engaged to him means something; it's a pact, a bond, a commitment between the two of you. You broke that commitment—and that is just plain wrong. Wrong wrong wrong.

The cab pulled up in front of my building. My little corner of the city was hardly glamorous, with its cramped bodega and dingy pizza parlor, squat brick buildings, dirty sidewalks. I hurried upstairs, slipped out of the dress, and ran myself a hot bath into which I poured every salt, oil, and foaming gel I could find. I made a cup of tea, put on a k. d. lang CD, grabbed the latest *InStyle* and my cell phone, and slid into the tub—*ahhhhhh*. Baths had been my refuge since I was a teenager, a way for me to escape the chaos of my family, a place to think, to soothe, to renew, to read. Of course, in those days I'd been reading Jane Austen and Edith Wharton, but we won't dwell on my literary devolution.

I was just getting into the perfect brain candy—a probing examination of Cameron's shopping habits—when my phone rang. I looked at the number: It was Arthur. *Oh God.*

"Hi, honey," I said, trying to sound casual as my heart thumped in my chest.

"Flatbush was so much fun—I had a wild boar samosa! How are you feeling, cutie?"

"All right. I'm taking a hot bath, getting ready for bed."

"My bathtub baby. How was your night?"

Here it comes, the Big Lie: "Uneventful."

"I missed you."

I could feel the tears about to come. Then another call came in: It was Josh.

No way I was taking that call!

"Arthur, there's another call, can you hold a sec? . . . Hello?"

"Hi, Shelley, it's Josh. I just wanted to make sure that you got home all right, and that you're okay."

Oh God, that voice. "I did, thank you. I am okay, I think, more or less, maybe less, but that's not your fault, it's—"

"Wait wait, stop right there. I had a wonderful time tonight, a spectacular time, but now that I know your situation, I won't ever call you again."

He had a spectacular time.

"Josh, can you hold on one sec?"

"Sure."

"Arthur?"

"I'm here."

"Amanda Walker wants me to take care of her children this summer." That was true. "Can I call you right back?"

"I'll hold, sweetie. Now that you're a practicing doctor I have to get used to these interruptions."

"Okay. . . . Josh?"

"I'm here, Shelley."

I plunged in: "I had a wonderful time tonight, too. Thank you."

We both made involuntary little purring-type sounds.

"Shelley, I would *love* to see you again."

Under the bubbles, the water got a little wetter.

"Josh, I think I better go now . . ."

"Good night, Shelley, and thank you again."

". . . Arthur?"

"Why are you talking in that throaty voice? Do you have a cold?"

I cleared my throat. "Um, gosh, I hope not. . . . So, it sounds like Flatbush was fun. What were the people like?"

"They were all very nice. Jennifer Wu used your ticket," Arthur said, a little too casually.

"Oh, she did?"

"I didn't want it to go to waste."

"Of course not."

"Shelley, you sound like you're jealous."

"Maybe I am, a little."

"Well, you have so much stuff going on in your life right now, I need a little backup."

"Why not invite a male friend?"

"Jennifer is great fun, Shelley, and our relationship is strictly platonic."

After what I had done, I couldn't believe I was challenging his innocent excursion. "I'm pretty exhausted, honey. Let's talk tomorrow."

"Love you, cutiepie."

I put down the phone and slid down into the water up to my neck—and then kept going, until I was in over my head.

14

THANK GOD FOR WORK. For the next few weeks I put men and sex and relationships out of my mind and concentrated on being a good doctor. I was seeing a lot of the patients I inherited from the disgraced Dr. Clark for the first time, and I was already getting new referrals. The office was a study in barely controlled chaos as an endless stream of children, parents, and nannies poured in. And then there were the phone calls and the paperwork. I felt like I was perpetually running twenty minutes behind and would never catch up. Thank God also for Candace, gatekeeper and child charmer, chief cook and bottle washer—you knew that no matter how hectic it got, she was managing things out front with acumen, aplomb, and opera.

It was Friday morning and I was sitting at my desk going over my schedule for the day. It had been a long week, but I found that no matter how exhausted I was when I woke up, when I got to work I was lifted right out of it. Of course, I had to keep up with the other doctors. As I had seen with Dr. Healy, there was a definite unspoken competitive edge in the relationships among us. If I needed further proof, Dr. Crissy Watkins appeared in my doorway, carrying a gift basket the size of a trashcan that was overflowing with gourmet goodies. I should point out that the path from the front desk to her office did not pass by my office—this was a show-off detour. As usual, Crissy was almost exploding with positive, well-scrubbed energy.

"Oh my gosh-golly, do you believe the size of this thing? Yikes!" she gushed, flashing that Mary-Tyler-Moore-sized smile of hers.

"It's amazing," I said, casually resting my chin on my fist, so that my Amanda-gifted gold bracelet was highly visible.

"Let's see—there's foie gras and smoked snails and salmon mousse and chocolate truffles and lemon curd and cornichons—and that's just the top layer! Goodness me, I guess my patients love me, they really love me!"

"It's pretty impressive."

"I'm sending the whole thing over to Safe Harbor, a shelter for formerly incarcerated, mentally challenged homeless women. I'm sure this will brighten their day right up!"

"No doubt," I said, trying to imagine the formerly incarcerated, mentally challenged homeless women politely sharing the foie gras and smoked snails.

"So, pal-o-mine, how's the kid business?" she asked.

"I'm very busy."

"I hear ya, sister! Do you ever feel like an ant crossed with a bee?"

"Hmmm . . ."

"Speaking of which, I better buzz off, my hive needs me."

One of my first patients was an eight-month-old boy, Christopher Wells. Christopher came from a showbiz family: His mother was a soap opera actress named Linda Simpson, and his father a producer on one of those glitzy prime-time newsmagazines. I loved those shows—they managed to stretch the definition of news to include juicy celebrity profiles and lurid investigations of billionaires' bitter divorces, all delivered with an air of breathless importance.

Since soap operas were one vice I managed to avoid, I wasn't familiar with Linda Simpson. I was expecting someone perky and pretty, but she was round-faced and bespectacled, wearing chinos, a blue oxford shirt, and no makeup. Holding her son, she radiated intelligence and seriousness. I think all babies are adorable, but I had to admit that Christopher, with round brown eyes and large dimples, was delectable.

After introducing myself, I asked how Christopher was.

"He's wonderful. He just got another booking today."

"A booking?"

"Yes, Christopher is a model," Mom said. "His agency calls him a supermodel, but I'm too modest to do that."

"Well, let's take a look at our little model."

Mom handed him over to me and then said, "Let me show you his book." She went to her carryall and lifted out an enormous leather portfolio. As I examined Christopher, she held it up and slowly turned the pages. "This is BabyGap. . . . Here's his Gerber commercial; it was a national. . . . Here's Charmin . . . Fisher-Price . . . Target. He's up for the new Spielberg movie. His acting coach thinks he has a special presence—she calls it 'celestial empathy.' It's the way he *listens*. So few babies know how to really listen."

I was glad there were child labor laws on the books, although young Christopher seemed to have suffered no ill effects from his punishing schedule, and he gurgled throughout the entire exam.

"Well, Christopher seems to be in the best of health," I said.

"I do have one concern," Mom said.

"Yes?"

"His nose."

"His nose?"

"Yes, his nose. I'm afraid it's beginning to look a lot like my original nose." She traced her finger down Christopher's proboscis. "See how broad it is here, and there's this little bulb on the end. I'd like to nip this in the bud. Do you know a good pediatric plastic surgeon?"

"Let me assure you that Christopher's nose is still in the early stages of development. His facial bones won't be fully grown until he is at least sixteen. It's impossible to tell at eight months what his nose will look like then. Plastic surgery at his age is out of the question."

"Well, one casting director commented on it."

"I don't claim to understand the finer points of the casting business, but I think criticizing the nose of an eight-month-old is absurd. Besides, I think he has a perfect nose."

Linda Simpson looked off into the middle distance, eyes unfocused, introspective and grave, as if she were contemplating a life-and-death decision. Then she gave the tiniest nod, to herself—a verdict had been reached. She turned and looked at me, her eyes filled with hard-won wisdom and bittersweet resignation. I almost applauded.

"Dr. Green, you're a woman of passion and conviction, and I trust your judgment. I only want what's best for Christopher. But when he hits adolescence, the competition gets really fierce, and if the nose isn't working then, it goes."

I assured her I would be happy to revisit the issue at that time.

In the midafternoon, I had just finished with a patient when the office intercom announced, "Dr. Green, call on line seven." I went into my office and picked up the phone.

"Dr. Green, it's Fred McNulty. Ginger is sick."

"What's the problem?"

"She has constipation and diarrhea."

"Mr. McNulty, those are mutually exclusive conditions."

"Well, she has them both, I swear."

I asked him to give me a description of the problem. "What you're describing is perfectly normal. Breast-fed babies sometimes strain, and then have explosive and watery bowel movements."

"Are you sure?"

"Positive."

"Well, shouldn't we be treating her for the constipation and diarrhea?"

"I *assure* you that there is no problem. No treatment of any kind is necessary. Ginger's digestive system is functioning just as it should."

"But she's constipated, and she has diarrhea."

There's something touching—and funny—about a worried father. When it comes to babies, dads are so much more helpless than moms. Especially when the baby is a girl.

"If you want to bring Ginger in, I would be happy to take a quick look at her," I said.

Dad breathed a heavy sigh of relief. "Thank you, Doctor."

I was hoping that Alison Young's lab work would have come in, but it hadn't. I had spoken very briefly to her father earlier in the week—he was quite brusque—and told him I would call today. I had wanted to wait until I had the results in hand, but thought I owed him the call in any event. I reached him at his office at Rockefeller University.

"This is Francis Young." He had one of those intimidating English accents that scream: *I'm very brilliant and very busy so please don't waste my valuable time.*

"Hello, Mr. Young, this is Dr. Green."

"Yes?"

"I'm just calling to tell you that Alison's lab work hasn't come in. I phoned the lab, and they told me they were backed up."

There was an exasperated exhale. "That is so typical of the American medical system. You people muck up *everything,* don't you?"

Since I was acutely aware of his wife's tragic misdiagnosis, I held my tongue. "I apologize for the delay, but please try to remember that I'm on your side. How's Alison doing?"

His tone softened slightly. "My daughter is not doing well, Dr. Green."

"Has she been out in the country at all in the last month and a half?" Since Lyme disease titers can take as long as six weeks to read positive, I wanted to double-check.

"No, she hasn't."

"Has she gotten any worse, in any way? Developed any new symptoms?"

"No, but she has pervasive malaise. I'm quite worried, Dr. Green. Unfortunately, I'm also very busy. I'm due to present a major economic study in Geneva in three weeks. My wife was the one who held the family together. Is my daughter going to be all right?"

"I certainly can't say this definitively without Alison's complete lab work in front of me, but her preliminary workup was normal, and so I am leaning toward a diagnosis of psychosomatic manifestation. I would recommend that Alison see a therapist. Mr. Young, I think your daughter needs someone to talk to about her feelings."

"She's been through an awful lot this year." He suddenly sounded deflated, and sad.

"Yes, she has. And that may be causing her current physical symptoms. I would be more than happy to refer her to a qualified psychiatrist, someone who has demonstrated the ability to help children in Alison's situation. In the meantime, I expect to receive the results of her lab work early next week, and I'll call you as soon as I do."

There was a pause, and I thought I detected a slight modicum of respect in his voice as he said, "Very well then, Dr. Green."

It was a stressful phone call, coming at the end of an exhausting week. In spite of it all, I was looking forward to the rest of my day. My last patient of the week was going to be the four-year-old daughter of a *major* movie star—of the male heartthrob variety—referred to me by Christina Allen. The family was living in a suite at the Pierre while Dad shot a movie in the east, and their secretary had phoned to tell Candace that the girl was being brought in by her mother. Celebrity slut though I was, I was determined to rein in my drooling, fawning tendencies and be the epitome of professional nonchalance.

But first I had a couple of mere mortals to see. I was in my office writing up notes when Candace appeared in the doorway.

"Your next patient asked me to give you this," she said, handing me the latest copy of *Elle Decor*. I opened to a page flagged with a Post-It. It was a spread on an immense downtown loft that had been done over in what the magazine touted as Future Retro by "beyond hot" interior decorator Suzie Buell. There was a picture of Suzie, who looked strikingly handsome, chic, and confident in gold flats, black slacks, a gold dragon belt, and a black silk shirt; her short golden hair and skin glowed. She was standing with one hand on her hip and the other resting atop an Art Deco bust of Greta Garbo that she had "scored at a divine antique shop I discovered in deepest Prague—my animal instincts come out when I shop. Grrrrrrr."

"She sounds like a tiger," I said.

"Well, the tiger stepped into a baby trap. Wait until you see her," Candace said.

I walked into the exam room to find two-month-old Blair Buell on the exam table and a frumpy, grumpy, puffy, chubby Suzie Buell standing next to her.

"Hello, I'm Dr. Shelley Green."

"And I'm a mess. I mean, *look* at me. I haven't slept in two months, I mean *not one wink,* I've gained fifteen pounds *since* the birth, my hair has gone lank, my skin sallow, I have heartburn, headaches, and hemorrhoids, I feel like shit 24/7. My career can't take it—I'm a power player and I look like a mental patient. There has *got* to be a way to make this baby sleep. I mean it, because I'm starting to hate her and that can't be healthy." She looked at me plaintively.

Ah, sleep. It's always a biggie when baby comes along. And for overachieving control freaks living heretofore perfectly controlled lives, it's gargantuan. They consider their inability to control the invariably chaotic early months of a baby's life as a personal failure.

"How is Blair?" I asked, more concerned with the baby than with her mom, who, with her wild-eyed desperation, could indeed have passed for a mental patient, or at least a beautiful TV actress playing one on *CSI*.

"Oh, she's fine, except that I'm afraid she has some rare neurological defect that won't allow her to get a good night's sleep."

"I doubt that. Almost all babies have very unsettled sleep routines for at least the first three months."

"Three months! I'll weigh two hundred pounds and be stark raving mad by then."

"Babies' brains are immature and disorganized, and you simply can't impose a schedule on them."

"My friend Didi swears her little Benjamin slept like a dream from day one. Didi swears she hasn't missed a single night's sleep since the day he was born."

"Trust me, Benjamin is the rare exception. Now, may I examine Blair?"

"Of course."

Blair was a delightful infant, with thick dark hair and a ready smile, who looked as if *she* was getting plenty of sleep. As I examined her, Mom kept up a running monologue behind me.

"The problem is, I don't do pills, I simply *do not do* pills. They're a slippery slope, and I've seen too many people—rich, famous, *smart* people—slide into the valley of the dolls. Not Suzie Buell, not when she's got Fran Templer's library to do."

I knew from reading the gossip columns that Fran Templer was New York's ultimate society and fashion icon, a woman of a certain age, whom Yves St. Laurent had pronounced "the chicest woman in the world."

"I mean do you know what it *means* to be doing Fran Templer's library?" Suzie Buell said. "It's like the president asking you to redecorate the White House—except Fran Templer is much bigger than the president in this town. And do you think I can let Fran Templer see me looking like this? She'd *fire* me—and I wouldn't blame her. Would you let a mental patient redo *your* library?"

"Do you have a baby nurse?"

"Of course I have a baby nurse. I have three. And, by the way, my husband hasn't touched me in a month. And I don't blame him. *I* wouldn't touch me. Unless I had a mental-patient fetish."

"Blair looks absolutely fine."

"Nothing neurologically weird going on?"

"Absolutely not."

"This whole screaming-in-the-middle-of-the-night thing is normal?"

"Perfectly normal. Babies get hungry."

"So Blair is just a regular kid?"

Considering her mom and her milieu, regular wasn't the first word I'd use, but I bit my tongue. "She's right up there with apple pie."

Suzie Buell broke into a warm, enormous smile—all her hyperactive angst melted away, and she was just a mom. "Oh, thank you, Doctor. Isn't she the most beautiful baby you've ever seen? Oh, who gives a damn about sleep when I've got my little angel?" She picked up her baby and cradled her in her arms, rocked her back and forth. "My sweet little angel girl, my little dream, my baby girl, my love bunny." She leaned down and rubbed noses with Blair—mother and daughter cooed with delight. Then Mom looked up at me with her exhausted eyes. "Oh all right, Dr. Green, if you *absolutely insist,* I'll get my doctor to write me a scrip for some sleeping pills. But nothing heavy. Didi swears by Ambien."

I told Suzie Buell that I wouldn't recommend a pill as long as she was breast-feeding, and she told me she was about to switch to formula anyway. So I gave her my blessings.

As I headed down the hall, I heard, "Dr. Green, call on line three." I ducked into my office.

"Hello."

"Hi, Shelley, it's Amanda."

"Hi, how are you?" I asked.

"Busy doing nothing, as usual. So, I heard you ended up going to the benefit with Josh."

I felt my blood run cold. Did she know, had Josh broken his pledge, was the news of our tryst all over the Upper East Side? And was she calling me at work just to gossip? That would be a very bad sign.

"I did go. Dr. Marge says going to benefits is the best advertising the practice can buy."

"Did you have a good time?"

"I was completely intimidated at first, but then I said 'what the hell' and relaxed."

"My spies tell me you're a terrific dancer. But Josh said you were tired and that he put you in a cab home on the early side."

God bless his little WASP heart.

"Yes, he did."

"Well, maybe you'll have better luck with him next time."

"Amanda, I'm engaged."

"I never let that stop me. Just kidding. I can't wait to meet your fiancé; I'm sure he's wonderful, and a very lucky man. Listen, I'm calling to see if I can lure you out to East Hampton next weekend to get the lay of the land."

"That sounds terrific, Amanda."

"Wonderful. I'll send a car to pick you up at your apartment at nine next Saturday morning. Maybe I'll plan a little social something for Saturday night. Ciao."

I had never been to the legendary Hamptons, that string of towns on the eastern end of Long Island that were a playground for the rich, had legendary beaches, and had recently become Hollywood East, celebrity central. Although I was excited by the prospect of seeing the Hamptons, there was definitely a slight undercurrent of iron fist in Amanda's velvet-gloved invitation. And eager as she was to meet Arthur, he wasn't included. I had already learned that on the Upper East Side perks come with a price. Besides, I had other things on my mind, namely that I was one patient away from meeting the child of a Major Movie Star, a hunk who'd been named *People*'s Sexiest Man Alive *twice* in the last five years.

Outside the exam room, I picked up a chart and read that my next patient was fourteen-year-old Nicholas Fielding-Gray, whose father was a vice president at Shearson Lehman and whose . . . other father was senior counsel at Merrill Lynch. Hmmm, Nicholas has two daddies. I'd seen same-sex parents during my residency, but these were my first gilded gays.

Nicholas sat on the exam table, a big, gangly boy in the middle of an adolescent growth spurt—his wrists poked out of his shirtsleeves, his pants were too short, his general appearance was of a healthy, somewhat disheveled teenager bursting at the seams. His dads, on the other hand, were two bright, buff, handsome men in their late thirties, impeccably dressed in conservative suits.

"Hi, I'm Dr. Shelley Green."

"Hi, Mark Fielding."

"Allan Gray."

"Just call me Nick."

"Before you say another word, was that Suzie Buell we saw in the waiting room?" Fielding asked.

I nodded.

"What happened to her? She looks like a mental patient," Gray said.

"Mental patient or not, she's brilliant," Fielding said.

"We want her to redecorate our townhouse, but she's got a three-year waiting list," Gray said.

Nicholas squirmed and rolled his eyes.

"And she's doing Fran Templer's library," Fielding said reverentially.

"Which is like being asked by God to redo heaven," Gray said.

"Except that Fran Templer is much bigger than God in this town," Fielding said.

Nicholas, looking mortified, explained, "Dr. Green, we moved here from Houston last year and Mark and Allan are pathetically starstruck."

Fielding gave his son's hair an affectionate muss. "We found him a terrific therapist."

"She treats six Rockefeller kids," Gray said.

"And are you liking your new home?" I asked Nicholas.

"Definitely. New York is cool."

"Why don't we get started with your exam?" I suggested.

"Mark, Allan, would you mind waiting out in the waiting room?" Nicholas asked. After they had left, he said, "They have big-time hover issues. It's an overcompensation thing."

"And how's school?"

"Dalton is great. Except, well . . ."

"Yes?"

"Mark and Allan. They kind of embarrass me."

"Because they're gay?"

"Oh no. Having gay parents is way cool, there are a bunch of them at Dalton. But Mark and Allan are just so *straight*. You know, corporate. They never loosen up. I mean, they show up at my soccer games in polo shirts and tassel loafers, with a little wicker basket filled with perfect little sandwiches. It's gross. They're the Stepford Dads."

"Have you talked about it with them?"

"I tried, but they don't get it. My therapist is helping me accept them as they are."

"That's probably wise."

Nicholas's exam showed him to be in the best of health.

"Does my penis look normal?" he asked anxiously.

"Perfectly normal," I assured him.

"What about those little bumps on my, um, scrotum?"

"Small fatty deposits. All males have them."

"I was worried they were cancer, or herpes."

"You have to have sexual relations to contract herpes. Have you?"

"No. But I've sure thought about it."

"Is there anything you'd like to talk about concerning sex?"

Nicholas hesitated, looked at me with a wary, appraising eye, and then said, "I swiped some condoms from my dad's nightstand and I've been teaching myself to use them. You know, just in case. I mean, I made out a little with Claire Bookman at Serendipity."

Nicholas was at an age when all children develop a preoccupation with sex, and a big part of a pediatrician's job is learning how to win their trust and how to speak to them honestly and openly.

"Claire Bookman and I are going to the movies on Saturday night—you never know what might happen," Nicholas said with an endearing mix of bravado and insecurity.

"Well, Nicholas, you know that there are risks associated with unprotected sex. There are numerous sexually transmitted diseases."

"I don't think Claire Bookman has any sexually transmitted diseases—she goes to Chapin."

I stifled my smile. "Going to a certain school, *any* school, won't protect a person from disease. And there is also the risk of pregnancy. Condoms can break."

Nicholas sat there, digesting this information. After a few moments, he said, "All right, I hear you. And I think I have a solution."

"Yes?"

"If things get intense with Claire Bookman, we'll stick to oral sex."

I felt it was important not to cast myself in the role of prudish naysayer. All that would do is end communication between us. Teenagers have sex. *Beginning* of story.

"Well, Nicholas, that's a decision to be made by you and Claire, but I don't think it's one the two of you should make lightly. And there *are* diseases that can be transmitted by oral sex."

Nicholas took this in and sighed. "I guess I have to be a responsible guy, don't I?"

I nodded.

"That's what the Stepford Dads are always telling me, too."

"You have your whole life ahead of you, Nicholas. And if you ever want to talk to me about any of this, just call."

As I was leaving the room, Nicholas blurted out, "Dr. Green, Claire Bookman is *wicked* hot."

I turned and looked at him—smiling, eyes sparkling. I wasn't sure what to say . . . so I just smiled back.

Before seeing the Tinseltown tot, I ducked into my office and did a quick check in the full-length mirror on the back of the door. Considering I'd been going nonstop since 8 A.M., not too bad. I'd worn a new beige pantsuit and taken extra care with my minimal makeup. I took a deep breath, stood up straight, and headed for the exam room.

I'd seen pictures of the missus in the tabloids and knew she was no glamour-puss, but I was still taken aback at how dressed down she was: sweatpants, running shoes, a shapeless cotton top, a baseball cap, no makeup. I could see popping out for coffee incognito on a Sunday morning in Malibu in that outfit, but walking around the Upper East Side? The management of the Pierre must be appalled. Did I mention her face and hair? Plain and stringy.

"Hello," I said. "I'm Dr. Shelley Green."

"Hi," she said distractedly. Her four-year-old daughter sat on the exam table, looking precious and a bit bewildered by life. Wearing a crisp yellow jumpsuit, she was much better dressed than her mother. Mom was standing behind her, hovering over her in what was almost a protective crouch. There was a small pile of books on the exam table beside the girl, and I quickly scanned the titles: *The Wind Farm Imperative*, *The Kabala Conundrum*, and *Madame Bovary*. Hmmm.

"And this must be Tia," I said. Tia looked as if she was unsure how to respond. I swore she looked dazed and confused. Maybe Mom had been reading to her from *The Kabala Conundrum*.

Mom wrapped her arms around the girl and leaned over her. "Yes, this is Tia. We're here for our booster shot, we don't need an exam, what percentage of paper does this practice recycle?"

"Um, I don't know the percentage."

I was treated to a look of self-righteous condescension. "Our pediatrician in Santa Monica recycles *one hundred percent* of her paper. Doesn't she, Tia?" Tia nodded. Mom stroked her hair. "It would be nice if we could leave Tia a planet, don't you think?"

"I do."

"Well, it's not going to happen by itself."

"Would you like me to find out the percentage of paper we recycle?"

"At this point, it doesn't really matter."

It had mattered thirty seconds earlier, but I kept my mouth shut. All I could think was, that hunk lives with this? No wonder he was so fond of shooting epics in distant locations. I mean, this woman should be raising goats on a farm in Vermont—and I happened to know that her husband paid $17.5 million for their Pacific Palisades house, which had once belonged to Goldie Hawn, who bought it from Bea Arthur.

It was pretty obvious that she didn't let anybody get close to her daughter, so I decided just to do my job as best as I could. "I've got Tia's shot prepared," I said.

Mom pushed up Tia's sleeve and then, to my astonishment, pushed up her own sleeve. "Tia and I are in this together."

"You don't actually want a shot, do you?"

"My husband and I immunized ten thousand Sudanese children. It was my Christmas present to him. That and a hybrid Hummer."

"That was a very wonderful thing to do."

She nodded her head nobly. "Barbra cried when I told her."

The mention of The Great One's name gave me a little shudder of excitement—I mean, forget *Six* Degrees of Separation . . .

Doctors, doctors who treat movie stars' children
Are the luckiest doc-tors
In the world

"We're going to be a very brave girl," Mom said to Tia, who looked up at her anxiously.

I approached the exam table. I was determined to make some sort of connection with this poor child, who had her father's gorgeous blue eyes.

"Hello, Tia," I said, and smiled.

Tia looked at me, and just as a smile was beginning to spread across her face, Mom clamped her hands over the girl's ears and hissed, "We discourage strangers from approaching Tia. There are stalkers out there, kidnappers, neurotic, needy women."

I didn't have to look far to find a neurotic, needy woman. One who had just insulted my professionalism.

"I am hardly a stranger. Tia is my patient, and while she is in this office her welfare is my responsibility. It's a responsibility that I take very seriously. Before I can administer the shot, I have to examine Tia to make sure she has no illnesses or infections that would lower her immune system and make her more prone to significant side effects," I said firmly, looking Mom right in the eye.

Mom tried to hold the eye contact and couldn't. "I knew that," she said with an offhand shrug.

As I examined Tia, Mom watched intently, leaning forward with wide eyes and bated breath, as if her daughter were made of porcelain and might shatter into a thousand pieces if I touched her too hard.

"She looks just fine," I said.

Mom stroked Tia's face and said, in a baby-talk voice, "We're weady for our schwot now."

I swabbed Tia's upper arm with alcohol and said in my gentlest voice, "Don't worry, Tia, this will be over in a second, and it will keep you from getting sick." Tia's face relaxed, and I could actually see a flicker of trust. Mom, on the other hand, was wincing in terrified anticipation, like she was on an airplane that was about to crash.

I pricked Tia's skin. "All done," I said.

For a split second she seemed fine—then Mom cried "Oww!" and Tia began to cry. And then, I kid you not, Mom began to cry, came around the exam table, sat on it, and took Tia's hand. I just stood there flabbergasted as they sat there holding hands, crying in unison.

If this had been a low-income clinic, I would have called Child Protective Services—but this wasn't a low-income clinic, just a low-sanity one.

I ignored Mom and said, "Are you all right, Tia?"

Tia, who had stopped crying, nodded in a remarkably self-possessed way and then looked at her mother in anticipatory concern, as if she knew what was coming next. Tears were still streaming down Mom's face. "This always happens to me when I'm away from my psychiatrist and my Kabala guide and my yoga master and my colorist, I fall apart—and yes, I *do* know I have a narcissistic attachment to Tia and that I use my alliance with her as a defense against my feelings of marital inadequacy, but it's not easy being married to my husband, knowing every woman in the world wants to sleep with him and that half of them have, and I'm the one who's supposed to hold the whole show together—the houses, the staff, do you know how much *paperwork* there is—and then the causes and the parties and the clothes and I'm supposed to be so goddamn level-headed and *intellectual,* I mean let's get real, he didn't marry me for my looks, and why isn't the Paxil making me happy, I want to be happy, I have everything, I *have* to be happy."

Tia stroked her Mom's hand. "Is okay, Mommy, is okay."

"Oh, Tia, you love me . . . don't you?"

"I love Mommy." Tia turned to me. "Kleenex?"

"Of course." I handed her a box and she pulled out several tissues and handed them to her mom.

"Here, Mommy." Mom blew her nose and wiped her eyes. She suddenly looked tiny and sheepish. "*Good* girl, Mommy *good* girl," Tia said. Then she stepped down off the table, took her mom's hand, and calmly led her out of the room.

And then, as if someone had turned a switch, the week's exhaustion flooded over me, and I retreated to my office. Olga, a stout middle-aged Russian woman, was waiting to give me a head and neck massage. Candace had come up with the idea of bringing in a masseuse on Friday afternoons to help the doctors and staff decompress from the week. You could always tell who had been kneaded, because they walked around with calm smiles while the untouched still had harried faces.

"Boy, am I glad to see you," I said. Olga smiled—she neither spoke nor understood more than a word or two of English. As she went to work I concentrated on breathing deeply and exhaling with a sigh. I had a brilliant med-school professor who always claimed that deep breathing was the most powerful therapeutic tool in the world, but since it was free and didn't come in pill form, people rarely used it.

Dr. Marge appeared in my doorway. She had definitely had her massage because she was wearing a benevolent, if slightly sad, smile.

"May I come in?" she asked.

"Of course."

She sat across from me. "I just did something I never do."

"What's that?"

"I canceled a social engagement at the last minute." Dr. Marge was famous for her ability to work all day, go home, change into some fabulous outfit, and go out to an opening night or a dinner dance, where she charmed and sparkled. Though she said it was half about drumming up new business, Candace told me that in fact she loved the social whirl, loved the dressing up, loved seeing her name in print. "Carolyn Roehm asked me up to Litchfield for the weekend. She was sending a car, but I called her up five minutes ago and told her I simply couldn't make it, that I was coming down with something."

"You're not feeling well?"

"I feel fine . . . physically." There was a pause while I wondered whether or not to pry. "Shelley, you're not picking up your cue." Dr. Marge had a certain light, deft touch and what I thought of as a distinctly European charm, understated and wry. She was one of those women who never raised her voice or lost her cool. Sort of my mirror opposite.

"Why did you cancel the weekend?"

"Because I couldn't stand the thought of two days of superficial chat, shopping for overpriced antiques, and nature walks. Is there anything more overrated than trees? I mean they grow everywhere, they're basically enormous weeds. This American reverence for them is so jejune. I see the hand of God in Michelangelo, in Mozart, in Chateau LaTour '67, but in some monstrous weed? Please."

I moaned.

"Isn't Olga marvelous?" Dr. Marge said.

"Mmmmm."

"Listen, my husband is out of town, yet again. Can I entice you over for a little light supper? We can discuss your arrangement with the Walkers."

The invitation was delivered in the kindest terms, and I felt it would be unwise to refuse it.

"I'd love to come over, if it's not too much trouble."

"Of course not. I'll make us an omelet. We'll have a cozy chatty evening and be in bed by ten."

"Sounds wonderful, I'll be ready in about fifteen minutes . . . ooooh, Olga, you just released the knot of death."

15

DR. MARGE LIVED on Central Park West, in the Trump International Tower. It was a lovely summer evening, and as we walked through the park—abloom with flowers and young lovers—Dr. Marge was in a reflective mood.

"I remember when I was your age, just starting out. Every day felt like a new adventure. Every patient gave me a little thrill of expectation. Children are wondrous, and surprising . . . it's their innocence, their openness." She looked around the park and then at me. "I miss my sons terribly." I sensed she wanted to say more, and so I said nothing. "But they don't miss me. They're young men now, and the last person they're interested in is their mother. It's an old story, and you know it's coming, but still . . . motherhood is very important to me."

"I look forward to meeting your sons," I said.

"They're both delightful—smart and considerate and charming. And very independent," she added with a rueful little laugh.

"Independent is good," I said, thinking of Ira, still living at home at age twenty-nine.

"May I confess something to you, Shelley?"

"Of course."

"I'm bored."

"Bored?"

"With the practice. I know you're probably the last person I should be telling this to, but you're a very sympathetic soul, do you know that?"

"Thank you."

"After almost twenty-five years, I'm bored to tears with sore throats, rashes, vaccines, not to mention the ruthless insurance companies and endless regulations. And to top it all off, the maddening epidemic of hyperparenting has tried my patience beyond measure. I want a new challenge."

A young skateboarder zoomed by, flew up a rise, twirled around, and flew back down.

"Doesn't that look exhilarating? That's the feeling I long for!"

We came to the carousel, with its grand old painted horses, calliope music, and happy children. We stood and watched as it went round and round, its young riders delighted and awed, squealing and waving. There was something timeless about the scene, as if we were in the Central Park of a hundred years ago. It was reassuring. No matter how complex the world had become, no matter how neurotic and stressed today's parents were, children will still play and run, skip and jump, will still be filled with curiosity and joy.

"When I first came to New York, this was one of my favorite places. My sons loved it. My husband and I would bring them here every Saturday morning. And then we'd take them to Rumplemeyer's for milk shakes. Rumplemeyer's is gone now, too. Oh dear, there I go again. Maudlin Marge. Enough. Tell me how you're doing, Shelley," she asked as we continued over to the West Side.

"Well, I'm thrilled to be at Madison Pediatrics, thrilled by the work, and, to be honest, thrilled by the world of the Upper East Side."

She gave me a meaningful look. "Be careful, Shelley. The wealthy and privileged always look out for themselves. Make sure you look out for yourself. Retain a healthy sense of skepticism."

We reached Central Park West, just above Columbus Circle. The gold-clad tower of Trump International loomed over us. "I know, it's tacky, but my husband insisted we move over here after the boys went off to college. As you know, he makes his living spotting consumer trends. It's a very image-conscious field, and this address wows his South American and Asian clients, which is where the money is these days. He's in Miami Beach now, at the Delano."

We entered the building, passed deferential staff, and headed for the elevators.

"Does your husband miss your sons as much as you do?"

The elevator arrived and we stepped in. Dr. Marge pushed the button marked 25.

"Not as much, no. He's always been a very busy man, but he and the boys are great friends, and that makes me happy. The three of them go on ski trips together. I tag along, but I don't ski, so I end up alone, reading a book by the indoor pool." The elevator doors opened and we headed down the wide hall. "Nouveau as this building is, I must admit that the views are spectacular, and so are the services—it's almost like living in a hotel. After a long day at work, I really appreciate being able to call down my dinner order."

She unlocked the door of her apartment and we walked into a large foyer that opened onto a vast room surrounded by a window wall, with stunning views of the entire park. Just as I was taking in the décor, a naked young woman with long blond hair and implanted breasts that stuck out in front of her like two enormous, gravity-defying accoutrements, walked across the space. She was carrying a can of soda. She saw us, popped open the can, and said casually, "Hi, girls."

Just then her identical twin entered, identically undressed and implanted.

"Awesome view," the twin said.

Then they giggled.

Dr. Marge went whiter than a bleached sheet.

"Do my babies want their daddy?" A middle-aged man, also naked, carrying a cocktail, appeared. He saw us and stopped, looking like he'd ingested a large fish.

You know that expression "time seemed to stand still"? Well, I lived it—there was a fraught pause that couldn't have been more than a few seconds long but seemed eternal.

Finally Dr. Marge said, "Herbert, this is Dr. Shelley Green. Shelley, this is my husband, Herbert Mueller."

Herbert Mueller swallowed hard and managed, "What a pleasure."

"Hi," I said.

"What happened to Connecticut?" he asked plaintively.

"I imagine it's still there," Dr. Marge answered, in a voice drier than the Sahara. "Now, aren't you going to introduce us to your friends?"

"Oh . . . of course. Dr. Green, my wife Marjorie . . . this is Tiffany-Dawn and Brianna-Jasmine."

"We're the Polson twins," Tiffany-Dawn said, as if that explained everything. Then she bit her lower lip as she pieced things together.

Brianna-Jasmine was way ahead of her, and said, "Wow, this is heavy."

And then they giggled.

16

I SAID A QUICK GOOD-BYE and left, ending what were surely the most excruciating moments of my life, not to mention Dr. Marge's. My heart went out to her, never more so than when she called me at around eleven that night, sounding surprisingly sober.

"Shelley?"

"Hi, Marge."

I waited, wanting to let her take the lead, to avoid consoling or questioning unless I sensed that she wanted it.

"Thank you for your discretion," she said.

"You can count on it."

"I've moved into the Lowell," she said. "It's a quiet residential hotel on East Sixty-third."

"Please let me know if there's anything I can do," I said.

There was a pause and then she said, "Well, I'll see you on Monday, then."

"You sure will. Dr. Marge, I enjoyed our walk across the park today."

"So did I. You have an innate kindness, Shelley."

"You haven't played Scrabble with me yet, I'm ruthless."

She laughed, and it sounded so good. And then she said: "Have you ever seen anything so ridiculous in your life as the breasts on those two? They looked like lethal weapons."

"Battering rams with nipples."

And then we were laughing: "Awesome view"—and then howling: "We're the Polson twins." When we finally wound down it felt like a healing breeze had blown over us.

There was long moment of silence and then Dr. Marge said, "Good night, my friend."

17

THE NEXT DAY was Dad's sixty-fifth birthday, and Arthur and I were heading out to Jackson Heights for what Mom called "a *petite little family soiree*"—which meant two things: a) Mom had signed up for a French course at the Learning Annex; and b) there would be forty screaming relatives packed into their cramped, airless apartment. This was the first time I'd seen Arthur since my own *petite soiree,* and I was *un peu* nervous. We'd made plans to get together several times, but each of us had canceled for one reason or another, and I was always secretly relieved. I needed to put a little distance between me and my indiscretion.

Arthur showed up at my apartment in, surprise, his dress-up uniform of baggy corduroys, a denim shirt, a retro tie with a stain on it, and a tweed jacket. Seeing him induced a massive wave of guilt, which I disguised by throwing myself into our kiss.

"Wow," he said. Then he stood back and looked at me. "You look terrific."

"So do you," I said.

"But I think you should start eating again," he said. And in that instant he became the mouthpiece for the Green Family behemoth. The mood was broken.

"Arthur, I don't want to eat more. I feel better at this weight."

"Okay, pumpkin, okay. As long as you're doing it for the right reasons, not just to impress a lot of shallow Upper East Siders."

"The Upper East Side has no monopoly on shallow people. Why, I bet I could even find one or two out in all-hallowed Brooklyn."

Why were we falling into this predictable pattern of bickering?

Because I think we both understood that our relationship was less secure than we'd imagined, that there was a new uncertainty about our future together. I suppose if we had been more evolved people, we would have discussed these feelings openly.

But we weren't. So we bickered.

I wondered if I should come clean about Josh. It was never going to happen again—it was a one-shot aberration, a wild uncharacteristic explosion of pent-up desire. But telling Arthur about it would only cause undue pain and unnecessarily complicate our relationship. When it comes to the feelings of others, I've never been a believer in absolute honesty.

"Time out," Arthur said.

"Time out," I agreed.

We exchanged half-hearted smiles and I busied myself neatening up the already neat apartment.

"I got your dad tickets to the Mets," Arthur said.

"Perfect. I got him a flat-screen TV."

"My God, that must have cost you a fortune," Arthur said.

I redoubled my faux neatening. "He's wanted one for years. And he's the only father I'll ever have. It's something I wanted to do." I felt my resentment growing. Why should I have to justify buying my dad a nice present?

Arthur plopped down on my bed with a sigh. "You're absolutely right, Shelley, and I apologize. It's a wonderful present, and it's going to make him very happy. You know what we need?"

"What?"

He took my hand, pulled me down on the bed, rolled on top of me, and kissed me hard and long. This was uncharacteristic. And I liked it. We began to make love and for a second I thought maybe it was going to be different, but it quickly turned into the familiar old choreography. I should have done something a little wild, a little un-Shelley, or un-old-Shelley, but I didn't, and the moment passed, and we worked our way to a predictable completion, and it was fine, really . . . well, better than fine actually—because while my body was in bed with Arthur, my mind was in that loft with Josh.

18

ON THE SUBWAY ride out to Jackson Heights, Arthur was relaxed, almost expansive, his male pride assuaged. I slipped my arm through his and enjoyed our easy compatibility, the comfort of being close to him. I'd been taking a lot of cabs lately, and being on the subway felt a little strange—this was, after all, how I'd spent my entire life before I was pulled into the world of Madison Pediatrics.

This was my first trip in months back to the neighborhood where I'd grown up. Jackson Heights is a nice place, filled with low-rise brick apartment courts built in the 1920s and 1930s. Leafy and safe, it has undergone a marked renewal since I was a kid, fueled by an influx of gay men and Indian immigrants, but it's still another universe from Manhattan. As Arthur and I walked from the train to my building, I couldn't help comparing the middle-class people we passed, the workaday mood, with the panache of the Upper East Side.

Our apartment was in one of those old brick buildings with a courtyard. The hallway—its tiles yellowed and cracked, its walls coated with too many layers of cheap paint—was old-fashioned and quaint at best, dreary and depressing at worst. As we rode up in the creaky elevator, I realized I did feel different—I felt like a visitor. This wasn't my home anymore. And, more importantly, I didn't want it to be.

We could hear the party noises as soon as we stepped off the elevator, and a smile broke out across Arthur's face. In some ways he was at his best with my loud, emotional family—they seemed to relax him. I'd met Arthur's folks several times. They were somewhat condescending academics, intellectuals with a Midwestern reserve. Arthur loved New York with the passion of a transplant, and my family was part of that passion.

I'd gotten a bit dressed up for the party, in heels and a knit burgundy skirt-and-sweater set I'd found at Bloomingdale's. I'd been careful with my makeup and new hairstyle. The truth was I wanted to impress the Green Family behemoth with my success.

"Shelley, what happened to your hair?" were the first words out of my mother's mouth after she opened the door. "And, Arthur, oh, don't you look handsome!"

I couldn't stop myself, "What, Mom, you don't like my hair?"

She put a hand on her hip and appraised me. "Well, it's . . . different. It certainly looks . . . expensive and *au courant*. Likewise the outfit. And the weight loss. My, we have changed. I'm afraid you're going to find this party much too Breughel-esque for your taste, now that you live in Degas-land. We're just peasants reveling after a hard week in the fields. But we have our downtrodden nobility."

Mom hardly looked downtrodden or noble in her party togs: an eggshell-blue satin cocktail dress, matching heels, an exploding-star rhinestone brooch the size of a dinner plate, rings and bracelets galore, her trademark chandelier earrings, and serious makeup, including lips lined in magenta and foundation that stopped cold at her jawline and looked like it had been applied with a paint roller. Her hair had spent the afternoon in curlers and then been sprayed to a near-bulletproof consistency. Just so that the glamour wasn't too blinding, she topped it all off with her ubiquitous glasses-on-a-string.

Behind us, the party was a jammed-in mass of cousins, aunts, uncles, in-laws, all yelling and eating, usually at the same time. I wanted to pull Mom out into the hallway and plead: "Mom, every message I got from the day I was born was 'Please, Shelley, study hard, make something of your life, do well, lift us up, make us proud,' and now that I'm doing just that, what do I get? Snide remarks."

But I didn't pull her out into the hallway. I choked down my frustration and disappointment. It gets easier with the years, but it never feels good.

"Now, Arthur, you look the same, thank God. Come in, come in, eat, drink, be merry." Arthur was immediately sucked into the middle of the maelstrom. Mom and I were alone in the entryway.

"Shelley, you'll excuse the humble digs, and I'm sorry there's no caviar."

"Enough, Mom," I said firmly.

"I'm so proud of you, Shelley. And you look lovely."

This was Mom's modus operandi: push me as far as she could, and then when I pushed back, switch gears.

"I got Dad a flat-screen plasma TV, forty-eight inches," I said, reaching into my purse and pulling out the TV's glossy brochure. "It's being delivered on Tuesday."

Mom took the brochure and glanced at the pictures. "Oh, Shelley, what a beautiful, beautiful gift. I can't even imagine what you must have spent. And I've wanted new carpeting for years now, but never mind, it's the thought, and Daddy loves to watch his ball games, and I've got my *Live from the Met,* if he'll ever let me watch it, you are the most wonderful daughter any father could ask for."

Now I was getting both messages in one sentence. Was it any wonder I was conflicted about a few issues in my life?

It was beginning to feel a little claustrophobic in the hallway, what with Mom bearing down on me, the tchotchke cabinet on one side, the woven Judaica wall hanging on the other. But she wasn't finished with me yet.

"Your brother brought *a woman* to the party," Mom said, lowering her voice conspiratorially, sneering out the words.

"Would you have felt better if he'd brought a goat?"

Much as Mom bemoaned Ira's seedy habits and unexplained absences, the one thing she feared more than his winding up in the gutter was his actually finding a nice girl and moving out of the house.

"Shelley, I can live without your sarcasm at a moment like this. Hell hath no fury like an ungrateful child . . . and it seems I have two of them. I could use a little support right now, is that too much to ask?"

"Mom, if you think you're going to have my support in keeping Ira an emotional adolescent, you're wrong."

Mom looked at me as though I'd just plunged a knife in her heart.

"I'd go kill myself, but you just did it for me," she said.

When I was little, Mom joined a neighborhood theater company, but she only lasted a week before she quit, claiming her part was too small. At home, she could be the undisputed star of the show. I've often wondered if things would have been different for Ira and me if Mom had been able to work out her instincts for dramatic suffering in a more appropriate environment than our apartment.

Just then I heard a familiar voice call, "Shelley!"

I looked over Mom's shoulder and saw Christina Allen coming toward us.

"That's her!" Mom hissed.

"Mom, she's a friend of mine, she's a doctor."

"I don't care if she cures cancer, wins the Nobel Prize, and gets her face on a postage stamp, *I-don't-like-her.*"

Christina looked casually smashing in blue jeans, black flats and belt, and a drapey green velvet shirt.

"Mrs. Green, Miriam, I love your family, everyone is so warm and funny and wonderful. . . . Why, you could cast a whole production of *Fiddler on the Roof* without leaving the kitchen. And your apartment is so . . . authentic. As for your son, he's authentic, too. You did a wonderful job raising him."

Even Mom couldn't resist this last compliment. "Why, thank you. Well, I'll leave you two doctors to talk shop," she said, before walking away with a parting, "Suss."

"'Suss'?" Christina asked.

"You don't want to know."

Christina gave me a hug. "Shelley, you look wonderful. And I meant that—you do have a terrific family. You should see what *my* family's parties are like—they stand around getting drunk but pretend they aren't, and all they talk about is stocks, horses, and how much they hate Hillary Clinton. It's deadly. *This* is fun."

I smiled—only Christina's fresh eye could make me appreciate my screaming brood. "They're nice people," I said. "I love them."

"And they love you. You should hear them talk. They're so proud of you, Shelley."

"Oh, Christina, you don't know how much it means to hear that."

"I met Arthur . . . ," she said.

"And . . . ?"

"He's very nice . . ."

"And . . . ?"

"Well-spoken . . ."

"And . . . ?"

"And he's no Josh Potter."

"Christina, we're engaged."

"I know you are, and I think that's quaint, but . . . well, let's not go there right now, because we'll be there in a minute. I have a proposition for you," she said with a sly smile.

"Yes?"

"An old friend of mine, Lucy Clarke, she's a lawyer-banker, hideously brilliant, just snagged her dream job, head of international something-or-other for B of A, but it's way the hell in Sydney, Australia. Long story short, she wants to keep her New York apartment and is looking for someone to sublet. It's a divine co-op right around the corner from our offices. One catch: She has a macaw she's devoted to. In return for taking care of the bird, you get the apartment for nothing but the maintenance fee, which is like nine hundred dollars a month."

Nine hundred dollars for a divine co-op on the Upper East Side? I paid a lot more than that for my tiny studio.

"Christina, Arthur and I just signed a lease on an apartment in Carroll Gardens."

"Isn't that somewhere in Brooklyn? Now that is quaint, not to mention tragic. I know a lawyer who could have you out of that lease in the time it takes for the foam on a mochachino to melt."

"But, Christina, I'm engaged."

"You may hate me for what I'm about to say, but I'm going to say it anyway. This is your time. A lot of very exciting doors are opening for you. If you don't at least dip your toe into the big glamorous world to see if you like it or not, you may regret it down the line. I mean, look at you, Shelley—you're a dish. And you've got real charm. I know for a fact that Josh Potter is interested in you. You don't want to be sixty-five looking back, full of *shoulda-woulda-couldas,* wishing you'd at least nibbled at the fabulous smorgasbord that was spread in front of you."

I looked over her shoulder and caught a glimpse of Arthur.

"Arthur isn't going anywhere, Shelley. I'm sure he's a great guy, but he'll wait for you. In fact, if he loves you he'll understand. I have a couple of back-up men in my life, guys who'd marry me in a minute. And it may happen, but if it does, I want it to be on my terms. We're accomplished women, Shelley, making a lot of money. We don't need men in the same way earlier generations of women did. We've earned the right to call our own shots." She ran her fingers through that thick black mane and shook her head. Her face softened into a warm smile. "I'm sorry if I'm coming on too strong, but I'm just really passionate about women owning their power. I grew up in a family of right-wing WASPs who don't even think we should have the right to control our own bodies, for Christ's sake."

"Oh, Christina, I don't know. I can't stand the thought of hurting Arthur."

"You're a dear heart, Shelley Green." Just then Ira slithered up behind her and slid his arm around her waist. She snuggled back against him and purred, "And so is your little brother. In addition to certain other attributes."

I guess when some women take control of their lives and make their own choices, they choose men like Ira. Speaking of Ira, his face looked very . . . glowing and, well, oddly smooth.

"Hi, Sis," he said.

"Hi, Ira. You look good."

"Hey, thanks. I owe it all to my plastic surgeon here."

"It's just a light peel and a little Botox," Christina said.

"At his age?" I asked.

"It's never too early to start. Speaking of which, Ingrid will be here in six weeks. Have you decided what you want done?"

"I'll take care of your daughter, no fee, and I'll just bank my procedures for when I feel ready. If that day ever comes," I said.

"I could do amazing things with your lips. And a peel would leave you as luminous as a teenager," Christina said.

"We'll see," I said. "I better go find the birthday boy."

Christina leaned into my ear and whispered, "Meet me at my office tomorrow at noon. We'll take a quick peek at Lucy's apartment." I hesitated. She took my hand and squeezed it. "It's just a look."

"All right."

As I walked down the hallway, I heard from behind me, "Ira, this coat closet is so sexy, come on."

"Oh, baby."

I looked over my shoulder just in time to see the closet door close behind them. Then I turned and headed into festive chaos.

Dad—midsized, paunchy, balding, with a New York pallor and big, sad brown eyes—stood in the middle of the living room surrounded by the behemoth. He was lapping up the attention. God knows it happened rarely enough. Dad's parents had lived through the Depression and encouraged their son to dream small: a government job, a steady paycheck, a decent pension. Dad never told me if he had other dreams, and I never asked, but he had long ago made peace with his lot. And it wasn't such a bad one, all in all. He loved people, loved to walk his route, and if any profession really did have a downtrodden nobility, it was delivering the mail day in day out. I was proud of him.

"Shelley!" he cried, enclosing me in a bear hug. Then he took my face in his hands and kissed me.

"Happy birthday, Daddy."

"Oh, my little girl," he said, and his eyes filled with tears. "Do you believe your old daddy is sixty-five. And you're a doctor, just like you always said you'd be, just like we all wanted. And you look beautiful. Doesn't she look beautiful?!" he screamed.

There was exuberant assent from the room, and suddenly I was the center of attention. Questions, compliments, kisses were flying fast and furious. I was back in the belly of the Green Family behemoth.

And you know what? It felt good. I was about to tell Dad about his present, was reaching into my purse for the brochure, when:

"*Quiet, everybody! I have an announcement to make!*" Mom was standing on a chair shouting at the top of her lungs. "*I said QUIET EVERYBODY I HAVE AN ANNOUNCEMENT TO MAKE!!*"

The room slowly quieted, filled with excited expectation, all eyes turned to Mom. She took a minute to revel in it.

"Thank you. I just wanted to remind everyone that *my* birthday is October eleventh." Explosive laughter. "Seriously, I want to tell you all something very touching and beautiful." The room grew absolutely silent—and Mom's expression grew absolutely beatific, tears welled up in her eyes. "Shelley bought Daddy a forty-eight-inch flat-screen plasma TV for his birthday."

Great, Mom, thanks.

My budding anger was cut off by the orgasmic screaming that suddenly started, coming from the direction of the hall closet.

"*It's a Sony!*" I screamed over the screaming—and mercifully the cheers began.

19

AS PLANNED, I MET CHRISTINA the next morning at her practice. Unlike the child-centric design of Madison Pediatrics, Lazansky & Allen Plastic Surgery Associates had a waiting room that looked like a suite in a very expensive, trendy hotel—everything was done in rose and beige, there were low geometric couches and armchairs, soft lighting, abstract art. And forget *Family Fun* and *Ladies' Home Journal*—here it was *Town & Country, W,* and *Maxim.*

"I love the quiet around here on Sundays," Christina said, leading me back into her office, which was also large, plush, and chic. She plopped down in her chair and put her feet up on her desk. I sat on the love seat. "That party was a blast. Your brother is a helluva nice guy. Listen, let me show you where we do our minor procedures. The big stuff is done over at Lenox Hill." Christina led me down a hallway and into a state-of-the-art mini operating room. It looked just like the ones on *Dr. 90210* and *Nip/Tuck.* "Sure I can't convince you to take a few shots of Botox, maybe a little collagen? It would take ten minutes."

"Not today."

"All right, let's go look at the apartment."

Lucy Clarke's apartment was in a small, distinguished prewar apartment house two blocks from Madison Pediatrics. Christina introduced me to the doorman, who was also distinguished and obviously took a proprietary pride in the building.

As Christina opened the front door of the fourth-floor apartment we were greeted by a loud, "Hey, baby, shake it, shake it."

"That's Harry," Christina explained. "He's sweet, but a little bit fresh." She walked over to a large standing cage. "Hi, Harry."

"Hey, baby, shake it, shake it." The beautiful, multicolored macaw hopped over and stuck his beak through the bars. Christina petted him. "That is so yesterday, that is so yesterday," he squawked.

"Watch it, buster, if you want to eat. Come meet him," she said.

"Hi, Harry," I said.

"Hey, baby, shake it, shake it."

He looked so adorable and comical, like a proud little man, all puffed up and full of himself. I was smitten.

"You been punk'd, you been punk'd," he squawked, putting me in my place.

"Lucy has an Ashton Kutcher obsession," Christina explained.

"I don't blame her."

Christina gestured to the apartment, "Well, this is it."

"Christina, it's beautiful." The expansive living room had classic proportions, lovely furnishings, built-in bookshelves, a fireplace, a large dining area, a view of leafy green treetops.

"Lucy has exquisite taste . . . in decorators. Check out the rest of the place."

The apartment had hallways, closets galore, crown moldings, a dreamy bedroom, a cozy study, an enormous bath that looked original, with black and white tiles and an old pedestal sink, a half bath off the foyer. The kitchen was charming, redone in an understated way, with a small banquette and table overlooking the gardens of the neighboring townhouses; a door led to the back landing and the service elevator. We walked back out to the living room.

"What do you think?" Christina asked.

"Well, it's basically my dream apartment."

"And it can be yours for nine hundred a month. Lucy is willing to commit for two years. And lest you think I'm Mother Theresa, I've been taking care of Harry for the last month and I'm over it."

The apartment felt buffered from the city outside, a refuge, an oasis. I imagined waking up here, making my coffee, eating my fruit and cereal, and then being at work in five minutes. And then coming home to this splendor at the end of a long day, running myself a hot bath or settling in for some TV on that oh-so-comfortable-looking couch. I realized with a stab of guilt that there was no Arthur in my scenario.

"Do you suppose it would be all right if Arthur moved in here with me?" I asked in contrition.

Christina hesitated for a second and then said, "I'd have to check with Lucy, but I don't see why not."

"That is so yesterday," Harry said.

"Out of the mouths of birds," Christina said.

20

ALISON YOUNG'S LAB WORK came in the next morning, and the results weren't what I had been expecting. She had an elevated erythrocyte sedimentation rate of 35—normal was less than 20. An elevated sed rate can be an indicator for a current or recent infection; it can also be an early marker for systemic inflammatory disease. I had prematurely assumed that Alison's symptoms were psychosomatic, had told her father that his daughter needed therapy, and now it looked as if there was in fact a physiological cause for her malaise, pallor, and weight loss. I felt like a fool and an idiot and—far worse—a bad doctor. I still felt Alison would benefit from therapy, but the simple medical fact was that she needed further tests to determine the exact etiology of the elevated sed rate.

I sat there at my desk with Alison's results in front of me, growing angry with myself. I vowed from the beginning of medical school that I would be a humble, methodical, and thorough physician. And now, less than two months into practice, I had rushed to judgment, let my emotional attachment to Alison overwhelm the caution and commitment to science that I had so diligently developed.

I allowed myself about thirty seconds of self-recrimination. Then I picked up the phone and called Alison's father.

"This is Dr. Green, Mr. Young. Alison's lab results have come in."

"And?"

"I owe you an apology. Alison has an elevated sedimentation rate."

He snorted in triumph. "This is exactly what happened to my wife! You American doctors think you have all the answers—not only that, you have them yesterday. But you're nothing but a bunch of bloody arrogant fools." He sighed heavily and I could hear the emotional exhaustion in his voice. "Mrs. Figueroa tells me Alison isn't eating and complained of a headache." There was a pause and the reality of the situation seemed to sink in. "So this might indeed be serious. Tell me some of the possibilities."

I explained what the elevated sed rate could mean, from something as benign as a recent infection to the possibility of an autoimmune disorder such as juvenile rheumatoid arthritis or lupus.

"How long have you been practicing medicine, Dr. Green?"

"I've been in practice for about six weeks."

"I see. And how many patients have you had with my daughter's symptoms?"

"Mr. Young, with all due respect, I'm not going to get into this with you. If you'd like to switch pediatricians, that is your prerogative. My plan at this point would be to get a definitive diagnosis. I'd like to see Alison one more time myself, since it sounds as if her symptoms have worsened in the last week. And I'd also like to make an appointment for her to see Dr. Charles Spenser, who is a specialist in childhood infectious disease and immunology."

There was a pause. "Let me think about this."

"Time is a factor here, Mr. Young. If you do want to switch pediatricians, I would be more than happy to supply some referrals. Otherwise, I was hoping I could see Alison either today or tomorrow."

He sighed heavily. "Alison didn't feel well enough to go to school this morning. She's at home with Mrs. Figueroa. I assume you have that number."

"I do."

"Very well. No doubt we'll be in touch." And then he hung up.

I'd done rounds with Dr. Charles Spenser when I was in medical school. He was one of the country's leading experts, brilliant and thoughtful. I called his office and was able to get an appointment for five thirty the next afternoon. Then I called Mrs. Figueroa, and she agreed to bring Alison in immediately. I asked Candace to tell my patients that I would be running about twenty minutes late.

Alison had the general appearance of being unwell. Her color was pallid, she was listless, her eyes were dull with dark circles beneath them, and she looked as if she had lost more weight. Mrs. Figueroa sat in a chair, looking worried.

"Good morning, Alison."

"Hi, Dr. Green." She tried to smile but couldn't quite manage.

"I understand you're not feeling any better."

She shook her head.

I brushed her hair from her face and cupped her cheek in my palm; her skin felt clammy. "I'm very sorry to hear that. But I'm sure we're going to get to the bottom of this, and that you're going to feel better again very soon."

"Daddy is upset at me for getting sick," she said.

"I spoke to your father, Alison, and he's concerned about you."

"He's delivering a very important paper in Geneva."

"Well, you're more important to him than any paper. And you're important to me. Now, can you tell me how you're feeling? Anything new in the last week?"

"I don't want to eat, or do anything, I don't want to go to summer camp."

"She just has no energy at all," Mrs. Figueroa said.

I performed a physical exam. Once again, there were no enlarged lymph nodes, no joint swelling or tenderness, and full range of motion. Her lungs were clear, there was no enlargement of the liver or spleen, and the neurological exam was negative. I was very glad that Dr. Spenser was being brought in on the case.

"Now, Alison, I've made an appointment for you to see another doctor tomorrow. His name is Dr. Spenser, and he's a very nice man and a very good doctor. If it's all right with you, I'd like to come with you to see him. Would that be all right?"

Alison nodded.

"Mrs. Figueroa, please give Alison two Advils every six to eight hours if her symptoms continue. Alison, drink plenty of fluids, and it would be good for you to try and eat something."

"I'll try."

"Thank you. I'll see you tomorrow at five thirty at Dr. Spenser's."

Alison nodded glumly. I gave her a hug, enfolding her in my arms, feeling her warmth.

"That felt nice," she said.

Back in my office, I looked over the day's schedule, as much to familiarize myself with it as to move my focus off of Alison. I'd had this problem during my residency—becoming emotionally invested in a patient to the point at which it became a potential drain on my energies. That was bad doctoring. I would move mountains to help Alison get better, but I also had a responsibility to my other patients.

Candace appeared in the doorway, looking worried. "Dr. Marge just came in, and she told me she's moved into the Lowell. I don't want to pry but my curiosity is killing me. Do you know what happened?"

"I don't. How does she seem?"

"Subdued, but composed. I knew there was trouble in that marriage. Didn't you go over to her place for dinner on Friday?"

"I thought you didn't want to pry."

Candace and I exchanged a glance.

"Message received," she said.

"By the way, Candace, how are you feeling?"

"I'm feeling terrific, stronger every day. Strong enough to be curious as hell about what's happening with Dr. Marge."

"How does the week look?"

"Intense."

"I have to leave here at five tomorrow. I'm going to meet Alison at
Dr. Spenser's."

"That sweet dear child."

"How's the CD coming?"

"My nephew is supposed to be working on it, but he hates opera.
I'm going to call him up and put some pressure on. I want one for Alison. Now let me go see if anyone needs to be rescheduled tomorrow."

My first patient that afternoon was five-year-old Bethany Clarkson, who was feeling "yucky." Bethany and her mother were visiting
from Charleston, South Carolina, and were staying at the Waldorf.
Her mother was friends with several of the practice's parents and
had used that connection to get an appointment. Claire had taken
her temperature and it was 101 degrees.

I walked into the exam room to find a forlorn-looking little girl
with blond hair and a pouty face. Although Bethany was clearly sick,
she was dressed for an antebellum garden party—poufed yellow
dress with lacy trim—and this was July in Manhattan. Sitting in a
chair was a bored, overweight teenage girl with frizzy blond hair
with dark roots showing, nails painted with glittery swirls, a pierced
lip, wearing a bulge-hugging T-shirt that read I'M HOT. She was chew-
ing a huge wad of gum. Probably a last-minute babysitter.

"Hi, I'm Dr. Shelley Green."

"Hi," Bethany said in a Southern accent. Nothing from the girl.

"I'm Dr. Shelley Green," I repeated.

This time the girl cracked her gum in response. I wondered where she'd gone to charm school—Riker's Island, maybe.

I turned my attention to Bethany. "So you're not feeling well?"

Bethany shook her head and made an exaggerated frown. "My dress *itches*," she whined.

"Don't look at me, I didn't dress her," the girl grunted. "I was supposed to be at Joey's today."

"She's from a nanny service," Bethany explained.

This wasn't the first time I'd seen a wealthy mother leave her child in the hands of someone I'd think twice about leaving my dog with. It was a strange phenomenon—one that I'd discussed with Dr. Marge and Candace—the way so many of these social women would blithely entrust a housekeeper who spoke no English, or an au pair who had been in this country for a week, or a nanny-service neophyte, to shepherd their child to something as important as a doctor's appointment.

"My shoes are tight," Bethany sulked.

"Well, here, let me take off the shoes." I did. "And would you like to take off the dress? We have a little robe you can put on."

"No."

"Now, Bethany, I'm just going to take a look in your mouth and ears. Is that all right?"

"No."

"Well, you do want to feel better, don't you? When did the fever start?"

"Yesterday."

I palpated Bethany's neck and shoulders and found her lymph nodes swollen. I asked Claire to draw blood. She did, and took the sample down to the lab to determine whether the infection was bacterial or viral.

Just then a young girl of about three came racing into my office, screaming in terror, and wrapped her arms around my legs.

"*Scared!!*" she wailed.

The force of her body flying into me almost knocked me off balance, and I took a step to steady myself.

"*Scared!*"

I reached down and cupped her contorted, bawling, quivering, terrified, crimson little face.

"What are you scared of, sweetheart?" I asked.

She gasped for breath and calmed down a fraction. "Doctor!! *Scary* doctor!!" Then she let loose a blubbery wail that brought forth copious saliva.

I felt terrible for her, but there was something comical and touching about her fear. I reached down and tried to lift her in my arms, but she squeezed my legs like a vise. I would have had more luck lifting an elephant.

"I'd slap the little freak," the babysitter said helpfully.

Dr. Cheng appeared in the doorway. The sight of him set off a fresh wail and a futile crouch down at my feet.

"There's little Margie," he said, leaning down, trying to disguise his embarrassment.

"*Scary man!*" Margie cried.

"Come on now, Margie . . . ," Dr. Cheng said.

Mercifully, Margie's mom walked into the room and pried her daughter off me.

"That's quite enough of that, Margie," she said firmly, lifting her daughter up. She turned to me. "I apologize. We're having a bad day."

She headed back down to Dr. Cheng's exam room.

"Thank you, Mrs. Fina," Dr. Cheng said to her. Then he turned to me and said sheepishly, "She doesn't like having her ears looked into." Then he grew serious and thoughtful for a moment, before exclaiming triumphantly, "Don't cry for me, Margie Fina!" Then he roared with laughter and rushed off.

Claire came back into the office and informed me that Bethany's blood had tested positive for a viral infection. These infections were extremely common in children her age and usually resolved themselves in thirty-six to forty-eight hours.

"Dr. Green, call on line four."

I picked up the exam-room phone—the voice on the other end spoke very fast in a very thick Southern accent.

"Hi there! This is Bethany's mom, I'm walking down the block to the office right this very second . . ."

"Okay."

"I'm almost there . . ."

"We'll be here."

"I'm walking into the building . . . I'm in the waiting room, I'm walking through the waiting room, down the hall . . ." Then Mom appeared, her ear still glued to the phone. *"Ta-da!"* she announced brightly, and expertly flipped the phone closed with one hand. In the other she was carrying at least half a dozen bulging shopping bags.

Bethany's mom was around thirty, slim, with streaked hair, wearing lots of makeup and flashy accessories. She gave an exaggerated sigh, plopped down the shopping bags, and exclaimed, "Well, here-we-are!" Then she opened her purse, took out a compact, flipped it open, and gave her makeup and hair a quick once-over. Finally she looked at me, as if for the first time.

"Liddy Clarkson, what a pleasure," she said, holding out her hand for a shake. She had a firm pulsing grip. "Is my baby girl sick? Boo-hoo. But I know the good doctor is going to fix you up in no time. Because we have a big day coming up on Saturday. It's the Friends of

Winterthur benefit lunch at the St. Regis, and Mommy is cochair. It's a *crucial* cause: The upholstery in the music room is positively disintegrating. Now, we have some very important decisions to make."

She reached into a shopping bag marked BONPOINT and pulled out three tiny outfits on satin hangers: a yellow Chanel-like suit, a full-length pink taffeta gown, and a black pantsuit with gold spangles. *"Un, deux, trois!"* she exclaimed. She hung up the mini-Chanel on the back of the door and the mini-taffeta on a hook on the wall. Then she turned to me and said, "Would you mind, honey?" before handing me the mini-pantsuit. Then she reached into a bag labeled PRINCES AND PRINCESSES and pulled out three pairs of sequined slippers and placed them on the floor in front of their respective mates.

"There now!" she exclaimed.

She stood back, hands on hips, and scrutinized each ensemble in turn, narrowing her eyes, lower lip jutting out, a low "mmm" escaping from her lips.

Bethany watched this whole performance with a look of defeated dread. The babysitter was chomping her gum and looking bored. I was beginning to feel like a fool, holding up the little black pantsuit.

"Mrs. Clarkson, Bethany has a viral—"

"Shhhh! Not now, sugar, I'm thinking. . . . Hmmm, I'm leaning towards the suit. Doctor, what's your opinion?"

"My opinion is that Bethany should be in bed, drinking lots of liquids, taking Advil, and eating chicken noodle soup if she feels up to it. She should be back to herself in two to three days."

Mrs. Clarkson jerked her head, as if startled. "What about the antibiotics?"

"Bethany has a viral infection. Antibiotics would be useless."

"Bethany has an infection, and I would like her to receive antibiotics."

"Mrs. Clarkson, the overuse of antibiotics, particularly in children, is creating new strains of resistant bacteria. This is a very real problem. Not only would antibiotics do nothing to lessen the course of Bethany's sickness, they might do her some harm."

I watched as she took all this in, and then, with a little shrug, tossed it all out again.

"I was always given antibiotics when I was a sick little girl and I don't think they did *me* any harm."

Mrs. Clarkson was clearly a woman used to instant gratification.

"I really would rather not prescribe any antibiotics for Bethany."

"Oh, honestly, Doctor, I have a very busy week ahead of me: Twelve *Du Ponts* are coming to the Winterthur benefit, and Bethany doesn't have an outfit! I don't have time to argue about antibiotics." She took the mini-Chanel off the door and handed it to the babysitter. "Would you help Bethany get into this? Doctor, would you have the front desk call in the prescription to a pharmacy near the Waldorf? Oh, Bethany, cheer up, you know what Mommy says: 'Glum little girls never get husbands.'"

"Mrs. Clarkson, this is a doctor's office, not a dressing room. And I am not prescribing antibiotics for Bethany."

She turned on me with a look of wounded incredulity. Underneath her wide-eyed façade, I could see the gears churning—and then click into place. She gave me a blazing smile that failed to disguise the rage behind it. "Everyone who is *anyone* uses Madison Pediatrics, so you must know what you're doing. I just hope Bethany doesn't *die,* that's my only concern. I guess there's really nothing more we need to discuss, then. So would you be so kind as to leave us alone so that Bethany can try on her pretty outfit? And don't worry, Bethany honey, Mommy has her own antibiotics she can give you."

During my residency, I'd come to the conclusion that there were some parents who almost instinctively raise their children with the right balance of nurturing and independence. The great majority of parents do their sincere best but tend to go slightly overboard in one direction or other. Then there are a small number of parents who are almost pathological in passing on their own unresolved neuroses to their children. Liddy Clarkson was the poster mom for this third group. By standing up to her on the antibiotics, I had already pushed the envelope, so I decided just to let her use the exam room as her personal dressing room. And I hoped that there was somebody in Bethany's family who was a little saner.

I wrote up my recommendations for Bethany's care, told her mother to call me with any questions, and left her to her fashion show.

My next patient was eleven-year-old Caleb Saltonstall. I saw from Caleb's chart that he and his parents, Marshall and Elizabeth, lived in Greenwich Village and had a second house on Monhegan Island, Maine. Under *Profession*, both had written "activist/environmentalist/philanthropist." I walked into the exam room to find Caleb, a skinny boy with longish blond hair and big green eyes, sitting on the exam table wearing baggy jeans, gigantic sneakers, a loose sports jersey, and at least a dozen rings and necklaces. He looked like a prepubescent pop-rock-rap-star wannabe. His parents stood on either side of him, looking worried.

"Hello, I'm Dr. Green."

"Marsh Saltonstall."

"Libby Cabot-Saltonstall."

Marsh and Libby were blond and fair, had handsome, open faces and tall, toned bodies. They both wore unbleached cotton shorts and shirts, and molded sandals. Looking at them, I could practically smell the Maine sea air.

"Hi, I'm Caleb," their son said with a knowing smirk.

"Nice to meet you all. I see that Caleb saw Dr. Clark six months ago for a check-up, which you passed with flying colors. Is there something that brings you in today?"

Caleb said, "No," while his parents said, "Yes."

"Well, maybe we should start with the yeses."

"Caleb won't eat," Libby said.

"I won't eat the crap you serve," Caleb said.

Mom tried to disguise her mortification with a little smile, but it came out closer to a twitch.

"We're vegetarians," Marsh explained.

"More like Nazitarians. They don't allow meat in the house. Or sugar. So I refuse to eat there. I mean, would you eat a lentil-tofu loaf? It tastes like moldy sawdust."

"But you're eating somewhere?" I asked.

Caleb smiled.

Dad looked at me, more in sadness than anger, and said, "We found a Big Mac wrapper in his book bag."

Mom closed her eyes, the better to absorb the blow. "Poison," she whispered.

"It may be poison, but at least it's edible. Which is more than I can say for your seitan kebabs."

"We were hosting a fundraiser for the Farm Animal Liberation Front—we're both on the board—and Caleb walked in eating a corn dog," Dad said.

"On a *stick*," Mom moaned.

"It was dee-licious," Caleb said gleefully.

I didn't think I should tell Marsh and Libby that one summer, when I was about Caleb's age, I had practically lived on corn dogs.

Marsh and Libby exchanged a glance, straightened up, and changed tack.

"We're worried about Caleb's cholesterol," Mom said briskly.

"And his liver functions," Dad added.

"We think tests would be appropriate," Mom said.

"Do you feel all right?" I asked Caleb.

"I feel great. Unless I eat one of Mom's kasha-cauliflower casseroles. They make me sick, for sure."

"Absent any symptoms, I don't usually recommend cholesterol and liver function tests for eleven-year-olds, but I don't see why we can't run them. My medical assistant will be in to take your blood."

Caleb sighed heavily and rolled his eyes. Then a little twinkle came into his eye.

"Mom and Dad eat roast beef," he said casually.

Marsh and Libby flushed a rare-roast-beef color.

There was a long silence.

"Once a year," Marsh squeaked with a little shrug, straining to be offhand.

"On Christmas Eve," his wife added.

"It's a Saltonstall tradition."

"Dating back to 1844."

"It's organic beef."

"Humanely raised."

"And slaughtered?" Caleb asked with mock innocence.

"Claire will be right in," I said, leaving them to their . . . beef.

Late that afternoon, Christina Allen popped in and told me that she'd spoken to Lucy Clarke in Sydney and that it would be fine with her if both Arthur and I took the apartment. She left me a set of keys so that I could show it to him. After seeing my last patient of the day, I called Arthur and told him the news.

"But, Shelley, we've signed a lease on the place in Carroll Gardens."

"We can get out of it."

"Do you think it's right to break a lease? That building isn't owned by some large corporation, it's owned by a family."

"Arthur, I will be more than happy to pay two months' rent on that apartment, to do whatever you and the owners feel is fair."

"Oh, I guess this is the way the rich operate—on a whim. Change your mind, write a check, and all is right in the world."

I took a deep breath. "It's a lovely apartment, honey, and I think we'd be very happy there. And there's a macaw, named Harry, who talks and is adorable. It's quiet and cozy and has charming views. Arthur, I think it would be a very romantic place for us to be together."

"All right, Shelley, I'll take a look at the place. But I don't feel right about just breaking a lease willy-nilly."

"How about Thursday night? Meet me here at the practice at about six thirty, and we'll walk over and take a look."

"See you then."

21

DR. MARGE WAS the consummate professional all week. She went about the business of being a pediatrician as if nothing upsetting was happening in her personal life. If anything, she seemed to be more focused, and my respect for her grew even stronger. I responded by treating her the way I always had. She clearly was not interested in discussing what had happened or its aftermath, and certainly not at work. On Wednesday, she surprised me by asking me if I wanted to grab a quick lunch with her. I accepted.

We went to a small café on Lexington Avenue, and she requested a quiet corner table in the back.

"I come here when I want to hide out. It's one of the less chic places in the neighborhood. Believe me, at most restaurants around here a half dozen of our patients or parents would come by and we'd spend our entire lunch hearing about their sore throats, potty training, and latest report cards. Some days I'm in the mood for all that. Not today."

The waiter arrived, and we both ordered salad nicoise.

"I asked you out for lunch, Shelley, to tell you that I'm thinking of taking a year's sabbatical."

I was so surprised that I just sat there speechless. Dr. Marge patted my hand.

"Don't look so shocked, dear girl, it's not the end of the world. And, in fact, I haven't decided for sure yet. If I do take a leave, it will mean an increased patient load for all the other doctors in the practice, so I want to discuss it with all of you before I make a final decision."

"Can I assume that this was triggered by . . . ?"

"It was certainly the final straw, yes. It turns out my husband has been leading something of a double life for some time now. We've been married for twenty-seven years, I suspected that on some of his long business trips . . . but nothing like this. I've filed for divorce, which he won't be contesting . . . unless he wants to find himself living in a refrigerator box." She picked up her folded napkin, gave it a sharp flick to open it, and put it on her lap. "So . . . suddenly I am faced with a yawning gap in my life. With the boys gone, I am essentially alone."

Our salads and coffees arrived.

"Do you have any idea what you'd like to do if you take a year off?" I asked.

"You know, when something like this happens to a woman, she has to be very careful—it can start a downward spiral. Bitterness is very unbecoming. Perhaps I'll go to Hungary for a year; they are in desperate need of pediatricians there. I've been helping to support a children's clinic in Budapest for more than a decade now, and I know they would be happy to have me. That would by my high-minded choice. Another part of me would like to do nothing but travel to all the places I've longed to visit: China, Africa, New Zealand. What I would really like most is to have a passionate affair, but that, sadly, cannot be booked through a travel agent. Isn't this salad marvelous?"

"Delicious. It would be absolutely fine with me if you took a sabbatical. I'll miss you terribly, of course, but I'll do my part to hold down the fort while you're gone. In fact, it seems to me that everyone is incredibly loyal to you and that you'd have universal support. Now if Candace was leaving, that would be another matter."

"Very true," she said with a smile. "Rest assured that my plans won't interfere with your summer with the Walkers. Amanda Walker is a real social force in this town and having her as a client is very good for Madison Pediatrics. Unfortunately, one must think this way."

"I understand."

"You do know, don't you, that Amanda has a reputation for being quite capricious? So stay on your toes. But, Shelley, tell me something about you. Have you set a date for the wedding?"

"Um, no, actually, we haven't. In fact . . ." I suddenly had a powerful desire to open up to Dr. Marge, to tell her what had happened and to get her opinion.

"Yes . . . ?"

"I don't know, I'm having some second thoughts."

"Shelley, you are going to marry this man. Probably have children with him. This is not a decision to make lightly. Take it from me."

"I almost slept with another man," I said simply—the words just came out, with no forethought. I felt instantly lighter.

It was Dr. Marge's turn to look shocked. Then she said, "This lunch just got a lot more interesting. Tell me more. And I promise you, my discretion matches your own."

I told her the story of my night with Josh Potter, leaving out some of the details, but none of the emotional turmoil. When it was over, Dr. Marge was quiet for a moment and then she said, "I'll give you my advice, but remember, it's my advice and it's your life and I believe each of us has to be the ultimate judge of what is right for us. I would think long and hard before tossing aside your Arthur. Yes, he sounds somewhat rigid, but he also sounds genuine. We women have to be very careful to protect our hearts, because in spite of all of our professional advances, we are still very different from men. We feel things more deeply."

Outside it had started raining, the interior of the restaurant grew dark and enfolding, there was classical music playing, Marge and I fell into an easy silence. An older couple came into the restaurant, well-dressed, understated. They had the comfortable familiarity that comes only with time. They were charming to the hostess, and after they were seated, the man reached over, took the woman's hand, and said something that made her smile.

I looked over to Marge—there were tears in her eyes.

22

I ARRIVED AT Dr. Charles Spenser's office at New York Hospital at five fifteen. I had no idea if Alison's father would be accompanying her, but I wouldn't be surprised if she showed up with just Mrs. Figueroa. Because it was the end of the day, the waiting room was almost empty. There was one boy, about Alison's age, wearing a cap to disguise his hair loss. I hoped he would be gone before she arrived.

I asked the receptionist if Dr. Spenser could give me a few minutes alone. I had faxed Alison's records over the day before, but I wanted to discuss the case with him briefly, and I also wanted to say hello. His blend of diligence, intelligence, and compassion had been a model for me during my residency.

The receptionist signaled for me to go back to his office. Charles Spenser was sitting at his desk, reading a chart. He was about sixty, tall, with thick silver hair and enormous vigor. A widower, he had moved to New York four years ago from Baltimore—where he'd been at Johns Hopkins—after his wife's death. His office was lined with awards, citations, and affiliations. When he saw me he broke into a warm smile and stood up. In spite of his fame and reputation, the man was completely down to earth.

"Dr. Green, look at you."

I felt a surge of pride as we shook hands. He knew how hard I had worked during my residency. And, of course, there was also the matter of my appearance, which was clearly a pleasant surprise to him.

"Thank you for seeing my patient on such short notice, Dr. Spenser."

"You're a practicing physician now. It's *Charles*."

His calling me Dr. Green had been a mark of respect; his asking me to call him Charles was a mark of friendship. I was being accepted, by one of the best, into the fellowship of Manhattan pediatricians. I felt my anxiety about Alison lessen—I wasn't in this alone. I smiled gratefully.

"So, how is the Upper East Side?" he asked.

"A world unto itself. The reality quotient can run a little low."

"I've no doubt. I've had a chance to look at Alison Young's chart. There's nothing I can tell you that you don't already know. Is there anything else I should know?"

I told him about Alison's mother.

"That's terribly sad," he said, "and the mother's misdiagnosis has obviously added to the family's pain."

"She's a lovely girl."

He looked at me. "We'll do our very best for her, won't we?"

"We will."

His intercom lit up. "Dr. Spenser, Dr. Green has a call on line two."

I picked up the phone. "This is Dr. Green."

"Francis Young here."

"Good afternoon."

"Alison won't be coming to the doctor's office."

"What?"

"I've decided to take my daughter to London for treatment. Quite frankly, I feel English doctors are superior."

"Mr. Young, I would implore you to reconsider. Dr. Spenser is a superb doctor."

"To be perfectly honest, Dr. Green, I simply do not have a great deal of confidence in you."

"When are you leaving?" I asked.

"First thing in the morning. My daughter is not well."

"I understand that. Does she have a physician over there?"

"Yes. She's being seen the day after tomorrow."

"Good. Will you be returning to New York?"

"Obviously that depends on her treatment, but I would certainly hope so. My work is in New York and Alison loves Brearley."

"Do you have a phone number over there?" There was a pause. "Until you tell me otherwise, Mr. Young, I am going to consider myself Alison's New York pediatrician."

There was another pause. "I appreciate your concern." He gave me his London number and hung up.

I sat there across from Charles Spenser, feeling my confidence, so recently boosted, plunging. Had I driven Mr. Young, and Alison, away? Had I failed—right in front of this wonderful and important doctor?

"Shelley, you handled that perfectly."

"No, I didn't."

"Listen to me. This is an unusual case, and it happened to land in your lap very early in your career. A sudden death like that plunges a family into shock, and it's not a shock that Alison or her father can recover from in eight months. You've been the recipient of some very strong aftershocks, so to speak. They're not easy to absorb, especially for a doctor like you. During your residency I saw over and over how much you cared. Well, we doctors have to remember self-care." He reached over, put his hand on mine, and gave it a reassuring squeeze. "You're going to have a wonderful career, Dr. Green, but you've got to find a balance. If there's one thing I've learned treating sick children, it's that life is tenuous. I've learned the value of laughter, and fun, and even indulgence. I don't know what's going on in the rest of your life, but I hope it's not all work. Because if it is, ironically, your work will suffer. You've earned the right to have fun, too, Shelley Green. Will you promise me you'll try and do that?"

I managed a nod and a quiet, "Yes. And thank you."

Dr. Spenser clapped his hands and rubbed them together vigorously. "Well, we've both got many miles to go before we sleep!"

And with that, we stood in unison.

23

DR. SPENSER'S ADVICE stayed with me. I was still finding my rhythm as a practicing pediatrician. I felt I had done a poor job handling Alison's father, and that the consequences were still undetermined. All my life I'd disguised my insecurities behind my hard work. Once I was out in the real world of medicine, there was nowhere to hide. It was a serious responsibility, and I was definitely still on a learning curve. He was right—I shouldn't, couldn't, let my career consume me. The more well rounded my life was, the better a doctor I would become. His words were just what I needed to renew my commitment to myself.

I was in my office late on Thursday, making notes on a chart, when Candace knocked on my open door. "You have a gentleman caller."

"Is he tall, dark, and handsome?"

"He's tall, fair, and looks like a keeper to me."

"Really?"

"Definitely. But what the hell do I know, I'm on my third husband. I think I finally got it right. This one loves me even as a one-tit wonder."

"Candace with one tit is better than most women with two."

"I bet you say that to all the breast cancer patients."

"Busted. Send in the keeper."

Arthur walked into my office, and said, "Boy, this is a long way from that clinic where you volunteered during your internship."

"Does that surprise you?"

"I knew it was going to be posh, but I didn't expect anything on this scale."

"It's a terrific practice, and I'm proud to be a part of it."

His face softened. "And I'm proud of you." He leaned down and gave me a kiss.

"Well, shall we go look at the apartment?"

"Let's."

It had turned into a glorious summer evening, and the Upper East Side looked like something close to paradise: Flowers bloomed in window boxes and planters, a canopy of green trees enveloped the streets, the people looked beautiful, the shops glowed, the architecture was graceful and stately. A little girl holding a balloon ran past us, laughing with delight; her proud parents beamed. I imagined living on these blocks, being that girl's doctor, having this neighborhood be my home.

The doorman remembered me and opened the door for us with a flourish. I smiled and said, "Thank you," trying to compensate for Arthur's awkwardness.

We walked into the apartment, and Arthur let out an involuntary gasp.

"Hey, baby, shake it, shake it."

"That's Harry."

I walked over to his cage. Harry strutted over to the bars and tilted his head down, presenting his crown for me to scratch.

"Is it legal to import macaws?" Arthur said. "Aren't they endangered?"

"This one certainly isn't."

"That's very glib."

"Oh, come on, sweetheart, lighten up. Look at this place. Isn't it beautiful?"

I wanted Arthur to share my excitement about this wonderful opportunity, to see it as a step forward in our lives.

"It's certainly very comfortable."

"Let me give you a tour."

I took him by the hand and showed him all around, every gaping closet and cozy nook, the classic bath, the kitchen with its banquette and view of hidden gardens, the little laundry room tucked in by the door to the service elevator. Arthur took it all in with a look of mild shock on his face. We ended the tour where we began, at the foyer end of the living room, looking toward the dreamy view of the leafy treetops outside.

"Well, what do you think?" I was sure that Arthur would be as captivated by the apartment as I was.

"I don't think I can move in here, Shelley."

"Why not?"

"I just wouldn't feel comfortable living in this kind of opulence."

"Arthur, this place is relatively understated. You should see Amanda Walker's."

"I'd rather not."

"Are you honestly saying that you don't want us to take this apartment?"

"Yes."

Although we were standing side by side, I felt a gaping chasm open up between us.

"You been punk'd, you been punk'd."

As I went over and petted Harry, a terrible sadness descended on me. The bird took an affectionate nibble on my fingertip.

"So long, Harry," I said.

Arthur and I rode down in the elevator in silence. When we got out on the street, it was dusk. I turned to him and saw that he looked pretty sad, too.

"I'm going to head back to the office to get a little more work done," I said.

"Do you hate me?" he asked.

"No, I don't hate you."

"Is it Carroll Gardens then?" he said.

"I don't know, Arthur. I need a day or two to think about this."

"What's that supposed to mean?"

"I'm honestly not sure."

He looked down, and I knew his male pride was absorbing the blow. My instinct was to reach out and touch him, comfort him, give in on the apartment. But I didn't. I stood my ground.

"Well, my train is in that direction," he said, gesturing toward Lexington.

"And I'm heading this way," I said, gesturing toward Madison.

We just stood there, in the sweet evening air, both of us tugged in two directions at once.

24

I HAD NO IDEA what to pack for a weekend in the Hamptons.
Should I go casual—chinos and jeans, pullovers and sneakers? Less
casual—slacks and skirts, sweaters and slip-ons? Un-casual—dresses
and sweater sets, heels and jewelry and makeup? As I struggled to
decide on Saturday morning, I could feel my social anxiety percolat-
ing. At the Walkers' Hamptons beach house I would be on foreign
turf, without the security and authority of Madison Pediatrics. Could
I hold my own, keep my mouth shut when I had nothing to say, be
interesting when I did talk, be friendly but not a butt kisser, suss,
pick up the right fork, and just generally not feel completely intimidated by people with a lot more money and breeding than I had? I
scanned the array of clothes tossed on every available surface of my
apartment.

I looked at the clock: 8:45! I had fifteen minutes to get myself together, and I was still in my bathrobe. I wished I could just bring one
of everything but then I would arrive with three suitcases for a one-
night stay.

My phone rang.

"Shelley, it's Amanda, and I bet you're standing there trying to figure out what the hell to bring."

"Oh no . . . well, actually, oh yes. Freaking out, in fact."

Amanda laughed, and I instantly felt better.

"Bring what you feel most comfortable in. We've been invited to dinner at Zana and Cotty Clay's place. It's a pay-your-dues dinner for me. She's the great pillar of old Hamptons society, and I suck up to her, well, basically because I'm a social whore and Zana Clay is one of my great role models. You can just goof on the whole thing. So bring a nice dinner outfit if you have one, and if you don't we'll go buy you one this afternoon."

"Amanda, maybe I should skip the dinner."

"Don't be silly, I wouldn't hear of it. You're my guest and believe me, that counts for something out here."

"Josh Potter won't be there, will he? I really don't think it would be a good idea for me to see him again."

Amanda laughed.

"There's no chance Josh Potter will be there. He comes from an old family, but he doesn't give a damn about the social game. For some neurotic reason, I do. Besides, I didn't even tell Josh we were coming out this weekend, so not to worry. See you in a couple of hours."

It was thoughtful of Amanda to call, but I had no idea what "a nice dinner outfit" was. And who was Zana Clay? Was she related to Fran Templer? So much for having fun. Well, there was no turning back now. I slipped into jeans, a cream oxford shirt, woven sandals, and a matching belt. Then I threw a little of everything into my bag and went downstairs to wait for the car.

It was a Mercedes sedan driven by a middle-aged Russian. I settled into the buttery-soft backseat with the latest *People*. I had to buy it when I saw Prince Harry on the cover. I have a thing for the Royal Family, and wayward Harry was my current fav. I loved reading about his exploits with drugs, alcohol, and casual sex. Someone should set him up with one of the Bush twins—they have so much in common.

It was a nice day, a little humid, with clear skies and temperatures in the bearable eighties. God knows I'd seen enough pictures of the fabulous Hamptons to have some idea of what they looked like, and I kept waiting for the scenery to improve, but all I saw was an endless panorama of housing developments and scrub pines. Finally we hit Southampton and got on the famous Montauk Highway, which isn't a highway at all but a mostly two-lane road with a lot of traffic. I kept looking for hints of the vast estates of people like Steven Spielberg, Jerry Seinfeld, and Calvin Klein, but all I saw were mini-malls and motels. Still, the farther out we got the prettier it looked, and the village of Bridgehampton was filled with lovely old architecture, interesting shops, and well-dressed people.

We went a few more miles down the Montauk Highway, turned onto a residential street and—wow!—suddenly we were in Oz. It really did look as if someone had waved a magic wand over the landscape, a magic wand that dispensed money, taste, and a lot of gardeners. There were perfect green lawns everywhere, and perfect flowerbeds and specimen trees, all surrounding enormous old shingled houses with wide porches and stately turrets. There were lots of long gravel drives and tall privet hedges, tennis courts and trellises, white paddock fences and creeping roses, carriage houses and peeks of hidden swimming pools. What was missing was people. I guess they were all holed up in their furnished basements chugging Buds and watching NASCAR. I rolled down my window and inhaled the sea air—it smelled like expensive salt.

We turned, and suddenly we were in an even richer area, which didn't seem possible. The houses grew farther apart and even bigger—I mean they were mammoth, some of them were geometric and swooping; they looked like airport terminals. I could see dunes in the distance, and I realized we were parallel to the ocean, and that these were the oceanfront estates I'd been drooling over for years in the Celebrity Homes sections of my favorite magazines. As I looked at these gargantuan houses, I couldn't help thinking how much work it must take to keep them clean—I could barely stay on top of my studio. And then my inner Arthur remembered reading about the thirty-eight illegal Hondurans discovered living in a one-car garage in Newark. Sticking to that same density, I bet you could fit the entire population of Honduras into one of these mansions. I probably shouldn't point that out to Amanda.

We came to a sign that said FOLIE D'OR and turned down a long drive. In the distance, atop a dune, sat something that looked more like a giant sculpture than a house. It was very Geary-esque, undulating across the dune, sheathed in shimmery blue metal.

We reached the front of the house. It had a vast circular drive, in the middle of which was an enormous abstract fountain that looked to me like three anorexic girls partying on Ecstasy, but maybe that was because *People* had a picture of Paris and a couple of pals at an after-hours club. There was parking for, oh, forty to fifty cars as well as a little helipad over to the side.

I got out of the car and found myself at the bottom of a wide set of steps. The brushed-steel front doors were etched with more abstract, Paris-on-Ecstasy-inspired shapes. Suddenly the doors opened all by themselves, and there was Amanda, looking surreally small against the gargantuan house.

"Shelley, welcome!"

We met halfway up the steps and hugged. Amanda looked fresh and adorable in crisp khaki shorts, a white V-neck T-shirt, and white tennis shoes. Even dressed that simply, she managed to give off that air of being superrich. I suddenly felt like I should have a bucket of cleaning supplies in one hand.

"Isn't it ridiculous?" she said, gesturing to the house. "Well, what do you want for thirty-two million dollars? At least if the stock market crashes, we can melt it down for scrap."

Amanda slipped her arm through mine and led me up the steps. When we reached the top, I looked through the open doors. Straight ahead—across a vast expanse and through a towering window wall—was a sweep of sea-grass-dotted dunes and the glistening blue Atlantic beyond.

"Amanda, that view is a dream."

"I don't even notice it anymore," she said, leading me inside. "How decadent is that?"

The main room was just slightly smaller than the main concourse at Grand Central Station. Outsized sleek, wavy furniture was set in about a half-dozen groupings. I suddenly realized why the rich are so thin: it's all the exercise they get walking from one end of their houses to the other.

A tall, lean, well-groomed—and, yes, that's code for gay—man, wearing a hip suit and carrying my suitcase, appeared.

"Shelley, this is Andre, he runs Folie d'Or, brilliantly—without him I wouldn't even be able to find the kitchen. Andre is from Russia, he's descended from the tsars, and I got in a bidding war over him with Henry Kravis. Andre will show you to your room."

"A pleasure," Andre said with a little bow and a charming accent.

"After you settle in, come find me," Amanda said. "I'll be out by the pool, or the tennis court, or the gym, or just page me on your Binky—Andre will explain it all to you. We're delighted you're here, Shelley, just make yourself completely at home."

Make myself at home? Oh sure, no problem—after all, my

apartment looks like the Bilbao Guggenheim, sits on ocean dunes, and comes with its own majordomo.

"Right this way, Dr. Green," Andre said, heading down a rippling hallway that had a marble floor and stainless steel walls. "Folie d'Or is divided into five sectors: central, master, guests, kids, and kitchen. You're actually the only guest this weekend, so you have this whole sector to yourself."

"Jeez, I've never had my own sector before. And call me Shelley."

Andre gave me a wry, knowing smile. "I'm actually descended from Russian peasants," he said.

"Hey, we might be distant cousins."

Andre led me into an enormous circular bedroom with its own curved window wall facing an elegant pool and the ocean beyond. Everything in the room was low to the floor: bed, dressers, couches, chairs. Maybe the Walkers had a lot of short friends.

Andre showed me the bath, which, thank God, did not have a window wall. It did, however, have a tub for six and a shower for twelve.

"This is wonderful, Andre, thank you."

"Oh, I haven't showed you the fun part yet: Binky." He held up a small gadget that looked like a cross between a remote control and a cell phone.

"Binky?"

"Yes, Binky. Amanda named it. Folie d'Or is a completely electronic, computerized house. Watch . . ." Andre pressed a button on Binky and the entire window wall turned opaque. "Should you want a little privacy. Or should you want to sleep late . . ." He pressed another button and the window wall turned black.

"That's amazing. How does it work?"

"The windows have two panes with a thin layer of colorless gas between them. This gas can instantly become opaque or black through a process called ionic pigmentation."

"Really?"

"That's what they told me," he said with an offhand shrug. "So . . . this button opens and closes your door, this one turns on your bath, here's where you program the water temperature, this button will adjust your bed to eighteen different positions, this opens the closets, this will set your wake-up call, this will allow you to call the kitchen and put in an order, this one controls the radio, this one will raise the TV up from under the floor, and this little screen is a computer with twenty-four-hour Internet access."

"Medical school wasn't this complicated," I said.

"It can be tricky. Anne Bass dropped Binky in the tub and her bed folded in two, Rush Limbaugh came on the radio, and the kitchen delivered two poached eggs with hot-fudge sauce. But don't panic— this little orange button is my direct line. If you need anything, just press it."

Andre left, and suddenly it was just me and Binky in the sector. I felt incredibly exposed with all the glass. I walked around the room trying to find a corner where I was hidden from the outside, but since the room was round I was out of luck. I wanted to make the window wall opaque and I pushed a button on Binky—a flat-screen TV began to rise up from the floor. Damn. I pushed it again and the TV retracted.

I started to unpack, but when it came time to hang up my dress I couldn't remember which Binky button opened the closet, so I just draped it on the bed. Then I sat on the edge of the bed feeling ridiculous. Could I really spend a big chunk of the summer here? Doubtful. You didn't have to be Mahatma Arthur to find Folie d'Or a bit much. I'd just have to find a diplomatic way to tell the Walkers that I didn't think the arrangement was going to work out.

But I was here now, and I decided, in the spirit of Dr. Spenser's advice, to make the best of it. I bounced on the bed a few times, trying to conjure up some carefree insouciance. It was all mine, my little playpen for the next twenty-four hours. So play, Shelley, play.

Just then Binky made a beeping noise and Amanda's voice came on, "Shelley, have you settled in yet?"

I picked up Binky. "Yes."

"Come meet Jerry."

"Where are you?"

"Walk out the door leading to the pool and turn right."

I stepped outside. The entire ocean side of the house was surrounded by a vast bleached stone patio, and sitting in a distant corner of it, practically in a different time zone, under a huge white umbrella, was Amanda. I began the trek, hoping my electrolytes would hold up. As I got closer, I saw Jerry Walker talking on his cell phone. He was about forty, not handsome, not homely, with a look that was somehow both lean-and-hungry and polished-and-pampered.

"Hi, Shelley, thanks for coming out. It's a real pleasure to meet you," Jerry said without getting off the phone.

"Thank you for having me."

"So I've got it all worked out with Marjorie Mueller about the summer. Listen, anything you want, anything at all, you let me know. You saved my daughter and I am profoundly in your debt forever, I mean that, for infinity." Then he turned his back and started to walk away. "You're kidding me, the pipeline's a go? That stock is going to triple on Monday. . . ." And then he was out of earshot.

"Jerry isn't really rude, he's just rude. It comes with the territory. Masters of the universe answer to no one. And that includes their wives," she said ruefully. "Yes, you could call me a Wall Street widow. But I'm not complaining. So, how about a drink or a snack? We'll be eating soon, then I thought you and I could pop into town for a little shopping." She pushed a button on her Binky, and within a moment a fresh-faced teenage girl appeared. "Maureen, this is Dr. Green. She'll be with us for the weekend. What would you like?"

"Lemonade?" I asked.

Maureen nodded and disappeared.

"Maureen's from County Cork. You can't get local help out here anymore, unless you want to pay them twenty-five dollars an hour. The Hamptons have a gush-down economy. Smith and Jones will be back from their riding lesson any minute."

Lunch began to unfold, and it was another surreal experience. Several Maureens appeared and deftly, silently, set the table as we sat there. Platters of chicken salad, shrimp, vegetable salad, bread, cheese, fruit, and cookies appeared. The kids showed up, and Jerry— with the phone crooked in his neck—was suddenly anxious and hovering.

"How do they look?" he asked me nervously.

In their white shirts and jodhpurs, Jones and Smith both looked as if they had stepped out of one of those Ralph Lauren ads.

"They look wonderful," I said.

"You sure? Don't you want to palpate their lymph nodes or any-thing?"

"How are you both feeling?" I asked the children.

"Fine, thank you," they both answered.

"Yeah, but there might be something insidious, like a brain tumor or a stroke, that they don't feel yet," Jerry said.

Amanda shot me a glance that told me this was Jerry's little rou-tine.

"Barring any complaints, I really don't think an exam is necessary at this time." I lowered my voice. "In fact, I don't think it's a good idea to worry Smith and Jones with hypothetical diagnoses."

Clearly Jerry wasn't used to people contradicting him, and he looked at me in shock for a moment, before saying, "You're brilliant." He turned his attention back to the phone. "So run those figures again."

The children were well behaved during lunch, but they rarely spoke except to answer their mother's questions. Amanda chatted about the local social scene and ate three grapes. Jerry spent the entire lunch standing and talking on the phone, occasionally reaching down and grabbing a shrimp. It was as if all four members of the Walker family lived in their own little independent, very wealthy, kingdoms. The Green Family behemoth they weren't.

"Well, Shelley, how about a little shopping?" Amanda said, getting up. "I need a hostess gift for Zana Clay, and you need a little dinner dress."

"Actually, I brought a dress out with me."

"Well, then you need *another* little dinner dress."

"I'll just run and get my purse."

"Oh, don't be silly, all the shops out here know me. They'll be happy to bill you."

We journeyed to the front of the house and got into a Mercedes sports car. Amanda even drove like a rich person, facing me, chatting away, giving the road an occasional offhand glance, almost like the car was driving itself. When we got to town, she slid into a parallel parking space with one breezy little twirl of the wheel.

The village of East Hampton was basically Madison Avenue by the Sea, except out here everything was shingled and gray, with lots of cheery trim and geraniums, and everyone's chic clothing was pastel instead of black, with lots of straw hats and sandals. Oh, and there was a windmill and a couple of pretty ponds. And that unmistakable fragrance—*l'eau de dough*—hung over the whole town.

Amanda led me into a boutique, and as she swept in, the whole store went still for a second. Then the shoppers returned to their perusing with exaggerated nonchalance—although I heard one woman whisper excitedly to another, "That's Amanda Walker!" Amanda made a beeline for a strapless satin midcalf dress with narrow multicolored horizontal stripes. It was absolutely stunning, like something Catherine Zeta-Jones might wear to a premiere.

"This is gorgeous, Shelley, try it on."

The owner, a chic middle-aged woman with pale skin, cherry hair, and matching lipstick, appeared.

"Amanda, how lovely to see you."

"Cecile, this is Shelley. We're mad for this dress."

"It's my favorite dress in the store," Cecile said.

I'd never worn anything remotely that flashy.

"But do you think it's me?" I asked.

Cecile gave me the once-over. "Yes," she pronounced.

"But aren't horizontal stripes fattening?"

"On you, they will be womanizing."

Womanizing?

Amanda handed me the dress. "March, young lady," she said, pointing to the dressing room.

I poured myself into the dress and managed to get it zipped up. It was tight. I stepped out of the dressing room.

"Wow!" Amanda cried.

"You look ravishing," Cecile gushed, and I noted that several of the other shoppers were looking on in agreement.

I looked in the mirror. There was no denying it was a beautiful dress—the design, the cut, the workmanship, the material—and that I did look sort of . . . glamorous in it. And it showed just enough of my cleavage to make me feel very sexy. But it didn't leave a lot of wiggle room, and I wondered if I could possibly sit down in it. Maybe I'd be better off in something a little less showy.

"I don't know, it's awfully . . . ," I began.

"It's awfully fabulous, and I'm buying it for you," Amanda announced.

"I couldn't possibly—"

"—stop me. Cecile, wrap it up, please."

There was no price tag on the dress, and I was sure it was in the thousands, but as we walked down the street Amanda told me that she got twenty-five percent off on everything in the store. The rich get richer. Or at least less less rich.

Amanda bopped into a fancy food shop and a suave, scrubbed—yes, that's code for gay—middle-aged man wearing a striped apron hustled over to us. "Good afternoon, Mrs. Walker," he said with a French accent.

"Hi, Henri. This is my pal Shelley. I want to put together a little basket of goodies for Zana Clay. Do you have anything new and fun?"

"Oh, yes, we have some delicious fun." He led us over to a pine hutch filled with jars and tins. "This is pomegranate in banana aspic from New Zealand. New Zealand, by the way, is the new Tuscany."

"Is it?" Amanda asked.

"Oh yes. And aspic is the new chutney."

"Anything else I should know?" Amanda asked.

"Ale is the new merlot. And some people are claiming that lunch is the new dinner, but that's absurd."

"It is?"

"Absolutely—breakfast is the new dinner."

Suddenly I caught a glimpse of Josh Potter out on the sidewalk—that hair, those eyes—he didn't see me! I dashed to the back of the store and hid behind the open panel of another hutch. There were baskets of bread everywhere. A young woman in a striped apron appeared.

"Hi, may I help you pick a bread? We have forty-seven kinds."

My heart was thumping so hard in my chest that I was surprised she didn't ask me to quiet down. "Do you have white?" I managed.

"White what?"

"Bread."

She looked at me uncomprehendingly. Then I heard it, from my hiding place behind the hutch door.

"Hi, Amanda," Josh said.

"Well, look what the cat dragged in," she purred.

"You didn't tell me you'd be out this weekend."

"It was a last-minute thing."

"Have you heard from Shelley?"

He asked about me!!!

"Are you all right?" the girl asked.

"Shhhh!" I hissed.

"You mean Dr. Green?" Amanda asked.

"Don't be coy with me, Amanda."

I couldn't let their little charade continue; it wasn't fair to Amanda. We were all adults, after all. So I joined them.

"Why, Josh, hi . . . hi-hi . . . *hi!*" I said.

"Shelley, your sly fox friend here has been keeping you to herself, naughty-naughty," Josh said. He was wearing slightly frayed khaki shorts—those legs!—and a wrinkled blue oxford shirt and some sort of very cool-looking thin leather bracelet.

"Shelley just arrived a little while ago," Amanda said.

"Well, welcome to the Hamptons," he said, and then he smiled, that wide guileless smile of his.

"Thanks," I said.

"So, what are your plans for the rest of the weekend?"

"Um . . . ," I stammered, as visions of Arthur intruded on my bliss. I could feel it coming, a guilt-fueled locomotive, unstoppable, Shelley's verbal vomit: "You know, I'm actually out here on a professional basis,

I'm really not out here to socialize, I mean look at me, I shouldn't even be allowed in the Hamptons without some kind of special permit, ha-ha, just kidding, not really . . ."

Josh put a gentle hand on my arm, "Shelley, you are exactly the breath of fresh air the Hamptons needs."

I took a quick breath and shoved Arthur out of my bliss. "That is the nicest thing anyone has ever said to me."

"We're going to dinner at Zana Clay's tonight," Amanda said.

"My condolences," Josh said.

The three of us laughed, and Henri glided up with a basket full of goodies. "Your basket, Mrs. Walker."

"Zana will go gaa-gaa," Amanda said. "Come along, Shelley."

"*Hasta la vista,*" Josh said as we left.

25

WE DROVE OVER to the Clays in a huge white 1950s convertible with enormous fins that felt more like a boat than a car. Amanda told me that she'd bought the car last summer at a Southampton charity auction after having "five glasses of champagne, four hits of pot, and three snorts of cocaine" and deciding it would be "a blast" to arrive at parties in it. After driving for all of two minutes, we turned down a lane that ran alongside a large empty field—"Empty fields scream old money," Amanda informed me—before reaching the house.

The place was colossal, looming, and covered with dark shingles. With its turrets, gables, porches, and walkways, it looked almost like a village unto itself, a spooky village where rich people kept their servants chained to the walls in some dark basement crypt. The grounds were neat enough, but there was none of that overdone obsessive-compulsive perfection that so many of the other places out here had.

The ghoulish theme continued when the front door swung open as we approached, revealing a butler who looked like he was about two hundred years old.

"Greetings," he intoned.

"Hi, Reginald," Amanda said.

We entered an enormous foyer that had an immense living room opening off to the right and an immense dining room to the left. The place looked like it hadn't been redecorated in fifty years, but every piece of furniture was beautiful, the lighting was romantic, and the overall effect was of old money that didn't feel like it had to prove itself.

Suddenly a woman appeared and crossed the foyer toward us. She was old, like her money, and skeletally thin, with a face that was both taut and craggy. She wore white linen slacks, a loose white linen blouse with the top three buttons open, gold sandals, a woven gold belt, and a clutch of long necklaces with large red stones. Her silver hair was short, swept back, and glistening, and she wore deep red lipstick that matched her necklaces. She moved with a strange gait— hips forward, head back, elbows bent, wrists dangling—that was both languid and tense. The total effect was both drop-dead chic and pretty weird, she looked like a *creature* of some sort, certainly a close relative of Homo sapiens, but somehow she'd taken an evolutionary byway and ended up, well, she'd ended up Zana Clay.

"Amanda, darling," she said in a deep theatrical voice.

"Zana!"

They air-kissed.

"You look adorable, *comme toujours*," Zana said.

"And you look divine, celestial, exquisite," Amanda gushed.

"Good girl," Zana said. Amanda handed her the gift basket. "Oh, how marvelous," she said, putting it on a side table without a second glance. She turned to Jerry. "And Jerry." Then she turned to me. "And . . ."

"Zana Clay, this is Shelley Green."

"It's nice to meet you," I said.

"How do you do, Shelley Gersh."

"It's Green."

"Oh . . . *Green* . . . Tell me, how do you spell that?" she asked.

The Shelley Green who'd gone to some pretty tough New York City public schools roared to my defense, ready to spit out, "That's right, bitch, I'm Jewish, you got a problem with that?" or maybe "That's right, freakface, I'm Jewish, and you look like the creature from the platinum lagoon."

But before my inner street kid could open her mouth, Amanda jumped in, "Oh, who cares how you spell it?"

"I suppose," Zana said mildly, as if she'd lost interest eons ago. She turned and headed into the living room. "Do come in."

As we followed her, Amanda leaned over to me and whispered, "I apologize for that."

Even though the living room was vast, it managed to be cozy, with four or five seating groups, and more soft lighting and wonderful old furniture. There was a fire going in the fireplace and that is where Zana led us. Three men got up; one woman remained seated.

"Cotty, you know Amanda and Jerry Walker. And this is Shelley Green."

Cotty Clay, who looked like he hadn't drawn a sober breath since the Eisenhower administration, was the opposite of his wife. He had let *everything* go, including his speech. He opened his mouth in greeting and sounds came out, "Haya walla, lapa flafluf snorkum." There were probably words buried in there somewhere, but they escaped me. Then he plopped back down in his armchair with a sigh of relief. Slack, ruddy-faced, wearing a strawberry jacket, he looked like a pink puddle.

"And this is Shirley and Blake Blake." Blake Blake? "And Owen Abbott."

Greetings were exchanged all around. The Blakes looked to be around sixty. Shirley Blake was a large-boned woman whose perfectly coiffed auburn hair framed a face that was, well . . . also large, enormous really; every feature was outsized. I found her homeliness sympathetic, and she had a smile that seemed genuine. Her husband was hale, hearty, and hammered, and punctuated every utterance with a piercing guffaw. Owen Abbott, the extra man, looked like an overgrown baby, with a perfectly round, pasty face and huge horn-rimmed glasses that made his eyes look like they were about to pop out of his head. He ran those peepers up and down my body and then licked his lips. I wondered if he had on diapers under his lime green slacks.

And I was worried about my social skills? The rich not only have more money than thee and me, they're weirder.

As if to confirm it, we all sat around while Amanda and Zana gossiped about other society women—I recognized some of the names from Page Six—and their husbands, riding instructors, personal trainers, and decorators, all of it elliptically, in a sort of code, in tones that oozed innuendo. I got the feeling that just about everyone was having an affair, hooked on Vicodin, drinking like a fish, a closeted lesbian, into S&M, or, gravest sin, had worn an outfit that made her look like a circus clown. Every once in a while Blake Blake would let out a rip-snorting guffaw apropos of nothing, Cotty Clay would blabber incomprehensibly, Shirley Blake would mention the Parish Museum benefit she was cochairing, and Owen Abbott would look at me, lick his lips, and announce, "I'm in bonds." Jerry had long ago retreated to a far corner of the room, where he was talking on his cell phone.

Then Shirley Blake came over and sat down next to me.

"The Blakes and the Clays go way back," she said, lowering her voice and rolling her eyes in Zana's direction.

"She's quite a character."

"Zana knows where every body is buried, probably because she shoveled the dirt on half of them herself. Amanda knows a hard social

truth: render unto Zana. I always found that whole whirl just too exhausting, not to mention meaningless, plus with my body, social
X-ray was never an option. So tell me, Shelley, what do you do?"

"I'm a pediatrician."

"No kidding. In town?"

"Yes."

"Goodness, this must be fate."

Here it comes, I thought. Her granddaughter has a sore throat,
would I pop over after dinner and take a quick look?

"I work at WNET. Last week we were brainstorming for new show
ideas, and yours truly came up with an idea for a show for new moms,
expecting moms, all moms. I want to call it *Baby Talk* and have a pediatrician be the host. We could do segments on making your own baby
food, cloth versus disposable diapers, all the milestones, postpartum
depression, everything." She grew animated as she spoke, and I found
myself sharing her enthusiasm for the idea. "I mean, we're still in the
early stages, but everyone loved the idea, and you are just the kind of
doctor I imagined as host."

"You're very kind. It sounds like an amazing opportunity, but I'm
very very busy, I just started practice. Wait! I know a doctor who
would be absolutely perfect. My boss. She's witty and warm and a
great pediatrician. And she has a very strong point of view. We're both
fanatics about the current epidemic of hyperparenting—obsessing
over every aspect of a child's development, trying to control what is
essentially uncontrollable, taking all the joy and spontaneity out of
having a baby."

"I love it! I want this woman's name."

Dinner was announced, and Zana stood up and ordered us all to
"Come to table." The dining room was another lovely room, and I
was placed on the side of the table facing the terrace and the glittering moonlit sea beyond. I was between Pink Puddle and Human

Guffaw, and across from Diaper Baby, who kept leering at me with his bug eyes and saying things like "Bonds are a universe unto themselves," "Bonds are the foundation of democracy," and "Bonds are hot!" I much preferred Pink Puddle's fascinating insights, such as "Lob wolly winkum snorks" and "Natum norky whush wank."

The fish course, sole with wallpaper paste—Amanda had warned me that Zana had the worst cook in the Hamptons—had just been whisked away when, suddenly, over Diaper Baby's shoulder, an apparition appeared in the window and waved at me. Actually it wasn't an apparition—it was Josh! I looked around anxiously; no one else had seen him. He gestured for me to join him outside. I shook my head. Impossible. He gestured again. I shook my head again. He made a pleading gesture. I tried not to break into a grin.

"Would you excuse me a moment?"

"Whassa lum."

I got up and made like I was heading for the powder room, but as soon as I was out of sight, I went into the living room, quietly opened one of the French doors, and headed out to the patio.

"What are you doing here?" I whispered.

"Looking for you," he whispered back.

"Well, you found me."

"How's dinner with the dinosaurs?"

"Pretty prehistoric. But I better get back in."

"Oh, don't be silly, they're all too sloshed and self-absorbed to notice." He took my hand. "Let's go for a little walk."

"Josh, this isn't a good idea."

"Says who?"

"My conscience."

"Tell her to mind her own business. Come on."

We stepped off the patio and into the night, surrounded by the soft play of dunes and sea grass, the sky full of stars and a silver moon, the Atlantic up ahead, all of it vast and iridescent.

Josh put his arms around me and we kissed.

"Why don't we lay down a minute?" he whispered.

"I can't," I whispered.

"Yes, you can."

He went back to the patio and grabbed a beach towel, then came back and spread it on the sand. We lay down, and for a moment I thought of the dinner party, how little time I had, how crazy this was.

But then Josh kissed me again and I forgot all that.

Within moments we were entwined, greedy, grappling with each other's clothing. I got his shirt open and ran my hands over his chest. He got my zipper down and tugged off the dress. I heard a rip, but who cares? Then we were naked in the night. I felt a wild jolt of freedom and I went with it. We explored each other's bodies with our hands and lips, and then he was inside me. He stopped and looked down into my eyes.

"Oh, Josh," I moaned, pulling him into a kiss.

And from there it was gentle and wild, tender and fierce—and Josh took me to a place I'd never been before.

We ended up sprawled out next to each other, holding hands, looking up at the stars.

God, it was beautiful out there.

And then we heard Zana Clay's voice echo down from the dining room and we looked at each other and started laughing, and we fought to stifle it and that only made us laugh harder. I felt like a little kid except I never ever did stuff like this when I was a little kid and it was so exhilarating.

"I've got to get back in there," I said, when we finally wound down. I slipped into my bra and panties, then held up my dress—there was a long rip running down one side. It was ruined. "Oh God, what am I going to do?" I said, suddenly panicky.

Josh slipped his shirt over my shoulders. "Wait here," he said, and disappeared.

I hugged his shirt around me. What had just happened between us took the intensity of our loft tryst and multiplied it by a hundred. And where did that leave Arthur and me? But the guilt was nowhere near as strong this time. Arthur and I would have to talk, take a good honest look at our relationship. I lay back on the towel and looked up at the stars. My body felt delicious, suffused with a warm liquid relaxation. It was okay. Being here. Doing what I had just done.

Josh appeared, carrying a metal toolbox. We smiled at each other, and he cupped my face, leaned down, and gave me a light kiss. Which was the most romantic moment of the night. Then he opened the toolbox and took out a roll of duct tape.

"Do you always carry a toolbox?"

"As a matter of fact, I do. I like to build things."

"And you're going to tape the dress up?"

"Gonna try."

"Do you have a plan B?"

"Do you have a plan A?"

"Good point."

Josh picked up the tattered dress. Thank God Amanda hadn't paid retail. He deftly turned it inside out, taped the rip closed, reinforced it with more tape, and then turned it right side out. "Put it on."

He put his shirt back on, and I got into the dress and he zipped me up. The tear, which began below the bodice and ran down one side, wasn't too very visible. I felt like I was in a sausage casing, but better a sausage casing than walking back into the dinner in my bra and panties. Josh stepped back and appraised his work.

"Good as taped," he said. "Just don't breathe."

"Thank you," I said.

"Thank *you*," he said.

We kissed again, lightly.

"May I come see you tomorrow?" he asked, looking into my eyes.

I nodded. There was a pause. "Well, I better head in."

"Enjoy the cheese course," he said.

I slipped in the same door I'd slipped out of, made my way to the powder room, and looked at myself in the mirror. My hair was all akimbo, my makeup a memory, but my skin was glowing and my eyes were shining.

I walked back into the dining room as quietly as I could and slipped into my seat, hoping the tape would hold.

"Steffi, you're back, we were growing *frantic* with worry," Zana Clay drawled from the far head of the table.

"I just checked in with the practice's answering service. Nervous habit."

"Make a habit of bonds!" Diaper Baby exclaimed.

The Human Guffaw guffawed.

But Pink Puddle topped them both with, "Forga fook fub norkum!"

26

I WAS AWAKENED the next morning by a tapping on my window. That sounds so quaint—"a tapping on my window"—like something that happens at a country cottage in a cozy English novel. Actually, it was a pretty hard rapping on my vast curved super-tech glass wall that was filled with gas blackened by ionic pigmentation. I was sound asleep, and at first I thought I was having a nightmare: Harry the macaw was pecking me to death because I was an adulterous slut. Thank God my Tippi Hedren moment was short-lived. I opened my eyes, realized where I was, and reached for Binky. I pressed a button, the wall instantly cleared and I was blinded by a direct hit from the rising sun. I buried my head under the pillow and pressed Binky again: Elevator music came on the radio. I pressed again and heard water running. Again, and the closet doors (finally!) slid open. By this time my eyes were adjusting to the light, and I lifted the edge of the pillow to see Josh standing outside, laughing.

I sleep in the nude, and so I gathered the sheet around me and got up. The bed was the size of a soccer field, so I felt like I was trailing

Melania Trump's wedding dress behind me as I walked to the outside door.

"Good morning, starshine," Josh said, giving me a light kiss.

"Mmmm," I managed.

"Toss on some clothes, and let's go."

"Go?"

"I made you breakfast."

"Here?"

"At my place."

"But what about Amanda?"

"You're not in prison, Shelley."

"True."

I turned and headed for the bathroom. Josh plopped on the bed.

"We have to talk about your taste in music," he said.

"Binky did it."

"That bastard."

"Shhhh—I don't want to get on his bad side."

"I can just see the movie: *Binky Goes Psycho.* Move over, Chucky."

Oh God—Josh shared my pop-culture passion, we were made for each other.

I brushed my teeth and got into jeans and a shirt, then Josh and I slipped—make that hiked—around the side of the house and got into his vintage pickup truck.

On the way over, Josh stopped for gas on the Montauk Highway. He pumped it and then reached into his pockets and came up empty.

"Shelley, I forgot to bring any cash or my wallet. Can you loan me forty?"

"Of course."

I remembered reading how the Kennedys were like that—they never carried cash. It was one of those charming, ironic, old-money quirks.

The drive took less than fifteen minutes. We crossed the highway and then headed east until we came to a sign reading STONY LEDGE FARM.

"An old friend of mine owns this place, rents me an old barn," Josh said.

It was a beautiful horse farm, with horses grazing on rolling green fields, split rail fencing, an enormous Colonial manor house, and smaller houses, barns, and stables tucked in here and there. Like the Clays', it wasn't overly groomed.

We bounced over the unpaved roads until we came to a small, secluded, converted barn.

"Well, here we are."

"This is wonderful."

The inside was one huge room, with an open ceiling, rafters, a basic kitchen at one end, a staircase up to a loft bedroom. The decor was masculine-minimal: a seating area with a simple couch, a couple of chairs, and a sprawling coffee table covered with books, magazines, and Scrabble; a framed vintage Polish-circus poster; a huge farmhouse table; a shelf lined with animal skulls. It was cool in an offhand way, if a little, I don't know, young maybe. Then I remembered that Josh's wife had left him for another woman, and it all made sense. Guy on the rebound, getting himself back together before setting up more permanent digs.

Two places were set at the table, which sported a jar filled with just-picked wildflowers and grasses. "Make yourself at home," Josh said, heading over to the kitchen. "I hope you're a coffee drinker."

"Drinker, no. Addict, yes."

He poured me a mug and brought it over. Then came the pitcher of fresh-squeezed orange juice and the fruit salad.

"Can I talk you into a couple of whole-grain blueberry pancakes?"

"You just did."

I sat at the table, watching him in the kitchen, and was surprised that I didn't feel more anxious.

"So how long have you lived here?" I asked.

"A little over a year. I was living out in Seattle when my marriage fell apart, and I decided to come back east. My family had a place out here for many years, and it feels like home." He spooned the batter into the frying pan. "There's really a lot more to the Hamptons than Amanda and Jerry's world." He smiled at me over his shoulder. "I'd love to show some of it to you."

My resolution to rethink my summer arrangement evaporated. "I'd like that."

"I've been doing a little volunteer work with the Peconic Land Trust, which is trying to save some of the farmland out here. It's not easy—the development pressure is intense. It's the same old golden-goose story, but we're having some success. I just convinced my old buddy Tom Hallowell, who owns this place, to put a development easement in place, which saves two hundred acres." He flipped the pancakes. "I'm sorry, is this boring?"

"Not at all." Was he kidding—boring? I could have sat there watching him for, oh, two weeks or so.

"You know, the world is such a mess, it gives me a sense of purpose to be helping save one little part of it."

He said this casually, and I couldn't help thinking of Arthur, who got so passionate when he was discussing his students. In comparison, Josh's idealism seemed almost like an afterthought.

He brought me over a plate with three perfect pancakes on it. "*Mange.*"

"These look delicious."

"You look delicious." He leaned down and gave me a little kiss—the smell of that pine soap. "Here's the butter and that's real maple syrup."

I took a bite. "Wow, these are so good."

"Made them from scratch."

"No way."

"Cross my heart." He brought his own plate over and sat. "So, tell me more about you."

"Well, I'm a Libra, and I love silly movies, rainy days, Thai food, and macramé."

"I'm sorry, my question was a cliché."

"No, it was sincere and nice, but I'm a former fat girl who has spent her whole life hiding behind books and wisecracks. It's a hard habit to break."

"You're awfully tough on yourself."

I looked down at my pancakes and wished I could have one-thousandth of the ease and grace that seemed to come as naturally as breathing to so many privileged people. Was it something they were taught at their fancy schools? Or was it simply encoded in their DNA?

"Relax, Shelley, you're among friends."

I looked up at him, and he was smiling at me, a warm kind smile. "Thanks, Josh."

There was a pause.

"So . . . ," he said finally.

"Yeah . . ."

"Would you like to take a little walk?"

"I should probably get back."

"Shelley, can I tell you something about Amanda and Jerry?"

"Sure."

"Amanda has a dark little secret—her father owns a Ford dealer-ship in Plattsburg, New York, which is ten miles past the butt end of nowhere. She comes from the cheerleader class. Oh, she masks it well, and she's a quick learner, but she's fighting like a tiger to win social acceptance. Yes, she's adorable and fun and generous, but it's all on her terms. And she'll change the terms without warning. As for Jerry, I've known him since the fourth grade, which is when he started buying and selling old coins. He made his first million by his sixteenth birthday. He lives and breathes money, and he loves every accoutrement that comes with it. Including Amanda. And a live-in pediatrician. I'm not saying he's not neurotic about his kids' health, but basically you're there for show. As long as you've got your cell phone and are within a half hour of their place, you can pretty much do whatever you want. Last summer they had a masseur out for the whole summer. And if the guest sector fills up with fancy socialites, you may find yourself moved to the staff sector."

While I appreciated his honesty, it made me feel a little diminished. "I'm not sure I wanted to know all that."

"I'm sorry. I guess what I'm really trying to say is: I like you, and I want to spend time with you."

That I did want to know.

We sat there quietly, awkwardly, for a moment. I wished I was one of those women who could trust moments like this—sweet tenuous moments—who could ride them out, fill them with tenderness and an unspoken understanding. But I wasn't. And so I said, "Josh, what's going on between us?"

He gave me another warm smile. "Well, there's definitely some major animal attraction."

"That there is."

"Beyond that . . . Listen, Shelley, the breakup of my marriage was pretty painful. I'm forty years old. To be honest, I'm not sure what I want, except that I want to have some fun. And you, my friend, are fun."

"I am?"

"Are you kidding me, Shelley? Don't you realize how spontaneous and wonderful you are?"

"I guess you bring it out in me."

"I know you're engaged, and if you want to stop at any time, I'll understand. But you're going to have to tell me to stop. Until you do, I'm going to keep coming. Because I want you."

And then we looked at each other.

And then we were up in the loft.

And, yes, it was just as good on a bed.

27

I'M NOT GOING TO PRETEND that it was easy to concentrate on work the next day. There was a phone call I knew I had to make, and after seeing my first half dozen patients, I made it, reaching Arthur in the teachers' lounge.

"How was your weekend in the fabulous Hamptons?" he asked.

"It was fun. There's a lot of money out there. The beaches are amazing. How was your weekend?"

"I went to the beach, too—Coney Island." Arthur adored Coney Island. In the early days of our relationship, we would go out there for Nathan's hot dogs, to ride the Cyclone, and to take long walks on the boardwalk.

"Oh. By yourself?" I asked.

"No, with some friends. Other teachers from school. We had a wonderful time."

"Anyone I know?"

"I think Jennifer is the only one you've met."

There was a pause—one of those terrible, sad pauses when two

people care about each other, but the truth of what is happening between them is almost too painful to face.

"Arthur, we have to talk," I said finally.

"Yes, Shelley, we do."

"Probably sooner rather than later," I said.

"Yes. Why don't we meet for dinner on Wednesday night? Somewhere neutral. Maybe Chinatown."

"Sounds good."

My next patient was Schuyler Merrill, a three-month-old girl. I
approached the exam room to find Schuyler's mother standing—
make that posing—in the hallway, talking on her cell phone, her free
palm on her hip, elbow out. It was a little after eleven in the morning, but Lee Merrill was done up to the nines in exquisitely tailored
slacks and blouse, gorgeous accessories, perfect rich-lady hair, and
artfully applied makeup.

When she saw me approaching, she pointed to the exam room
and mouthed, "She's in there."

I went in to find Schuyler accompanied by a middle-aged baby
nurse. I began my exam, expecting Mom to come in at any moment.
Instead, she stayed out in the hall talking on her cell phone. From
the snippets of conversation I was able to glean, she seemed to be
making arrangements for a trip to Paris.

Schuyler was an adorable infant who rewarded me with a big
smile when I tickled her tummy. The exam showed her to be in fine
health. I stood there waiting to give the news to her mother, who
showed no inclination to get off the phone. I went out to the hallway . . . and still she kept talking. Finally she looked up at me and
asked, "Did you want me for something?"

I felt like saying, "Did you want *me* for something?" but I began,
"Schuyler is a wonderful baby, in excellent—"

"Can you hold that thought for a second? . . . Lisa, I *need* to have suite 812—it was Jackie's favorite room in all of Paris, and Yves and Paloma are coming for tea. Just make it happen." She closed her phone. "Schuyler is a wonderful baby, isn't she? Which makes this all the harder."

"Makes what all the harder?"

"Doctor, may I speak to you in your office?"

"Of course."

Lee Merrill looked in the exam room for the first time and said to the nurse, "You can take her home now. Bye-bye, sweetie-pie."

When we were in my office, she took out a gold cigarette case and lighter and lit up.

"We really can't have smoking in here," I said.

"I'm going to ignore that," she said breezily, but with an iron undertone, before taking a deep drag. "Dr. Green, I need your help."

"Shoot."

"My baby bores me to tears. I don't care about her development, I don't care about her milestones, I don't care about her teething, burping, crying, crapping, I don't care about any of it."

I tried to disguise my shock. "I'm not sure I can help you develop an interest in Schuyler. Perhaps if you spent more time with her."

"Dr. Green, I care about refined people and exquisite things, I care about Vermeer and Faberge and Lagerfeld, but I *don't* care about that screaming little creature."

I had studied enough psychology to grasp that Lee Merrill was going through one of motherhood's unspoken truths: the phenomenon in which a new mother has a strong negative reaction to her newborn. The reaction is usually triggered by either jealousy, because the baby steals both the husband's and the world's attention from the mother, or claustrophobia—suddenly you're tethered to another person for the rest of your life and your emotional and physical freedom is curtailed in profound ways. My educated guess was that Lee Merrill fell into the claustrophobic category. Here was a young woman with grand worldly ambitions, and there's nothing terribly grand or worldly about a demanding infant.

"How does your husband feel about Schuyler?"

"Oh, he dotes on her. For ten minutes a day. My husband is a budding billionaire, meaning he works twenty hours a day. And grinds his teeth the other four. He bores me, too."

I was glad she was being honest. It provided some hope. Had she been in denial and simply acted out her feelings unconsciously, the baby would have been in deeper trouble. In addition, her admission showed that she was troubled by her feelings, another good sign. My responsibility here was to Schuyler.

I emptied loose change from a small glass bowl on my desk, and held out the bowl toward Lee Merrill. "Please put out that cigarette," I said firmly.

She looked at me for a moment, a little challenge in her eyes. I held her gaze. She took the bowl and snuffed out the cigarette.

"Mrs. Merrill, I appreciate your honesty in admitting your feelings about Schuyler. It took real courage."

"Thank you," she said.

"And it also showed that you care about Schuyler more than you may realize."

"I doubt that. She cramps my style," she said.

"That may be true, but the fact remains that you asked to speak with me. That indicates some guilt about your feelings toward her."

"Do you think so?"

"Absolutely. On some level, you know that your feelings and behaviors will harm Schuyler, and you want to protect her."

"I want to protect her from me?"

"From the more narcissistic aspects of your personality, yes."

She grew thoughtful, looked down, and smoothed out her slacks, even though they were already smooth. I resisted the urge to say more—these moments have to play themselves out.

Finally, Lee Merrill said, in a much calmer, more even voice, "Well, I'm not going to pretend I enjoy spending time with her. I wish I hadn't had her."

"But you *do* have her, don't you?"

There was another pause, and then she looked right at me. "I do, don't I?"

"Yes, you do," I said softly, kindly, firmly.

Lee Merrill exhaled with a deep sigh.

"So I suppose the question becomes: Where do we go from here?" she said.

"Yes."

"Any ideas?"

"I would suggest in the strongest possible terms that you begin to see a psychiatrist."

"You're a tough nut, Dr. Green."

"I'll take that as a compliment."

Lee Merrill fingered her necklace, checked her nails, bobbed her foot. "I'm not a mean person, I'm really not, I adore my friends, I tip well, I'm good to my staff—oh Christ, maybe I can think of Schuyler as a *friend* or something, I don't know. We could do the play date thing now and then. . . . May I please have a cigarette?"

I shook my head. She sighed in a mixture of exasperation and resignation.

"Do you have a psychiatrist you can recommend?" she asked.

"I do."

"I'm not making any promises."

"I'm not asking you to."

She became still and looked me right in the eye. "I'll tell you one thing I am *not* going to do. I am not going to cancel my trip to Paris.

But I will ask my husband's mother to stay with Schuyler while I'm gone. She loves her grandnana."

I told her I thought that sounded like a good plan and gave her the name of an excellent psychiatrist. Then I asked her to call me in two weeks to confirm that she had begun seeing her, scheduled a follow-up appointment for Schuyler in a month, and hoped for the best.

A little later I saw four-week-old Jeffrey Rubin, whose mother had brought him in with the complaint of colic. Francine Rubin, dark-haired and pretty, was dressed in chinos and an elegant silk blouse. She wore no makeup and minimal jewelry, and she looked very concerned.

Claire had weighed and measured Jeffrey. He had good color and seemed to be thriving. His physical exam was entirely normal.

"Dr. Green, he sometimes cries nonstop for three hours," Francine Rubin said plaintively. "Three full hours."

"How long has this been going on?"

"It started at about two weeks, and it's been getting worse and worse."

"Well, the first thing to do is rule out gastric reflux," I said.

"My original pediatrician did that."

"So I'm Jeffrey's second pediatrician?"

"Third, actually. The second ruled out milk allergy. So where does that leave me? Besides anxious and exhausted."

"And what did Jeffrey's first two pediatricians recommend?" I asked with growing trepidation.

"The first said I should try to calm and soothe him, but that if that failed, I could walk away. Can you imagine? Walk away from my own baby when he's screaming like that?"

"And what did the second pediatrician say?"

"He said I should strap Jeffrey to my front and *vacuum*. Have you ever heard anything so ridiculous in your life?"

"Actually, Mrs. Rubin, there is a lot of anecdotal evidence that vacuuming with a baby is very effective. The womb is a very loud place; a baby hears the sound of the blood rushing through the placenta. Mimicking that sound will soothe the baby."

"But what about the underlying cause?"

"If Jeffrey isn't allergic and doesn't suffer from reflux, then he is probably one of the twenty percent of infants who can't stop themselves from crying, particularly when they're tired. Evolution, in its infinite wisdom, made infants' heads small enough to pass through the birth canal. But there's a tradeoff—babies are born with small and highly disorganized brains. They have limited control of their muscles and senses. During the first ten weeks, babies' brains grow by twenty percent, and they begin to make the connections necessary for rudimentary control and learning. They cry when they need help. And when their needs have been met, they stop. But infants like Jeffrey are maturing a little bit more slowly. They have a difficult time gathering themselves, and these early months are very hard for them. The crying is often worst during the late evening, what we call the fussy time of the newborn."

"It's painful to watch."

"It is. But his brain will quickly catch up. In the meantime, I suggest swaddling him to your front, vacuuming the house, rocking him as you go, and perhaps try a pacifier. This regimen has proven itself very soothing and effective."

Mom went to her baby and picked him up. She nuzzled and kissed his face, and then turned to me. "There's just one problem, Dr. Green."

"Yes?"

"I have no idea how to use a vacuum cleaner."

We laughed. I assured her it was a pretty easy skill to master.

Josh called me just as the day was winding down—his voice ran through me like an electric charge.

"I miss you," he said.

"I miss *you*."

"How was your day?"

"It was interesting."

"I'd love to hear all about it," he said. I had a sudden vision of the two of us sitting down to dinner in a cozy neighborhood bistro, having a glass of wine, hashing over our respective days.

"How was yours?"

"Mine was pretty low-key. I took a run on the beach, and then a nice long swim. Did a little work on some shelves I've been building here in the barn."

I was getting the impression that Josh was a long way from a workaholic.

"Arthur and I are having dinner on Wednesday," I told him.

The mention of the dinner instantly made our conversation seem much more serious. There was something important at stake here.

"Okay," Josh said.

Sitting there in my office, what had happened between Josh and me over the weekend didn't seem quite real. It had been so unexpected, so intense, that I didn't quite trust it. If there was one thing I had with Arthur, it was trust.

"I'm sort of in limbo until then," I said.

"I understand."

There was a pause filled with . . . with I'm not sure what, some combination of desire and trepidation that I had never felt before.

"Do you think you'll be coming out here again this weekend?" Josh asked.

"I'm not sure. Amanda and Jerry want me there as much as possible."

"Well, I'll be here. Or there, if you want. Just keep me posted."

"I will, Josh."

"It was a fun weekend."

"It was a lot of fun."

We breathed in each other's ear for a minute.

"Guess it's time to hang up," he said.

"Guess so."

I hung up, but before I had time to sort out what I was feeling, Marge appeared in the doorway.

"I just got a call from a Shirley Blake at WNET," she said.

"About *Baby Talk*?"

"Yes. She wants me to come in next week and meet with them. I don't know what you told her about me, Shelley, but you certainly earned your agent commission."

"I intend to collect it."

Marge sat and crossed her legs. "It's a terribly exciting idea, isn't it?"

"It is. And perfect for your talents."

"Of that I'm not so sure, but I'm more than happy to go and talk with them."

"So, how's life at the Lowell?" I asked.

"Divine. When I'm not in a rage. They cosset you there, I feel like minor English royalty."

After the Incident at Trump International, I felt much freer with Marge—I mean, how could there be any secrets between us?

"How are your sons taking it all?" I asked.

"Well, obviously both Herbert and I are sparing them the gory details. We've simply told them that we've decided to separate and begin divorce proceedings. They actually don't seem too surprised. I suppose it's the wisdom of youth—or is it the wisdom of children into the true state of their parents' marriage? And now that I'm over the worst shock, I, quite frankly, am feeling a delicious frisson of freedom."

"That's what I like to hear."

"And this call from WNET was just what the doctor ordered, so to speak. So tell me, how is your man drama playing out?"

"Well, let's just say the weekend was amazing."

"My-my," Marge said. "Well, I can't wait to meet this chap. And patients are clamoring to get an appointment with you. All in all, young lady, you've taken to the Upper East Side like a fish to lemon."

"I think I'm in real danger of getting hooked," I said.

"That can be taken two ways," Marge said with a significant look.

"Don't I know it."

28

YOU PROBABLY WON'T BE SURPRISED to learn that Arthur and I had "our" restaurant in Chinatown, a steamy no-frills grotto six steps down, and even "our" dishes—prawns with mixed vegetables and tofu fried rice. In an effort to get the dinner off on the right foot, I let him order them both.

I hate to admit it, but I was a little disappointed at how relaxed and healthy Arthur looked, with color in his cheeks and bright eyes. He seemed to be taking this whole thing that we were going through—whatever it was—better than me. I was tormented with doubt, with second and third thoughts. Was I about to toss over a great guy in the name of a hot fling? How far could what I had with Josh go?

Arthur ordered a Chinese beer.

"But, Arthur, you never drink on weeknights," I said.

"Never say never!" he crowed, lifting the bottle and taking a virile, very un-Arthur-like slug, like he was in a beer commercial.

All right.

We sat there in silence. I looked around the restaurant, which was filled with large Chinese families talking, laughing, eating. Their chattering familiarity reminded me of the Green Family behemoth. I felt a stab of sadness. Arthur loved my family, and they loved him.

"So, Shelley," he said.

"Arthur."

We looked at each other and the bravado drained out of him like air from a tire. His shoulders slumped. It was his turn to look around the restaurant. This wasn't going to be easy for either of us. Mercifully, the food arrived. We each served ourselves, silently, with a strange formality. I took a bite of the tofu. He took a bite of the prawns. We ate in silence for a moment.

"How's the tofu?" he asked.

"It's good, they do good tofu here."

"They do do good tofu."

More silence.

"How are the prawns?" I asked.

"Excellent."

"Spicy?"

"Yes, but not *spicy* spicy."

"Good."

"Could be a few more prawns," he said, poking at his plate.

"That happens sometimes—not enough."

"It's annoying."

"More is better," I said.

"Not necessarily."

"No?"

"*Good* is better. Not more for more's sake," he said.

"I didn't say that. More *good*."

"More good *is* better."

More silence.

"Arthur, I'm having an affair."

"I know."

"You know?"

"Of course I know."

"How?"

"Shelley . . ."

Of course he knew.

I thought he was going to melt into a puddle of hurt and pity. Instead he took a big bite of prawn and said, "I'm having an affair, too."

"You are!?"

"Yes."

I felt some funny mixture of hurt, anger, relief, and amazement. It was the first time in a long time that Arthur had really surprised me.

"With Jennifer Wu?"

"Yes."

There was obviously a flirtation between them, but this . . .

We both took deliberate bites of our food and once again ate in silence.

Then we looked at each other: Now what?

And then we both smiled—little smiles, tiny tentative smiles, but smiles nonetheless. It felt like our engagement was probably unraveling, but we just couldn't hate each other, couldn't let it get ugly. We were friends. I felt a surge of affection for Arthur, followed by a surge of realization that what I felt for Josh was a very different emotion—less secure, less cozy, less comforting, but more intense, more exciting, sexier.

"I'm sorry I was such boring sex," Arthur said.

"You weren't boring sex," I said.

"Yes, I was."

"No, you weren't."

"You're a nice person, Shelley, but we both know I was boring sex. Jennifer told me I was."

"She did?"

"She showed me, too," he said with a knowing smile.

I felt a terrible stab of jealousy. Followed by confusion, even humiliation. I thought this dinner was going to be a dance on eggshells, with me pirouetting around Arthur's male pride, ego, and feelings. Here he was about to give me *Kama Sutra* lessons.

"Well, if you were boring sex, I was boring sex," I said.

No protestation was forthcoming. Instead, Arthur slugged down the rest of his beer, and gestured for another in his new beer-commercial way. I had a sudden urge to wring Jennifer Wu's scrawny neck. God, Shelley, look at thine own behavior—a physical transformation, hobnobbing with billionaires, sex on the beach—and you're upset because Arthur has a little bit of new confidence?

"Shelley, maybe we rushed things. You were consumed with becoming a doctor. I always felt like I was second in line behind your career."

"You did?"

"Yes, but I could accept that. Then you became a doctor, and I thought it would be my turn to go to the head of the line. Instead, I've felt like an afterthought."

"But, Arthur, I've only been a doctor for a matter of months."

"That's been long enough for you to change. I mean, look at you. You look like the 'after' on those cheesy makeover shows you watch," he said.

"Those women always come out looking like hookers. Are you saying I look like a hooker? Well, I must be an unemployed one, because who's going to pay for boring sex?"

Arthur laughed, and I realized how ridiculous I sounded. My frustration burbled up and . . . I laughed.

"Shelley, the way you look is just the physical manifestation of where you're going. You've moved into a world that I have no interest in being a part of."

"Let's not start that old argument," I said.

"Let's not."

And so we ate in silence. Actually, I'd pretty much lost my appetite, but I pushed the food around a little bit.

The bill came. Arthur insisted on paying it.

We walked up the steps into the colorful cacophony of Chinatown. Both Arthur and I looked around for a moment and then turned to each other. There were no more smiles, no bravado, no banter, just two people who had thought they were going to be spending the rest of their lives together—and were realizing that all that had changed. His eyes looked awfully sad, and I'm sure mine did, too. We both looked away.

"So, you're going to take the apartment?"

I nodded. "I'll call the owners of the place in Carroll Gardens."

"Okay."

I could feel tears welling up behind my eyes—I didn't want that. I took a deep breath.

"And your folks," Arthur said.

"I'll call them, too."

Then Arthur's eyes welled—he didn't want that, either.

"Okay, Shelley."

"Okay."

We sort of moved to each other, and then both pulled back, and then came together in a quick hug. Then Arthur turned and walked away down the street.

It wasn't until he was around the corner and out of sight that I realized I'd forgotten to give him back his ring.

29

I FELL INTO a kind of emotional netherworld. I needed some time to absorb everything. I called Amanda and told her I really couldn't come out that weekend. Much as I wanted to see Josh, I felt that the stakes in our relationship had suddenly skyrocketed, for me at least. That was what made me nervous: Had they skyrocketed for him?

On Friday morning, I called him from my office.

"Hey, I just got back from a run and swim," he said.

It must be nice to have a trust fund.

"Was the water freezing?" I asked.

"I go over to Louse Point, on the bay, where the water's much warmer. I can't wait to take you there. There are a couple of places where you can skinny-dip."

"I've never skinny-dipped."

"Oh, it feels wonderful."

"I bet."

"I love to do it at night—take a bottle of wine, a joint . . ."

I didn't tell him that I hated pot. I'd smoked it once with Ira when

I was fifteen, had a massive paranoia attack, and ended up eating seven cans of Pringles. No thanks.

"So, are you coming out this weekend?" he asked.

"I'm not, actually."

"I'm disappointed. So . . . I don't mean to pry, but how the hell did your dinner go?"

His voice was strong, there were no apologies. I liked that—he wanted me.

"It went well, considering."

"And?"

"And . . . we've decided to break off the engagement."

"Yahoo!"

I laughed.

"I'm sorry, I should probably say, 'That must have been hard. Are you okay about it?' But that's not what I'm feeling," he said.

"I'll accept the yahoo."

"Well, why aren't you coming out then?"

"I'm taking that apartment I told you about. I'm moving this weekend."

"Well, let me come in and help you. I've got my truck."

"Thanks so much for the offer, but actually I've already made plans for my folks to help."

I didn't want Josh to meet my parents yet. Not until I'd told them about Arthur, and they'd had time to accept it.

"But, Shelley, they're older."

"No really, they love helping, plus I think my brother is going to help, and I'm only taking my clothes and a few things, the new place is furnished, I'm giving most of my stuff away," I said. I didn't tell Josh that "giving it away" meant putting it out on the sidewalk with a FREE sign on it.

"You're just going to give away a whole apartment full of furniture?"

I realized that Josh really didn't grasp where I was coming from, financially, class-wise.

"It's a pretty small place. It was just my med-student crash pad," I said, trying to sound casual.

"Okay."

"Well, I've, ah, got a waiting room full of patients to see."

"All right, Shelley. If you change your mind about wanting my help, just call."

"I will."

"I'll miss you this weekend."

The phone call didn't do much for my insecurity about where Josh and I were heading, but fortunately I didn't have much time to dwell on it. I had patients to see.

Three-year-old Rebecca Whitney simply would not give up her bottle. I knew this because I'd had several phone conversations with her mother on the subject. I'd asked Dr. Marge's advice and she told me her technique, which I was now going to try.

Rebecca was simply adorable, slightly chubby, with masses of red hair, freckles, a round face, and huge green eyes. She sat happily on the exam table in a blue sundress, her bottle beside her, taking everything in with confident curiosity.

Pam Whitney stood nearby, beaming at her daughter.

"Hi, I'm Dr. Green," I said.

"Look what I can do," Rebecca said. She clapped her hands three times, snapped her fingers twice, and then repeated the sequence again . . . and again . . . and . . .

I jumped in. "You're very musical."

"Want me to sing?"

"I'd love that."

"You are the wind beneath my wings / You are the wind beneath my wings. . . . That's all I know."

"It sounded wonderful."

"I can dance!"

She clambered down off the table and began to twirl on the balls of her feet with her hands over her head, in a rough approximation of ballet. This quickly segued into a few shake-your-booty moves that involved a lot of hip action and head tossing.

"That was a quick overview of Rebecca's cultural life," Mom said.

"My leg fell 'sleep yesterday," Rebecca said, pointing to her left leg.

"Did you shake it to wake it up?" I asked.

"Noooo! I couldn't. It was snoring. Daddy snores. Daddy's silly. He walks like this when he wakes up." Rebecca lumbered around the room, as Mom and I laughed in delight. Rebecca was quite a little performer, but not in an icky, cutesy way. She just loved making people laugh.

"Now, Rebecca, can we talk about your bottle?"

Rebecca dashed back to the exam table, climbed up on it, and enfolded her bottle in her arms.

"You know I got a call from Mr. Bottleman today," I said. Rebecca listened intently. "He told me that there are a lot of babies in Bottleland right now, and that he's running a little low on bottles. He said that if any generous little boys or girls would send in their bottles for the babies, he would send them a big present."

Rebecca thought about this for a moment, and then turned to Mom. "Mommy, we have a lot of bottles we could send to Mr. Bottleman."

"Mr. Bottleman said that only the boys and girls who send in *all* their bottles will get the present," I said.

"Where's Bottleland?" Rebecca asked.

"Um, it's in . . . Bottleworld."

"What does Mr. Bottleman look like?"

"Well, he looks like, ah . . . a bottle. But he has legs and arms and a head, of course."

"And babies in Bottleland have no bottles?"

"There aren't enough."

"If we send our bottles I get big present?"

I nodded.

"Mommy, let's put my bottles in a big bag and send to Mr. Bottleman."

"We'll do that when we get home," Mom said, giving me a very grateful smile.

"I know what Mr. Bottleman is going to send me for present," Rebecca said. She turned to her mother. "American Girl doll you wouldn't buy me."

Back in my office I called the London number Francis Young had given me.

"Hello?" a woman answered in a crisp English accent.

"Hello. This is Dr. Green, Alison Young's New York pediatrician, calling."

"Dr. Green, what a pleasure. This is Jenny Burke, Alison's aunt. Alison speaks very highly of you."

"How is she doing?"

"Better now. But Alison had a sudden and terrible bout of joint pain and swelling in her knees and ankles. It was quite severe—she was in agony, poor child. Her doctor diagnosed juvenile rheumatoid arthritis and began her on a course of steroidal medicines. Her symptoms are much improved."

JRA. That seemed to make sense. It was consistent with Alison's early symptoms, with the elevated sedimentation rate, and with the sudden onset of joint pain and swelling. I had confidence in her doctors. Still, it was not happy news. JRA is a lifelong chronic disease. Its course was unpredictable and Alison would need careful follow-up and monitoring.

"Well, I'm relieved that a diagnosis has been reached, and I'm happy to hear that Alison is feeling better. Is she available, by any chance?"

"She is. Won't you hold on a moment while I go round her up? Oh, she'll be delighted to hear from you."

Maybe Francis Young was right to take his daughter back to England.

"Dr. Green, hi, this is Alison."

"Alison, you do sound better."

"I feel so much better."

"Your appetite is back?"

"Is it ever."

"And you have more energy?"

"Lots."

"I'm sorry you had to suffer with that pain."

"It was hard. But it's better now."

"Your father must be thrilled."

"He is. He's moved into a hotel so that he can finish his research. It's very important."

"I'm sure it is. Are you planning on staying over there for the rest of the summer?"

"Yes, until school starts."

"Will you please keep me posted about your plans?"

"Yes."

"Alison, I'm delighted that you're feeling so much better."

"Thank you, Dr. Green. I miss you." Her voice grew a little sad.

"I miss you, Alison. I'd like you to come in to see me when you get back."

"Bye now, Dr. Green."

"Good-bye, Alison. Before you hang up, could you put your aunt back on?"

"She's right here."

"Hello, Dr. Green."

"Mrs. Burke, I was hoping to talk with Alison's father. Just to check in."

"Well, I'm afraid my brother has decamped to a hotel and barely returns my phone calls. But he's been following Alison's progress."

"Could I ask you to call me if anything changes vis-à-vis Alison's condition?"

"Of course. And may I thank you on behalf of Alison's family for all the care you've shown her."

"It's my pleasure," I said.

After we hung up, I sat at my desk for a moment. JRA was such an unpredictable disease; its severity could range from mild to crippling. The fact that her doctor was treating her with steroids instead of a nonsteroidal anti-inflammatory indicated to me that her flare-up had been severe. Unfortunately, this could mean that Alison was at risk for a serious case of the disease. I was sure the British doctors knew their stuff and were monitoring her closely.

Why, then, did I feel a nagging doubt?

30

I SPENT SATURDAY PACKING. It was exhilarating, and sad. I'd spent the last five years in this tiny apartment, and leaving it marked the official end to an important part of my life. Arthur and I had spent many quiet evenings here, and now I was leaving him behind, too. As I filled a garbage bag with things that were too awful to even offer for free—over-the-hill stuffed animals and half-burned candles—I thought of all the nights I'd come home exhausted to find Arthur waiting to serve me a wonderful meal he'd made. Afterwards, he'd run me a bath, give me a back rub, listen, commiserate, offer helpful suggestions.

I got up early on Sunday morning, grabbed a few bags, and took a cab up to my new home. The streets of the Upper East Side were deserted and quiet, as if everyone was still sleeping or eating breakfast in bed. Ernesto, one of the courtly doormen, greeted me and took my bags.

I unlocked the door, walked into the apartment, and felt my body break out in goosebumps. This glorious place was going to be my home for the next two years. I couldn't ask for a better base from which to launch my career. I'd always felt it was my hard work that brought good things to me, but getting this apartment felt more like luck. For the first time in my life, I felt charmed. It was a giddy feeling.

"Hey, baby, shake it, shake it," Harry squawked in greeting.

"You want me to shake it, Harry baby, I'll shake it."

I went over to the CD player, found an Aretha Franklin disc, and slipped it in. "Respect" came on, and I started to shake my booty around the room. Moving with a freedom and abandon that surprised me, I danced into the dining area, around Harry's cage (he tucked his chin and looked at me with wide-eyed amazement), and then down the hall, into the bedroom, the study, the bathroom, back down to the living room, shaking and swinging, bopping and snapping and clapping, lost in elation.

And then the doorbell rang.

I opened the door, and there stood Mom and Dad. Mom was carrying a huge wrapped platter, and Dad was carrying a shopping bag and a cooler.

"I've got bagels, lox, herbed chèvre, Greek yogurt, papaya, and Cinnabons—for lunch lasagna, haricots verts, endive salad, and M&M brownies," Mom said, walking right past me. "Moving is hard work, we need to eat. . . . Oh my God, Shelley, this place is gorgeous!"

Dad smiled at me sheepishly.

"Mom, you weren't due until ten. It's eight thirty."

"Eight thirty, ten, what's the difference? Suss. Will you look at this living room . . ." Mom walked around with her mouth open, still holding the platter out in front of her.

"Hey, baby, shake it, shake it."

Mom stopped in her tracks. "What's with the bird?" she asked.

"He comes with the place," I said.

"Well, he broke my mood. For a moment there I was imagining

Marcel Proust and Jackie Onassis sitting side by side on that settee, discussing Sartre and Chopra. If this was *my* apartment, I would have *salons* every Thursday, just at dusk . . ."

It was so embarrassing when Mom got deep.

I took the platter from her and put it on the dining room table. "Would you like to see the rest of the place?" I asked.

"Pay no attention to your mother, she's filled with inchoate yearnings . . . ," Mom said, one hand resting on her chest, the other fingering the drapes.

"We want to see everything, Shelley. The place is terrific," Dad said, looking at Mom with wistful affection.

Mom made her way through the apartment as if she was in a dream, waxing poetic at every architectural detail and plumbing fixture. Dad was particularly impressed by the comfortable armchairs facing the television in the study. In fact, he tried one out, clicked on the TV, and found an early-morning discussion of the Mets' pennant prospects. Mom took away the remote and turned off the TV.

"Harold, this apartment is a spiritual experience, and you want to watch television?"

"Yes," Dad answered.

"After we eat." Mom took my face in her hands, and her eyes welled with tears. "Shelley, we are so proud of you, this apartment is your accomplishments made flesh."

"Flesh? An apartment?" I said.

"Don't be didactic. Has my Arthur seen this place yet? He's going to love living here. You'll have us for dinner once a week, we'll pick a day, Sunday works best for me. My Arthur will make magic in that kitchen," Mom said.

"Actually, Mom, Dad, there's something I want to tell you," I said.

"Uh-oh, I don't like the sound of this," Mom said.

Dad looked longingly at the TV.

"Maybe you better sit," I said to Mom.

"*Sit,* she says ominously. Goodbye Merchant-Ivory, hello film noir," Mom said, looking stricken. I knew I could count on her to turn this into a trauma in three acts. "Is my Arthur all right? Has he decided he's gay? I always suspected."

"Miriam, please, would you let Shelley talk?" Dad said.

"Oh, now it's two against one. I'm the villain. Well, I didn't turn Arthur gay, studies have proved—"

"Mom, enough!"

"I love you, Shelley," Mom said, turning on a dime, sitting primly, folding her hands in her lap, looking up at me with an expression of sincere, albeit exaggerated, concern.

"There's something I need to tell you both about Arthur and me," I began, just as the first tear rolled down Mom's cheek. "We've decided to end our engagement. I do not want to discuss this very personal decision with the two of you. I want you both to respect the fact that Arthur and I are adults, and we have come to this decision mutually, with clear heads, as friends."

Dad looked sad and worried, but he stood up and gave me a hug. Then he took my face in his hands and said, "I trust my baby girl." Then he kissed me and hugged me again.

Mom just sat stock still on the couch, tears pouring down her face.

"Mom, please . . . ," I said.

Mom waved a hand in the air, "I'm fine, Shelley, I didn't say a word. . . ."

"Mom, please stop crying."

She looked up at me and said through her tears, "You know, Shelley, this isn't all about you."

"You're right—it's about me and Arthur."

She turned to Dad. "See how she talks to me? This isn't film noir, it's *Psycho.*"

Dad wasn't about to take sides. He just shrugged and shot another yearning glance at the TV.

"Mom, Arthur and I have ended our engagement. Deal with it. I mean it. Either you cut this out right now, or I'm going to ask you to take your food and leave."

Mom looked down at her hands. When she looked up, she was dry-eyed and smiling brightly. "Oh, Shelley, this apartment is a dream come true, I'm so proud of you. Professionally. But come, enough talk, let's eat. We have a big day ahead of us. Harold, will you look at those built-in bookcases! Oh, there's *The Handmaid's Tale*—Margaret Atwood, *c'est moi*."

The intercom buzzed, and I went into the kitchen.

"It is your brother, Ira," Ernesto informed me.

"Send him up."

I opened the front door to find Ira standing there looking like a zombie, his shimmery clothes wrinkled, his face pale and slack, his eyes hidden behind large dark glasses.

"No loud noises, Shelley, and can you please bring me six aspirin and a glass of water." He walked right past me and lay down on the couch with a loud groan. "My head is exploding—no, it's imploding. And I thought *I* could party. Christina has the constitution of a marine."

I found some aspirin and brought him four.

"Thanks, Sis, you're the best. I'm in agony, and I think my schlong is going to fall off from overuse."

"Overshare. And, Ira, what are you doing here?"

"I came to help you move. Ohhhh."

"You're not going to be much help in that condition."

"I'll supervise."

"From the couch?"

"Good idea."

Mom appeared in the doorway. "Oh my God, my baby, my Ira," she wailed, rushing to the couch.

"Ma, please, keep it down," Ira groaned. Behind his dark glasses, I could see the look of satisfaction on his face.

"It's that woman. I knew she was trouble. Shelley, bring me a warm washcloth, not hot, not luke," Mom said, stroking Ira's forehead.

"The feet, Ma," Ira moaned.

"Of course. Oh, my Ira, my poor Ira." Mom pulled off his shoes and socks and rubbed his feet.

"Hey, baby, shake it shake it," Harry piped in.

"Shoot the bird," Ira groaned. "Ohhhhh, my poor head."

Well, my new apartment was losing its virginity. I went and got the washcloth, passing the study, where Dad was happily watching ESPN. When I walked back into the living room, Mom was sitting on a chair next to Ira, holding one of his hands in hers and looking like she was about to give him the Last Rites.

I handed her the washcloth, which she gently placed on his forehead. He let out an agonized sigh

"Some people are just too sensitive for this world," Mom said in a hushed voice. "And then evil comes along and preys on that vulnerability. If she were Marie Antoinette, I would personally behead that woman."

Since I'd seen this show before and knew what came next, I decided to be proactive. "Would you like me to run Ira's bath?"

Mom looked wounded. "Shelley, I'm his mother." News flash. "I know how my Ira likes his bath."

I left them to their fun and games and went into the study. Dad clicked off the TV.

"Shelley, why don't you and me drive down to your apartment and start bringing up boxes?"

"Good idea, Dad."

It was a cloudy morning, and as we drove downtown, Dad turned on his favorite radio station—the one that played classics sung by Frank Sinatra, Tony Bennett, Ella Fitzgerald. When I was growing up, I spent most Saturdays at the library, reading and doing homework, and Dad used to pick me up late in the afternoon and the two of us would drive out to Bay Shore for soft ice cream. We always listened to this same station. Dad would ask me a few questions about what I was studying, but most of the time we drove in a comfortable, loving silence, listening to the music and enjoying the fizzy, romantic, nostalgic mood it created. I felt that same mood today, and I loved my father all over again.

As we were crossing Thirty-fourth Street Dad asked, "Shelley, do you want to talk about this thing with Arthur?"

"Probably not, Dad."

He turned and looked at me, concern in his eyes. "Are you sure?"

"There really isn't too much to say. We've been growing apart."

I'd always felt unconditional love, support, and pride from Dad, but he'd never given me a lot of guidance. He had an innate modesty that was compounded by the fact that he was a mailman. Though he loved his job, I think he was also a little bit ashamed of the fact that he hadn't reached higher. He didn't feel comfortable being authoritarian, and he'd always left it to Mom and the rest of the Green Family behemoth to pile on the pressure and guilt.

On the radio Tony Bennett was singing "Someone to Watch Over Me."

"Arthur is an awfully nice fellow," Dad said, almost to himself. I knew he'd miss him.

"He is nice, but the truth is, Daddy, I want more. I love Manhattan, I love that apartment, I love making good money, I want to travel, have adventures, meet people. Does that make any sense?"

Dad patted my thigh. "Of course it does, sweet Shelley, and you deserve it. You're smart and you've worked so hard and look at how terrific you look. Ever since the day you were born you've been no trouble to your mother and me. I really couldn't ask for a better daughter."

While I appreciated his kind words, a part of me was a little disappointed that he didn't challenge or question my decision, even if only mildly. I wanted a chance to air my own doubts. Sometimes unconditional support isn't what a daughter needs, even if she may think it's what she wants.

When we got to my building, I hired the super to help me ferry most of the boxes down to Dad's car. We loaded up the trunk and the backseat and headed back uptown.

"Well, we got most of it," Dad said.

"I'll just pick up the rest during the week. It's really down to a couple of boxes and suitcases," I said. The truth was I had work to do to get ready for the coming week, and I couldn't face an extended melodrama with Ira and Mom. I wanted the whole crew out of my new home as soon as possible.

With Ernesto's help, we loaded all the boxes into the service elevator and then unloaded them onto the landing outside my kitchen door. We walked into the apartment, laden with boxes, to find Mom laying out the dining table.

"You're just in time for brunch," she said. "Put those boxes in the study for now."

Ira appeared, looking like an almost new man, bathed and pampered and gorgeous, wearing a terrycloth robe.

"Where did that robe come from?" I asked.

"I found it in the closet. Dad, take it easy with those boxes—remember your knees," Ira said, sitting down at the table. "Ma, this looks beautiful."

"I feed my family," she said with gushing modesty. "Here's your coffee, darling."

"Ma, you're the best."

Dad and I made three trips to get everything into the study, then joined Oedipus and his complex at the table. No sooner had we begun to eat when Ira's phone rang.

"Hello? . . . Hey, babe, how ya doing? That was some night last night."

Mom, looking stricken, jumped up from the table and busied herself with nothing in the kitchen.

"Meet you for brunch and a little hair of the dog? You know I'm there, hot stuff." He hung up and stood. "Listen, I've gotta split. I'll call ya later, Ma," he called to the kitchen.

"Ira, you're wearing a bathrobe," I said.

"So? Christina only lives six blocks away."

"You're joking," I said.

"Shelley-belly, it's an Upper East Side thing," Ira said.

"Take-off-the-robe," I said.

Ira put on his clothes and left.

The three of us sat there and ate in near silence. Dad tried to make conversation, but Mom didn't want her suffering interrupted. After about a half hour they left, leaving me with enough food for a month.

I spent the afternoon unpacking and trying to get the apartment's feng shui back to where it had been before the reenactment of my childhood hell. By late afternoon, thanks to Harry's delightful company and a lot of easy jazz, I felt pretty much back to center.

Just as I was lying down on the couch with *Star*, there was a knock on the door. If it was Ira, I was going to refuse him admittance.

It was Josh.

I opened the door and was in his arms for a long kiss.

"I'm sorry, I couldn't stay away," he said, when we finally broke.

"I forgive you."

"You're getting under my skin, Shelley Green."

"Ditto, Josh Potter."

He looked around, "So this is your new pad?"

"Yup."

"Nice," he said casually. I was a little disappointed at his lack of shock and awe, but then I remembered that he'd been walking into apartments like this his whole life.

"Hey, baby, shake it, shake it," Harry said.

Josh went to the cage and did an absolutely adorable little dance-in-place. "How's that, kiddo?" he asked Harry.

"That is so yesterday," Harry answered.

"Well, I tried."

Josh spotted *Star* and picked it up.

"I love intellectual women."

"I'm just taking a little break from Voltaire."

He plopped down on the couch, lean and lanky and nonchalant. I wanted to go and kiss him, but shouldn't we keep building the relationship, I mean we'd already established that the sex was good.

"Would you like something to drink or eat?"

"I am kinda hungry. What do you got?" He walked into the kitchen, opened the fridge, and perused its contents, completely at home. "This is a strange mélange."

"I love a man who uses *mélange*."

"I switched from Obsession. Mélange drives women wild."

"My parents brought the food."

He was already unloading stuff and within a minute was building himself a lox and herbed chevre sandwich. He sat at the banquette and dug in. I felt a flicker of pique at just how at home he was making himself.

"Could you hand me one of those ginger ales?" he said.

I got a can out of the fridge. "Would you like it in a glass, with ice?"

He nodded. "So, how did the move go?"

"Oh, it went fine. I've got a few more things to pick up this week, and it'll be all done. How's everything out in the Hamptons?"

"The summer deluge gets worse every year. On weekends I hole up at the farm and never venture forth unless I have to. Just getting a quart of milk can take an hour." He looked out the kitchen window at the verdant backyards. "This place really is sweet," he said in a proprietary tone. He finished his sandwich, left the plate on the table, came over to me, and took me in his arms. "Our little love shack."

He kissed me, and suddenly I didn't care how proprietary he was acting.

31

THE NEXT FEW WEEKS were good ones.

I was in a groove at work. Sometimes other doctors asked me how I could stand all the crying, temper tantrums, patient volume, paperwork, parental anxiety, incompetent nannies, and near chaos of a pediatric practice. In comparison to most medical specialties, it was indeed mayhem. But I loved it. I was going to be watching my patients grow up and helping them to gain their footing in the world. Then there was the spontaneity, honesty, and humor of kids, literally never a dull moment, even when I yearned for one. In some ways it was like being in the middle of an enormous, rambunctious family, and I had a certain place of honor and responsibility in the mix. I guess in some ways I was recreating the Green Family behemoth. It felt like home.

Another reason for my happiness was that Josh had been in and out of town a lot, staying at the apartment. He helped me settle in; he opened charge accounts for me at Sherry-Lehmann wines and the EAT Gourmet shop, put together a little "wine cellar," and stocked my larder with all sorts of yummy delicacies. We went out to eat a few times, to a very trendy place in the East Village, to a little Upper East Side bistro. One evening we took a long walk through Central Park. Josh was wonderful company—interesting, interested, and oh-so presentable. I loved the glances we garnered when we strolled down the street hand in hand. And, of course, we made love every day he was around. One Wednesday, I rushed home during lunch for a little afternoon delight. Me!

I spent another weekend out in the Hamptons, including one night when I slept over at Josh's barn. For the first time in my life, I felt I was achieving a balance between work and play. Everything seemed to be falling into place. And I seemed to be falling for Josh Potter.

On Friday afternoon I was in a state of delicious exhaustion. I sat in my office to catch my breath. I only had a couple of more patients to see, then Olga, then home. The Walkers were in Nantucket for a week, so I was spending the weekend in town, and going out to the Hamptons the following Friday. The per diem they were paying me was astronomical, and I was grateful. The Sherry-Lehmann bill alone was $1,100, but having good wines around was sine qua non. Josh also liked to have good marijuana around. In fact, he seemed to take a toke or two just about every day, but I didn't care—it made him affectionate and funny, horny and cuddly. Unfortunately it didn't do much for his cleaning skills: Most days I came home to an unmade bed and unwashed dishes. We would have to discuss that.

Candace appeared in my doorway. "Look what my nephew just dropped off!" She handed me a copy of *Opera for Kids*.

"Congratulations!" The CD cover was a digitally composed photograph of an ornate opera house, its seats filled with diapered babies with blissful smiles on their faces. It was clever, fun, and very professionally done. "This looks sensational."

"He did a good job. He made me a gross, and Dr. Marge said I can sell them from the front desk."

"Time to negotiate my cut."

"You're holding it."

"Do you think opera will help with my next patient? She's sixteen."

"Doubtful."

Aurora Tanner was a shy, attractive young woman who was accompanied by her conservatively dressed mother. Aurora sat rigidly on the exam table, clearly intimidated in her mother's presence. I discussed general health concerns with the two of them, and then asked Mom to wait out front while I finished my exam. No teenager is going to open up with a parent present.

Aurora visibly relaxed when her mother left. As I listened to her heart and lungs, peered into her mouth and ears, palpated her neck and groin and kidneys, and tested her reflexes, I asked her about school, her summer, her interests, and her friends. We quickly developed a rapport. She was a bright girl, but I sensed that she was holding something back.

"Well, Aurora, you seem to be in fine health. Do you have any special questions or concerns you'd like to talk about?"

"No, I don't," she said.

"Are you sure? Anything you tell me will be completely confidential. And I would hope that I could be of some help."

She shook her head, but a blush rose in her cheeks. "All right, there is something," she blurted out.

I waited for her to continue, but she didn't. "You know, I was your age not so long ago, and I can promise you that nothing you tell me will surprise me."

"Dr. Green, my parents aren't tolerant people."

"I would never repeat what you tell me in confidence to anyone."

Aurora looked down at her hands, and after gathering her courage, she asked, "Have you ever met a sixteen-year-old who was uncertain of her sexuality?"

"Of course I have," I answered.

When she looked up at me, her eyes were filled with tears—of relief, confusion, and fear. "I feel attracted to other girls, Dr. Green."

"Aurora, those feelings are absolutely normal."

"They are?"

"Of course they are. Sexuality isn't hard and fast, for anybody. I'm heterosexual, but I had crushes on other girls when I was your age."

"You did?"

"Oh, yes. Intense crushes."

"Do you think I'm going to be gay when I grow up?"

"I think your sexuality will sort itself out in the next two years or so. Have you been sexually active at all?"

"No."

"Don't rush into anything. But be true to yourself."

"But my parents think gay people are sick."

"I must tell you, Aurora, that I disagree with your parents. But I understand your fears and concerns. Would you like me to refer you to a therapist?"

"My parents would never let me see a therapist."

"All right. Just know that you're not alone, Aurora, and that your feelings are perfectly normal. Is there one special girl you're attracted to?"

A little smitten smile played at the corners of her mouth. "There is someone. I don't know her personally, but I just think she's *sooo* cute."

"That's wonderful."

"It's Ellen Degeneres."

"*Ellen?* Oh God, I have a huge crush on her, too!"

"You do?"

"She's the most adorable thing on the planet."

"When she dances I melt," Aurora said.

"I die."

And so it went, we laughed and swooned and bonded over Ellen. Aurora promised she would call me if she needed to talk to someone. I knew that if she were gay, dealing with her family would take a lot of courage.

"Thank you for opening up to me, Aurora. You're a brave girl."

"Thank *you*, Doctor," she said. And then she hugged me, a quick spontaneous hug that seemed to surprise her. She stepped back, proud of her hug, eyes bright, looking like a different girl from the one I had met ten minutes earlier.

My last patient of the day was an eighteen-month-old girl whose mother was a semi-famous folk-rock singer and songwriter, who had been a pretty big star in the seventies and whose tunes popped up in car commercials and continued to earn fat royalties. I had read in one of the celebrity magazines that Mom, whose songs fell into the elegiac-hippie-catchy category, had adopted a child in her late forties because "my life needed a rambunctious rainbow." Mom was famous for her long flowing hair, long flowing dresses, and appearances at every peace march from Bangor to Beverly Hills.

I walked into the exam room to find Mom dressed in a midcalf skirt of gorgeous beige cashmere, a beige silk shirt, a wide leather belt, and a vest jewel-embroidered with Native American symbols. Oh yes, and cowboy boots. And then there was her jewelry: matching turquoise-and-diamond earrings, necklace, and bracelet. (Yes, turquoise and diamonds in the same pieces.) The total effect was a little disjointed: Park Avenue meets Woodstock at the Grammy Awards. Sage, her daughter, sat on the exam table, held by a young Hispanic woman.

Mom fixed her limpid blue eyes on me. "You must be Dr. Green. What an honor." Those eyes bored into me. "You're a healer, I can see it in your face, in your eyes . . . in your soul."

"I try my best. And this is Sage?"

"Yeeesss," Mom said with enough gushing love to turn *yes* into a three-syllable word. She took her daughter's face in her hands and looked at her with infinite wisdom and adoration. "Oh, my little Sage, my old soul, my dear sweetness. And this is Maria, Maria full of grace."

Maria nodded and smiled.

Sage was a darling, if somewhat bewildered, little girl, who offered no resistance to my exam.

"Sage looks fine," I said.

"Sage and I do have one little issue," Mom said, tossing her mane for emphasis.

"Yes?"

"The whole potty training thing. You see, I just don't *do* poop. And I'm sending Maria down to Guatemala for two weeks. Her mother has a tumor the size of a basketball—"

"A baseball," Maria corrected earnestly.

"Thank you, Maria. Her mother has a tumor the size of a baseball in her stomach."

"In her chest."

"Thank you, Maria. In her chest. She's a beautiful, soulful woman. I sang to her on the phone . . . she cried . . . I cried . . . we cried together. Then she threw up. Chemo in Guatemala is very iffy. Anyway, I'm sending Maria home for two weeks to be with her mother. And Sage and I are going to my ranch in Montana, and without Maria I'm a little bit freaked out about the whole poop thing. . . ."

"Could you be a little bit more specific?"

"Well, I don't do the whole diaper thing, it's just . . . not in my repertoire," she said in an exasperated, almost petulant voice. "And I just can't get Sage to poop on the potty."

"Well, Sage is only eighteen months. Very few children take to the potty before two."

"Yes, but Sage is a very special child."

"I'm sure she is, but toilet training is a matter of muscle control, neurology, communication between the brain and the body. Most children her age aren't biologically or psychologically ready to control their bowel movements."

Mom took this in with wide eyes, and then said, "Do you believe in miracles, Doctor?" I hesitated. "Because I do. *Fervently.* Sage is a miracle. She was born in a South Texas trailer park to a twelve-year-old illiterate speed freak with six priors for everything from prostitution to falsely soliciting contributions for Ronald McDonald House. Then the universe brought Sage and me together, and now she'll inherit my co-op in the Hotel des Artistes, my Montana ranch, and the copyrights on my songs. So do you see why I believe in miracles?"

I could certainly see why Sage might.

"Doctor, I bought Sage a beautiful, hand-painted potty. Maria places her on it."

"And how does Sage respond?"

"Like a little angel. A confused, frightened, and very constipated little angel."

"Putting that much pressure on a child before she's ready is not a good idea. That's why you're seeing the constipation."

"Doctor, we're talking to each other, but are we *hearing* each other? I don't *do* diapers. They mess with my muse."

So many of the parents I saw at Madison Pediatrics were tightly wound control freaks, but at least they were straight about being unnerved by the uncontrollable demands of child rearing. This woman was clearly dishonest with herself, but that was her business. My goal was to help Sage through what could be a difficult transition for a toddler.

"Can't you find a temporary baby nurse for the two weeks Maria will be away?"

"Maria is family, she lives in my heart and in Sage's heart. Besides, my lifestyle is very free—I stay up all night making music, I'm a home nudist, a lacto-vino-vegan, I chant, and I love my boy toys."

"I see."

She suddenly grew quiet, looking down at her manicured hands with the profoundly pensive, wistful expression I recognized from her album covers. "This whole baby thing is heavy."

The sixties may be long over, but their legacy lives on.

I had an idea. "You know, I'm a big fan of your music."

She gave me a saintly smile, took my hands in hers, and said, "Sister."

"You know what my favorite song of yours is?"

"Can you pick just one?"

"It isn't easy, but I just love 'Walk Into the Wind.' Those lyrics are so beautiful . . . would it be completely inappropriate for me to ask you to sing just a snatch of it?"

"Inappropriate? It would be a gift." She ran her fingers through her luxurious mane, shook her head like a fine thoroughbred, and sang in that lush, lovely voice of hers:

Walk into the wind
Fly up to the sun
This is your moment, child
Don't wait
Give what you take
And love what you hate
Love what you hate
Love what you hate . . .

The words hung in the air for a moment, and I gave Mom what I hoped was a significant look, before moving my gaze to Sage.

Mom slowly broke into a knowing grin, "Oh, honey, you are a sly one—I stepped right into that trap, didn't I? Well, I wrote that song and let me tell you: It is *not* about poop. It's about a skanky surfer dude I picked up on the Santa Monica pier and hauled over to the Chateau for a weekend of sex, booze, and 'shrooms. Nice try, but nope—nada poopy for this rock goddess."

I smiled sheepishly.

"But I'm hearing you, Doctor. This potty thing could fuck up Sage's head. I don't want to blow it. . . . Wait, I have an idea! I met Maria when she was my maid at this sweet little pseudo-eco-resort in Guatemala. Me and Sage will check in there for the two weeks, and I'll just hire a driver to take Sage over to Maria's whenever she needs changing, it's only about five minutes away. It's kind of a whole beautiful circular thing. I'll get a song out of it! Plus I'll get my brains screwed out by the Guatemalan pool boys." She looked at me in triumph. "You see, Doctor, everything happens for a purpose, even poop."

I wished them a good trip and reminded Mom one last time of the dangers of trying to force a child into using the toilet before she is ready.

I plopped into my office chair, and Olga went to work on my neck and shoulders.

As I was beginning to unwind under her ministrations, Marge appeared in the doorway. She looked exhausted, but not in a too-many-glasses-of-wine way. Ironically, she had sobered up over the summer.

"May I?" she asked.

"Of course." She came in and sat down. "How are you?"

Marge got a wistful, faraway look in her eyes. "I'm tired—physically, emotionally, spiritually."

"It's been a rough time for you. Why don't you take a week off and fly to Paris?"

"I honeymooned in Paris," she said, ending that line of conversation.

"Have you heard any follow-up from your meeting at WNET?"

"Just a courtesy thank-you call from Shirley Blake."

"But you felt the meeting went well?"

"I didn't pull my punches, Shelley, I let them know exactly how I feel about hyperparenting and a range of other issues. They taped me. I probably came on too strong."

"I doubt that. You always deliver your punches in a velvet glove."

"Well, Shirley Blake is a nice, smart lady, and I wish her well with the show no matter what happens."

I wanted to do something to help Marge through these hard times, but I knew that just like with my patients, there was a limit that needed to be respected. Still the kernel of an idea took hold. I filed it away for later exploration.

"And how is everything with you? You look radiant, but you always do these days." I smiled. "So, it's still going great guns?"

"Yes," I replied.

"It makes me happy to hear that."

"He's awakened a sensual side of me that I didn't even know I had."

"Yes, but that only goes so far. I hope that an emotional connection is developing."

"Well, yes, I think so."

"You think so?"

"Well, to be perfectly honest . . ."

"Yes?"

"Oh, it's nothing."

"Shelley, dear, trust me, it's not nothing."

"Well, it's just that he's a former actor, and sometimes I wonder if, you know, he's so handsome and polished, and I just wonder . . ."

"Is it real?"

"Well, yes, I guess that's it."

"My advice, and take it for what it's worth—as you well know, I'm hardly an expert on men—is to pay attention to your instincts. If this is something you're sensing, don't ignore it. But on the other hand, it could just be your own insecurities. Remember, Shelley, you've come a long way in a short time. When I first met you, you had very little social confidence."

"That could be it. I mean we have a great time together, we definitely click. But sometimes it's hard for me to believe someone like him could be interested in me."

Dr. Marge looked at me, studied me, in a way that I found slightly unnerving, but then she smiled, leaned across the desk and grasped my hand.

"Shelley, I would have no problem believing that any man could be interested in you."

She was so kind that for a split second I thought I might cry.

32

IT WAS MONDAY MORNING and my first patient of the week, twelve-year-old Jeremy Winslow, looked terrible. A livid rash of poison ivy ran up both arms, across his collarbone, and licked at his neck. Why then did his expression hint at some secret satisfaction? Jeremy was a skinny boy, with a thick shock of jet-black hair and rectangular black glasses that made him look both hip and nerdy. His mother, a stylish fashion executive in her midthirties, stood nearby, looking worried and confounded.

After introductions, I said, "Well, Jeremy, it looks like you stumbled into a patch of poison ivy."

"It's everywhere at that stupid camp," he said in a tone of petulant disdain, pushing his glasses up his nose. Jeremy's combination of precocious intelligence and irrepressible boyishness made him instantly endearing.

"Jeremy has some issues with going away to camp," his mother explained, her patience clearly stretched to the breaking point.

"I hate camp, I hate the country, I hate canoeing and archery and crafts. They're all stupid."

"Jeremy, both your father and I work all day, and Manhattan in the summer is no place for a child."

"Mommy, look at me. Do you really think it's worse here than at that stupid camp? Besides, I love New York in the summer. It's all cool and deserted."

"Your father and I spent a lot of money for that camp, Jeremy. It will build your character."

"We sit around a stupid campfire with weird, hyperactive counselors singing lame songs. What kind of character is that going to build? The only useful thing I learned there is how to identify poison ivy."

"When did your rash first appear?"

"Two days ago. The camp nurse is retarded, so I came home. And I don't want to go back, ever."

I examined his poison ivy. It was in its first full blush, and from its distribution up Jeremy's arms and across his upper chest, it almost looked as if he'd grabbed a leaf and rubbed it on himself. "I'm going to give you a prescription for cortisone cream and an antihistamine for the itching. You should respond to the treatment in a few days, although the rash will take longer to clear up completely."

"Well, there goes camp," Jeremy said in triumph.

"Jeremy, I'm sure you wouldn't be the first camper to have a case of poison ivy. There's no problem with him returning to camp, is there, Doctor?" Mom asked me hopefully.

"Mommy, of course there's a problem. I can hardly move my arms. I can't paddle a stupid canoe with my feet."

I hated to wade into this one. And while I didn't see any medical reason for Jeremy not to return to camp, I couldn't help being on the little guy's side.

"Jeremy, your father and I simply don't have time to look after you."

"I can look after myself. There's a Brazilian music concert at Town

Hall tomorrow, I'll catch up on some off-Broadway shows, I haven't been to the Museum of Natural History in almost a month, I have tons of books to read, the Walter Reade is having a Fellini retrospective. I just hope I can find the time for everything," he said, pushing up his glasses.

Mom couldn't suppress a proud, rueful smile.

"That camp was very expensive," she said, one last halfhearted plea.

"You can deduct it from my allowance," Jeremy answered. Clearly he'd thought of everything.

"Doctor, what do you think?" Mom asked.

"Medically, I don't think there's any risk in Jeremy's returning to camp. But, as he points out, there are a lot of activities he won't be able to participate in." Jeremy looked at me, eyes bright, trying to suppress his smile at our complicity.

Mom clapped her hands together. "Okay, I see which way this wind is blowing. All right, young man, you can stay home, but I'll want to know your whereabouts at all times."

"Of course, Mommy, I'll just carry my cell phone. And thanks," he said, pushing up his glasses and grinning at both of us.

Later that morning I took a call in my office.

"Shelley?"

"Yes." I didn't recognize the voice, but it was very cultured.

"This is Serena Van Rensselaer. Do you know that you're the hottest pediatrician on the Upper East Side?"

"I doubt that."

"Point being, my sister Tatiana and I are both pregnant. I'm four months, she's three—I've always been one step ahead of poor Tati—and we want you to be our pediatrician. So, can we do a prenatal lunch? Say a week from Saturday? La Goulue? Noon? See you there, can't wait."

And with that she rang off. Talk about entitlement! I was miffed at her presumptuousness. But I didn't underestimate the value of Serena and Tatiana Van Rensselaer to my career. They were New York's It Sisters, notorious party girls who dated their pedigree back to the Cavemen and had worked their way through most of the major young movie stars before settling down into high-profile marriages with blueblood investment types. Their lives were chronicled with breathless adoration by Suzy, Page Six, and E!

I walked down to Dr. Marge's office. She was sitting at her desk getting ready for the week.

"Serena Van Rensselaer just called me," I told her.

"You've made a name for yourself very quickly."

"It's all because of you."

"I may have passed you the ball, but you've run with it. That outfit is lovely, by the way," she said.

"Thank you—I love Fendi."

"Must have cost you a fortune."

"It was on sale. Besides, I consider it an investment."

"I hope you're saving some of your salary."

"Of course I am," I fibbed.

I had a wonderful new hobby: shopping. When I was feeling overwhelmed by the pressures at work, or unsure of my relationship with Josh, or felt my persona needed a pick-me-up, shopping was a tremendous release. Just thinking about hitting the stores filled me with a charged anticipation, almost a high, and now that I could afford nice things, the Upper East Side became like a big candy store—only instead of Snickers and M&Ms, I was now gorging on Fendi and Blahnik. My wardrobe was growing by shoes and dresses.

Dr. Marge looked at me with concern and a hint of skepticism. "Shelley, you seem a little, I don't know, keyed up lately. You've got a very full plate. How are you handling it all?"

"I'm shopping as fast as I can," I said with a too-loud laugh. Wanting to change the subject, I asked, "Can you come over for dinner a week from Friday?"

"I'd love to. Are you having a party?"

"It'll just be me and Josh, Amanda and Jerry Walker, you and . . . maybe someone else."

"I'm intrigued," Dr. Marge said, standing up, "and I'm running late."

Back in my own office I called Alison Young in London.

"Francis Young here," her father answered.

"Hello, Mr. Young, it's Dr. Green in New York. I'm calling to see how Alison is doing."

"She's doing very well, thank you. The doctors over here in England are very knowledgeable . . . and thorough."

"Have you made any definite plans for returning to New York?" I asked.

"Actually we'll be returning next week. Alison is eager to get back."

"Well, that's good news. I hope that you'll both come in and see me."

"My sister may accompany Alison over. I have a symposium in Singapore that I'm preparing for."

"Well then, I hope Alison and her aunt will come in to see me."

"Dr. Green, I'm very satisfied with the medical care my daughter is receiving. She's gone from being a sick child to an almost healthy one. It's just her left knee that still hurts. I don't want any boats rocked."

"Mr. Young, if Alison is going to be on long-term steroid therapy she will have to be followed very carefully."

"I'm well aware of that fact."

"May I speak to her a moment?"

"She's out in the yard." He sighed. "All right, hold on."

Every time I spoke with Mr. Young, my empathy for Alison increased.

"Hello, Dr. Green," Alison said.

"It's wonderful to hear your voice. And I look forward to seeing you. How are you feeling?"

"Pretty good, thank you. But I'm a little swollen, in my face, and my left knee, too."

I wasn't surprised. Cushingoid features—a rounding of the face, fatty deposits around the neck—were a common side effect of steroid therapy.

"Any other changes?"

"Well, I'm gaining weight."

This was another common side effect. There were a host of others, including thin skin with easy bruising, loss of muscle mass, and headaches and dizziness, but I didn't want to worry her by asking about them. I'd see her in person soon enough. I was concerned about that left knee.

"Anything else you've noticed?"

"No, not really."

I was fairly confident that Alison would need a tapering regimen, a slow decrease in dosage, down to the absolute minimum required to control her JRA, followed by close monitoring and an increase in dosage as needed.

"You can afford a few more pounds," I said.

"I've gotten addicted to Bounty bars. I'm going to bring a case back with me," Alison said.

"You better save me one, or there'll be a mutiny over the Bounty."

"Dr. Green, that is the worst pun I have ever heard."

We shared a laugh.

"See you soon, Alison."

Alison sounded well, but I knew that she faced a long-term struggle.

JRA at its worst could be devastating. And I was still troubled by a gut feeling that there was a stone I had left unturned in her case.

My next call was to Dr. Charles Spenser.

"Hello, Dr. Green," he said in his warm baritone.

"I'm calling for two reasons. First, Alison Young is apparently doing well over in London. They diagnosed JRA and have her on steroids. But I'm just not absolutely convinced that's the correct diagnosis. She's coming back to New York early next week."

"Please, bring her in to see me."

"Thank you so much. Second, would you like to come over for dinner a week from Friday?"

"I'd love to, thank you."

Now I just had to hope that my matchmaking instincts were right.

I was very curious to see one of my afternoon patients. Make that two of my afternoon patients. I was seeing my first set of identical twins. They were five-year-old boys, Matthew and Zachary Miller. Candace had informed me that their mother was "major-league neurotic." I was so used to hearing this warning that I asked her to save time by only telling me when a parent *wasn't* neurotic. She assured me that Mrs. Miller really was in the big leagues.

I walked into the exam room to find Matthew and Zachary sitting side by side on the exam table, in their street clothes. They were adorable, with enormous brown eyes and round faces framed by bangs. And they were indeed identical—down to the expressions of stoic petulance on their faces, which were accentuated by their determined sucking of their right thumbs.

"Hi there," I said.

They both looked at me with identical blank expressions.

Mrs. Miller herself was a mixed message in jeans, a T-shirt, old loafers, messy hair—and enough gold jewelry to finance four years at

Harvard. She rushed over to me, upset and embarrassed, and said sotto voce, "Doctor, may I speak to you outside, please."

We walked into the hallway.

"I can't get them to take their thumbs out of their mouths, *ever*. It has something to do with my breasts, doesn't it? They want my breasts back, they have an abnormal breast fixation. What woman will ever marry them now? Or will they be gay? Is it a prefellatio manifestation?"

"Mrs. Miller, please, can we discuss this after the exam?" I walked back into the room and Mom followed. "Matthew, Zachary, I'm Dr. Green."

Once again they looked up at me with unchanged expressions of complete disinterest, thumbs planted securely in their mouths.

"Would it be all right if I examined you both?"

They shook their heads *no* in perfect unison.

Mrs. Miller continued her sotto voce commentary: "It's not autism, they get straight As at school—do you think it could be Asperger's? By the way, did I tell you they won't *talk* to me? *My* mother *never* talked to me. She left my father, yanked me out of Nightingale-Bamford, remarried, and moved me to Captiva without saying a word. Can you even begin to imagine how *traumatic* that was? I was a happy, healthy five-year-old, and suddenly I'm on an island with a stepfather I barely know. That's when I started *my* thumb-sucking phase. You couldn't *pry* my thumb out of my mouth. They ended up putting it in a cast for six months. It won't come to that with Matthew and Zachary, will it?"

"Mrs. Miller, may I speak to you in my office for a minute?"

We went into my office and she sat across from my desk, distracted and fidgety. This woman screamed attention deficit disorder.

"Mrs. Miller, can we discuss your sons' thumb sucking for a minute?"

"That's what I'm here for. Is casting an option? I like your outfit. It's Fendi, isn't it? We just bought a place in Millbrook. Tally-ho, ha-ha."

"Casting is not an option. In fact, it hasn't been used for some years, and I'm sorry that you were subjected to it. It's important to remember that sucking is instinctual for a child and often begins right after, or even before, birth. In fact, some babies are born with sucking blisters on their wrists or hands. A baby who sucks its thumb is actually a self-soother, which can be a sign of healthy independence and self-sufficiency. Matthew and Zachary are, however, beyond the age when a child should need this primitive reassurance. For them, it's clearly a retreat from anxiety, a regression to infancy."

"Are you saying that my children are anxious?" Mrs. Miller asked.
"Yes."

She thought about this for a moment and then asked, "Was the Fendi on sale?"

"Aversion tactics such as casting or the application of a bitter coating will only heighten their anxiety. The same is true for nagging or threats. In fact, the more negative attention you give the thumb sucking, the longer it's likely to last. It will turn into a battle of wills, and the twins will have an even greater need for the stress relief that the thumb sucking provides."

"I've been there. Down on Captiva, my thumb was my only friend."

"That must have been a sad and difficult time for you," I said, sensing an opening.

Now that the attention was firmly on her, Mrs. Miller calmed down. A look of girlish self-pity came over her.

"It was very sad, and very hard."

"Yes. That's why we want to help Matthew and Zachary. We don't want them to be sad."

"No, we don't."

"So I would recommend not paying too much attention to their thumb sucking. You could try buying them baseball gloves, tennis rackets, even video games. You want to get them involved in activities that force them to use both their hands."

"I'm going to do that, I'm going to do just that. And I'm going to discuss it with my psychiatrist."

"You haven't already?"

"We've been concentrating on me."

I asked Mrs. Miller if she wouldn't mind waiting in my office for a few minutes. I walked into the exam room to find the twins acting like normal rambunctious five-year-olds. Their exam was punctuated by wisecracks, competitiveness, and general precocity. I didn't mention the thumb sucking.

Mrs. Miller appeared, and the boys immediately stuck their thumbs back in their mouths. I held my breath, waiting to see how she responded. She walked behind the exam table and stood between her sons, putting an arm around each. "Come on, Matthew, Zachary, let's go ride the carousel."

"Will you all come back and see me in a month?" I asked.

The twins—and their mother—all nodded their heads in perfect unison.

Later, after seeing my last patient of the day, I called Josh, who was out in Amagansett.

"It's me," I said.

"Hi, cutie."

"So, the dinner is on for a week from Friday."

"Fun. Let me cook."

"You talked me into it. How about that incredible cod Provençal you made for me?"

"It would be my pleasure."

"Is all well out there?" I asked.

"Fine. I get a little bored when you're not around."

"The Van Rensselaer sisters want me to be their pediatrician."

"Serena is a pistol," he said.

"Do you know her well?"

"Oh, no, no. Just from around. Same circles. You know."

"Yes, of course. Same circles."

We hung up and I sat there in my office. The practice seemed to have suddenly gone quiet. Almost eerily quiet. For a moment I wasn't sure what to do with myself. And then I had a sudden overwhelming urge to go shopping.

33

IF MADISON AVENUE was my candy store, Barneys was that great big bonbon in the sky. I dashed over, and as soon as the doorman opened the gates for me and I stepped inside the store, I felt a combination of relief and tingly anticipation. There was something so calming about all the luxury—all those beautiful scarves and sweaters and shoes and dresses—and it was exhilarating to know that with a little swipe of plastic they could be mine.

I headed downstairs to the cosmetics floor. I didn't really need any more makeup, but then again I didn't not need it either. I passed the La Vie en Rose counter.

"Hello, would you like to try the La Vie en Rose Cellular Treatment line?" a very nice woman with a French accent asked.

"Thank you," I said, sitting on a stool.

She gave my face a quick scan. "You have lovely skin, and we want to keep it that way."

She began applying all sorts of luscious creams to my face, neck, and eye area, all the while explaining to me in her soothing French accent how the Cellular Treatment line worked with my dermis to renew and regenerate my cells. I'd been through medical school but had a hard time following her scientific spiel. Still, it felt comforting to be ministered to like this, and I could feel myself beginning to relax, but in an elated way, if that makes any sense. After all, the music was playing, and all around me people buzzed about with that peculiar energy that spending unholy gobs of money creates.

After lathering me with creams, the lovely French lady applied a little color, some lipstick, mascara.

"Voilà!" she pronounced.

I looked at myself in the mirror. My skin was absolutely radiant, the makeup subtle but very effective.

"*La belle mademoiselle*," she pronounced. Arranged on the counter beside her was a small city of jars and bottles. She gestured to them with French insouciance. "You will take them all, yes?"

In addition to skin care and makeup, she had mastered the art of the rhetorical question.

I looked at myself again in the mirror. My skin did look amazing, all plumped up, smooth, vibrant, alive—was I actually watching the continuous cellular renewal in progress?

"Of course I'll take them all."

Six hundred dollars later, I headed up to the shoe department on the third floor. This wasn't a pleasure trip—I *had* to have a new pair of shoes for my lunch with the Van Rensselaer sisters. In fact, I probably needed a whole new outfit, but I might as well start with the shoes.

The women's shoe department at Barneys was becoming my Shangri-la. The erudite young salesmen, the comfy banquettes and couches, the cool but warm decor, the music, the flattering lighting, it all cocooned me in giddy adrenaline.

A tall, languid salesman approached. He looked like Italian royalty with his dark hair, dark eyes, and fabulous dark suit.

"Good afternoon," he said. "May I help you?"

"I'm looking for something elegant but afternoony."

"Ah—a lunch?"

"Yes."

"Have you considered Balenciaga?" he said, waving his hand in the direction of an exquisite display.

The shoes were amazing, multicolored high-heeled slip-ons with diamond cutouts. But they were very dressy.

"Do you think they're too elegant for a lunch?" I asked.

"Is there such a thing as too elegant?" he asked.

Another master of the rhetorical question.

"May I see this one in a seven?" I said.

With a courtly little bow he departed. I sat on one of the darling little couches and looked around at Barneys's usual complement of chic New York women, rich out-of-towners and their compliant husbands, and wildly overdone Russian-Mafia wives.

I spotted a tall, lean man facing away from me, wearing a beige linen suit. He was with an Asian woman who was holding up a shoe. He turned and our eyes met.

It was Arthur.

It took both of us a moment to register who the other was. And then there was a tentative, awkward beat before he came toward me. He had a flattering new haircut that brought out those beautiful gray-green eyes.

"Shelley . . ."

"Arthur . . ."

Another awkward pause.

"You look, ah . . . *terrific*," he said.

"So do you."

I exhaled and looked around, faux casual.

He exhaled and looked around, ditto.

"So . . . ," he said.

"Yes . . ."

He shrugged and semi-laughed. "Funny meeting you here."

"No, funny meeting *you* here."

"I know. Me in Barneys," he said wryly. "I'm with Jennifer. She, um, her family, I mean, own some office buildings in Hong Kong."

"Oh."

"Shelley, I owe you an apology."

"You do?"

"Yes. I was an overbearing, self-righteous asshole. I saw everything in black and white, was rigid and politically correct to the point of being a closed-minded prig. People with money are still people, and a lot of them are very good people."

"They are."

"You wanted something in life, and I made you feel guilty about it, and I'm very sorry."

"Oh, that's okay, Arthur. I was pretty bullheaded, too."

"No, you weren't. You were wonderful."

He looked down.

Then we both asked at once:

"How's the practice?"

"How's school?"

We both laughed, kinda.

"Practice is good, going well . . ."

"School's good, going well . . ."

"Good."

"Good."

He buttoned and unbuttoned his jacket, stopped abruptly, and asked in a rush, "And your relationship is . . . ?"

"Still there, still a relationship, yup-yup . . ."

"Good . . . good . . . lucky guy."

"Lucky girl."

"No, Shelley, you made your luck. I admire you so much."

"Thank you, Arthur."

"And the family, how's the family?"

"The family's good. I mean, the family's the family."

"Will you give them all my very best?" he asked in a wistful voice.

"Of course I will."

He looked down again. So did I.

"Okay then . . . ," he said.

"Okay . . ."

Jennifer Wu walked up and slipped an arm through Arthur's.

"Shelley, hi," she said.

"Hi, Jennifer."

Arthur winced.

"Well, we better get going," she said. "We're heading downtown to a gallery opening."

"Great. Nice to see you both."

Arthur and I looked at each other. Then they turned and walked away.

The salesman appeared with my shoes. I bought them.

And another pair.

34

THE WEATHER OUT in the Hamptons on Saturday was dramatic, even romantic in a *Wuthering Heights*–y way: warm, humid, overcast with a high gray sky and an ocean breeze. Josh wanted to take me out to Montauk in the afternoon to show me "his" Hamptons. I felt like I should clear the excursion with Amanda. With Binky's help, I located her in the gazebo, which sat atop a dune in a secluded corner of the estate. I trekked up there to find her lying on a massage table, naked except for a tiny towel draped across her bottom, being kneaded by a very buff young black man wearing a white T-shirt that looked like it had been sprayed on.

"Shelley, this is Derek, he of the magic hands."

"Hi, Derek."

"A pleasure," Derek said with a smile.

"Amanda, is it all right with you if I take off for a couple of hours?"

She looked up at me. "Absolutely not." We looked at each other for a moment before she laughed and said, "Just kidding. Sure, the kids are off on a balloon ride with Ellen Barkin and her brood. Where are you going?"

"Oh, just out with Josh."

"It's not fair—you've got a career you love, and you're sleeping with one of the world's great hunks. I've got more make-work than I can handle and a husband who's absent even when he's present. Speaking of make-work, don't forget to be back in time for my little cocktail do."

"That should be fun."

"I'm sure it will be—just two hundred of my nearest and dearest. I've flown in Pedro from London to style me. He does Madonna and Fergie, and were there ever two women who needed it more? We're going to be drenched with celebrities. Who says I'm not leading a meaningful life? Run along, Shelley, Derek has a job to finish."

After a welcoming kiss, Josh and I rode in silence, listening to U2. I was coming to love the scenery out on eastern Long Island: the flat landscape dotted with potato fields, the charming villages, the towering dunes, and everywhere the sea itself—sometimes caught in little glimpses at the end of a lane, sometimes wide, immense, blue-green, sometimes lapping the sparkling coves of the bay.

This was my first trip out to Montauk. The land grew hilly and markedly less tame as we drove; the grassy dunes seemed to take over, and sand licked at the sides of the road, driven by the wind. Josh turned off the highway before we reached the village. We drove down a winding side road until we came to South Fork Ranch, which undulated up a small hill and looked like it should have been out west: rustic fencing, old wooden buildings, the whole place scruffy and very un-Hamptons.

Josh turned to me, "Ever been horseback riding?"

I had mortal fear of getting on a horse. "No."

"Willing to try?"

"Umm . . ." He leaned over and kissed me. "I've always wanted to try."

"That's the spirit," he said.

There were horses everywhere, grazing, hitched up, walking around corrals. Horses look so pretty from a distance. Up close, they're huge. And their teeth are gargantuan. And they do bite. What if I got chomped? Thrown? Trampled? I suddenly wished I were on a nice cozy walking tour of Brooklyn.

Josh took my hand. "Don't worry, it's fun and easy. I ride here all the time."

A middle-aged ranch hand, unshaven and craggy, came over, and before I knew it we were saddled up. Well, the horses were saddled up, Western-style. As we walked over to them, Josh assured me that my horse, a brown speckled mare named Maisie, had a considerate, easygoing nature. To me she looked like a fur-covered climbing wall. I got up on the small block, stuck one foot in the stirrup, and flung myself up.

And then we started moving—with the emphasis on the *we*. With every step that Maisie took, my body shook, slid, shifted, or bounced in the saddle. It wasn't pleasant. Up ahead Josh sat tall and confident. Why wasn't he bouncing around like a sack of potatoes? It wasn't fair.

He looked back at me. "How're we doing?"

"Great."

We were heading through dunes toward the ocean.

"Ready for a little canter?"

I remembered reading somewhere that it was actually easier to gallop than walk on a horse—it had something to do with aerodynamics, or maybe it was just that no one could hear your screams over the hoofbeats.

Josh took off like the wind. There was one beat—just one—when

Maisie stopped, and I thought she was going to be considerate and drop dead.

Nope.

She flew.

I grabbed onto the reins and the saddle horn and squeezed my legs tight as Maisie scaled a dune. We came to the top and she paused. It was a long, steep way down to the beach.

"Maisie, let's walk, *please!*"

She pretended not to hear me and took off down the dune. It was like being on the Cyclone—except Maisie didn't have a safety bar. I closed my eyes and clenched my body and held my breath and tried not to scream. It didn't work.

"*Ahhhhhhh!*"

And then Maisie stopped. I was still alive. I opened my eyes. We were on the beach. Josh's horse was frolicking at the edge of the surf. He hadn't even noticed my death-defying descent.

"That was intense," I managed, gulping air, my heart racing.

"Why don't we take a little breather?"

"You talked me into it."

We trotted up the sand to the edge of the dunes, dismounted, and hitched the horses to some dune fencing. The beach was deserted out here, except for a few figures speckled in the distance.

Josh took my hand and led me up a little path until we came to a sheltered gully in the dunes. We sat side by side.

"That was a blast," Josh said.

"It was. Now, is there a car service that can take us back to the ranch?"

He put his arm around me and pulled me close, kissed the top of my head.

"You're good for me, Shelley Green. It's been tough since my marriage broke up."

"It was very painful?"

"Yes, in many ways."

"So you moved back east."

"I did indeed. Back to the nest, not that the nest was still around. Both my folks are dead. My sister lives in Rome."

"What did your dad do?"

"He worked for the family company. We manufactured high-end stationery."

"Is it still operating?"

"No. Dad sold it to some conglomerate when I was about eleven. My folks were pretty self-absorbed. They traveled a lot, entertained a lot, spent a lot," he said, a rueful edge creeping into his voice. "Luckily there was a trust set up, so my sister and I get the income from that. It gives me a little breathing room until I decide what I want to do next."

"Are you looking for a job?"

"Jobs and me don't hit it off too well. Never have."

He gave a little shrug, and suddenly he reminded me of one of my entitled patients.

"Are you and your sister close?" I asked.

"Christmas-card close. We have dinner when she's in the States, which is about once every three years. She's a nice girl, but she's four years older, and we were both sent away to school. We just never developed much of a relationship."

I marveled at how much distance money and privilege could create in a family. I suppose when you're not dependent on each other for survival, something fundamental shifts. Give me the Green Family behemoth any day.

A light rain started to fall.

"Do you think we should head back?" I said.

"No, I think we should stay right here," he said, leaning in for a kiss.

For some reason I didn't quite understand, intimacy with Josh didn't appeal to me right at that moment. I think it may have had something to do with his remark about getting a job. I loved Josh's ability to have fun, but was it a one-sided coin? Plus, we didn't have a blanket, and the thought of rolling around in damp sand wasn't too tempting.

"Amanda asked me to make sure we got back in time for her cocktail party," I said.

"You know, I heard that Jerry's been sleeping with some woman he met out in Silicon Valley."

"Really?'

"Yeah, she's some business hotshot, very accomplished, but married, too. To tell you the truth, it's not the first time he's strayed."

"Does Amanda know?"

"Amanda's no fool. But she won't do anything rash. Being Mrs. Jerry Walker is very important to her."

The rain picked up. One of the horses whinnied.

"Let's go *around* the dune on the way back," I said.

Josh dropped me back at Folie d'Or, and then headed home to change for the party. I had pretty much mastered Binky, and I ran myself a hot bath and listened to Erykah Badu as I soaked.

When I got out of the bath, the rain had stopped and the sky was clearing, the gray giving way to the promising orange of early dusk. It was turning into a perfect evening. I slipped into a cream linen cocktail dress and matching sandals.

Josh appeared at the outside door, showered, shaved, and looking almost impossibly tall and handsome in faded jeans, his thick, brown leather belt with the gold buckle, well-worn brown cowboy boots, and crisp white shirt.

"You look sensational," he said.

"And you look like a dream walking."

"Walking into a nightmare maybe. Let's hope this party is bearable. Did you see the army out there?" We peeked around at the patio. There were at least twenty young caterers scurrying around setting up tables, bars, and buffets.

Josh picked up Binky. "Let's call Andre and get the lowdown. . . . Andre, *amigo,* Josh Potter here."

"Who let you on the premises?" Andre answered.

"I snuck in with the caterers."

"No doubt with the lemons."

"Now, now. Listen, I'm with Shelley."

"I adore Shelley, but I'm rather busy right now, a.k.a. beyond frantic, so can we have this chat another time—say, never? . . . The raw bar goes . . . No, not there! Three-quarters of an inch to the left!"

"We just wanted to know what kind of crowd to expect."

"The divine Mrs. W. is an alchemist, so expect Zana Clay *and* Russell Simmons. But the real excitement is that *Fran Templer* is expected!" Andre literally swooned on the words.

"No kidding?" Josh said. "Thanks for the info, Andre. . . . Well, Shelley, this may be fun after all."

"I've never seen a picture of Fran Templer. What does she look like?"

He thought for a moment. "Let me put it this way—she's indescribable, but you'll know her when you see her."

"I can't wait."

We made our way to the house's central sector. The cavernous room looked dazzling and elegant. Its main window wall had been retracted, so indoors and out were seamless, the room giving way to the patio and then to the dunes and the sea beyond. There were hundreds of candles everywhere, many in simple standing candelabras, but also on every surface, and outside they were on the ground, encircling the perimeter of the vast patio and lighting the boardwalk that led down between the dunes to the ocean. The effect was magical, sparkly, bright, alive—I felt my pulse pick up, my adrenaline soar.

Josh led me out to the patio, which was set with three bars, three lavish buffet tables I wasn't going to get within ten feet of, and the perfectly positioned raw bar. The early arrivals were milling about in small clutches. We were approached by a handsome waiter carrying a tray.

"Champagne?"

We each took a glass and sipped as Amanda appeared.

"Well, look at the lovebirds. What hath I wrought?" she said dryly. She was wearing a little lettuce-green dress that glittered, a white leather belt, white high-heeled miniboots, and geometric white jewelry. Her hair was swept up and back. The whole look was futuristic and retro-sixties, original and striking.

"Amanda, you look totally amazing," I said.

"That's what I get paid for. Be on best behavior—*Town and Country* and *InStyle* are both coming. We've got a rocking mix, kids: J.Lo, Nina Griscom, Spielberg, Blaine Trump, Chris Rock, Aerin Lauder, Darren Starr, and, hold on to your sanity—Fran Templer!"

Guests started to pour through the massive front doors, past a phalanx of suited security guards wearing earpieces.

"Time for me to be a hostess twinkly," Amanda said, and disappeared.

Within minutes the space was jammed with the most beautiful collection of people I'd ever seen. Josh seemed to know at least half the crowd, and we were soon in the middle of a small group who definitely came from the Old-Money side of things. The women were tall and sleek, and had long hair they flicked. I noticed that they all semi-flirted with Josh in a knowing way that made me a little uneasy.

I looked around and saw J.Lo and Colin, Chris Rock and Kim

Cattrall, Zana Clay and . . . was that chic older woman at the raw bar Fran Templer? I was determined to get a look at this icon before the night was out. In fact, I think you could say my determination was inching into obsession.

"Is that Fran Templer?" I asked one of the young women in our group.

"No, that's Mica Ertugan. I saw Fran Templer a little while ago. I think she's sitting inside, with Muffie Potter Asten."

Muffie Potter Asten? Do rich people change their names to be more rich-people sounding?

"I'll be right back," I said to Josh, and took off in search of my prey.

I went inside and scanned the twenty or so seating areas. There were chic older women dotted about, how would I ever know which one was Fran Templer? I went up to a chic younger woman.

"Have you seen Fran Templer?"

"She was here just a minute ago, with Mercedes Bass."

"Mercedes? Not Muffie?"

The young woman looked at me, appalled, and then turned away.

I took off through the sea of chicness and hipness, brushing past Diddy, Uma Thurman, Billy Joel—who cares about any of them? Seen one celebrity, you've seen them all. I had to find Fran Templer.

Then I spotted Shirley Blake—a beacon of hope.

"Shirley, it's Shelley Green."

"Shelley, how wonderful to see you."

"Listen, have you seen Fran Templer?"

"Yes, I have, we were just chatting. I think she took off toward the master sector; Amanda put in a stainless steel bidet and Fran wanted to take a look at it. Listen, everyone at the station was crazy about Dr. Marge Mueller."

"What's Fran Templer wearing?" I could feel myself starting to sweat.

"Oh God, Shelley, I never notice things like that. I think it was black. Or was it white?"

"Well, what does she look like?"

"Fran? Fran looks like Fran."

Big help. I took off down the long and winding hallway toward the master sector, my heart pounding in my chest. A chic older woman suddenly appeared at the end of the hallway and started coming toward me—slinky and haughty and sheathed in a black-and-white dress. Eureka!

As she drew close I exclaimed, "Fran!"

"I beg your pardon?" she said, aghast.

"Ah, um, aren't you Fran Templer?"

"I most certainly am not. I haven't spoken to Fran Templer in twenty years: She insulted my soufflé!"

And with a huff and a puff, she slinked away.

I continued on my dogged way down the hallway. The enormous master sector had several seating areas filled with people—I frantically scanned for Fran and didn't see any likely candidates. I dashed down the short hall that led to the master bath—it was filled with a small crowd gawking at the bidet as Amanda stood by proudly—but no Fran!

I was starting to feel dizzy, so I made my way back to the bedroom and plopped down on a small chair by an open door that led out to the patio. Just outside the door, on the patio, facing away from me, smoking cigarettes, were two young women who had stopped by to say hi to Josh earlier. I could overhear their conversation.

"Did you get a load of Josh Potter's new meal ticket?"

"I wonder where they met—a B'nai Brith mixer?"

"She's two tits with a bank account attached."

"Josh would fuck a wall if he had to."

"You'd know."

"Don't start."

"Get real, Marina, you'd take him back in a heartbeat."

"Not if he crawled . . . although he is unbelievable sex."

I closed my eyes and concentrated on taking deep breaths.

I felt a hand on my shoulder. "Shelley, are you all right?"

I looked up. Amanda was standing there. My first instinct was to pretend that everything was fine, but her concern seemed genuine.

I shook my head.

Amanda reached down and took my hand. "Come on." She led me across the bedroom and into her dressing room, which had a small sitting area. She closed the door behind us and led me over to a pair of chairs.

"Shelley, what happened?"

I told her what I had overheard.

"Those jealous, anti-Semitic bitches," she seethed. "Marina Ames was madly in love with Josh, and he left her because she's shallow, manipulative, and dull. Hell hath no fury like a debutante dumped. And to be perfectly honest, Shelley, if Josh Potter was looking for a meal ticket, he could find one with a lot more money than you. As for that despicable B'nai Brith crack, anti-Semitism is a dirty little not-so-secret out here. Until a couple of generations ago, the Hamptons were almost exclusively gentile. Wealthy Jews started moving in and some assholes like Marina still haven't accepted it. At this level of society, you're swimming with sharks." She stood up. "Hey, come on, let's have a little fun." I hesitated. "Come on, it's payback time," she said, taking my hand and giving me a little tug.

Amanda led us out onto the patio and right over to Marina Ames.

"Marina, hi, I'm so glad you could come," Amanda said with a big smile.

"Hi, Amanda," Marina said, ignoring me.

"Have you met Shelley Green?"

Marina deigned to glance at me. "We have."

"Shelley is doing so many incredible things with her life. She's a fantastic pediatrician, and *everyone* is taking their kids to her. And she's been networking with Shirley Blake at WNET on a very exciting television project. And we won't even get into her romantic life. . . . So, Marina, what are *you* doing with yourself these days?" Amanda asked, wide-eyed.

"I'm busy," Marina said with a little shrug.

"I know you wanted a job in the fashion industry. Did anything pan out?"

"I'm still looking."

"It is a tough business, but don't give up. What about projects, volunteer work, weren't you studying Italian for ten minutes?"

Marina looked around uncomfortably.

"A pet maybe?" Amanda asked.

"I'm allergic."

"Are you? I know that feeling. Come on, Shelley, there are all sorts of fun people I want you to meet. Who knows what magic you'll cook up?"

As we weaved our way through the crowd, I couldn't help wondering: Why would anybody want to swim with sharks?

35

IT WAS TUESDAY MORNING, and Alison was sitting on the exam table. Her aunt, a tall, handsome Englishwoman in her midthirties, stood beside her. I tried to disguise my alarm at Alison's appearance. Her face was round and bloated, and I could see a developing "buffalo hump," fatty deposits building up around the nape of her neck.

"Alison!" I said.

"Dr. Green!" she said, holding out her arms.

We hugged.

"Well, you two certainly have a mutual admiration society," her aunt said with a laugh.

I turned to her. "Dr. Shelley Green, what a pleasure."

"Jenny Burke, and the pleasure is mine."

"How was your flight?" I asked.

"The food was gross," Alison said.

"Well, I'm just glad you have an appetite. And when does school start?"

"In two weeks. I can't wait!"

"What are you looking forward to most?" I asked.

"Seeing my friends, especially Lucy Franks; we're *best* friends."

"I'm sure she's looking forward to seeing you."

"Oh, she is. I called her yesterday, she's at her country place up in Connecticut. It's on a lake. When I visited we went out in a canoe and paddled all the way across. Lucy was wonderful when Mommy . . ." Alison's voice trailed off and her face grew sad. She looked down at her hands.

Jenny Burke and I exchanged a glance. She put her arm around Alison.

"Well, that's how you can tell when someone is a really good friend," I said. "They're there when you need them."

"Lucy's mother is very nice," Alison said, still looking down at her hands.

"Tell me how you're feeling, Alison," I said.

"I'm feeling *pretty* well, not great. I mean, my energy and appetite are better, and my pain is better, but I look funny."

Alison's exam showed the early stages of Cushing's disease. She had been on steroids for six weeks now, long enough for some of the other side effects to begin, but she had been spared the worst of them: muscle weakness and wasting, peptic ulcer, infection.

"Well, Alison, you're doing okay," I said. "I do want you to see Dr. Spenser, who is a wonderful man. After you see him, I'd like to begin tapering you off the steroids. Your swelling will go down then."

"Won't my pain come back?"

"We'll monitor that very carefully. Juvenile rheumatoid arthritis is a chronic disease, meaning that you may have it for a long time. My job as your doctor is to make sure that we manage it in the very best way that we can."

Alison nodded her head gravely, and said a simple, "Thank you."

"You're a brave girl, Alison."

"We have to make the best of what happens to us. That's what my mother would want me to do. She didn't like complainers."

"She'd be proud of you."

"I always want to make her proud." Alison looked down and said in a quiet voice, "That way Mommy stays alive."

I looked at her aunt. She had tears welling in her eyes. She took a deep breath and stood up straight. "Well, Alison, are you ready for our back-to-school shopping jaunt?" she asked brightly.

Alison nodded and got down off the exam table.

"Plaid is very in this season," she informed me.

"Is it?"

"Yes. According to Lucy, and she's very stylish."

"Well, then, I suppose Burberry's will have to be our first stop," Jenny said.

When they were gone I called Dr. Spenser's office and set up an appointment for the following week. No sooner had I hung up than it hit me!

I rushed down the hall, through the waiting room and out onto the street. I looked down toward Madison Avenue—and there, just about to turn the corner, were Alison and her aunt. I ran toward them.

"Alison! Alison!" I called.

They turned.

I reached them, panting.

"Dr. Green, are you all right?" Alison asked.

"When did you visit Lucy Franks in Connecticut?"

"Um, it was in May, the third weekend, I think."

"Where was your father?"

"He was away for two weeks, in Russia."

"And did you notice a bite or a rash when you came home?"

Alison thought for a moment.

"You know, I did have a little itchy bump on my leg. But it went away."

I hugged her tight. She looked bewildered.

"Alison, can you come back to the office for just a moment? I want to take a blood sample."

Alison nodded.

We took the blood and Claire sent it off to the lab. Then I told Alison and her aunt that I was almost certain that she was suffering from Lyme disease, and that a course of amoxicillin would cure her.

36

THE LAB TEST came in on Friday morning and confirmed my diagnosis. I sent the amoxicillin prescription over to Alison by messenger and called her aunt with instructions to begin tapering Alison's steroids. My happiness was tempered by the fact that I hadn't reconsidered Lyme disease after the first two tests came in negative and her father mistakenly assured me that she hadn't been out of the city in the spring. What gave me the most peace of mind was the knowledge that Alison should have no lasting effects from her steroid regimen. I looked forward to being her pediatrician for years to come, to watching her grow and develop into a wonderful young woman.

I had just seen my last patient of the week, and was getting ready to head home. Josh was at the apartment cooking. He had driven in late in the morning with the just-caught fish. My confidence in our relationship was shaken, and I was hoping this dinner would restore it. It was the first thing we had done as a team, and I viewed it as something of a test.

Christina blew into my office, breathless as usual, gorgeous as usual in a black slip dress and sling-back black heels.

"Shelley, how the hell are you?"

"Good, and you?"

"Sensational," she said, sprawling on the love seat and crossing those endless legs. "I'm on a wicked Friday night buzz—Ira and I are going to Pastis for dinner and champagne. You know, Shelley, we're practically family."

"We are?"

"Well, things are moving in that direction."

"They are?"

I tried to disguise my shock. I assumed that to Christina, Ira was basically a boy toy.

"He's coming over to China with me next week to pick up Ingrid."

"He is?"

"Shelley, don't look so surprised. I think you underestimate your brother. He's charming, funny, original, and I think he has some very good ideas."

"Like Power Papoose?"

"He sold the whole ten gross on eBay, to a wholesaler in Latvia. But has he told you about Vacculift?"

"Vacculift?"

"Yes, it's a nonsurgical face-lift that works on the same principle as those vacuum storage bags."

"Okay."

"It's basically an airtight shower cap with an opening on top for a vacuum cleaner nozzle. You put on the cap, hook up the vacuum, turn it on for twenty minutes, and—as our slogan says—'Vacuum the Years Away.' How brilliant is that?"

"*Brilliant* isn't the first word that comes to mind."

"It's incredible for those big nights out, just sucks your wrinkles up-up-and-away. Lasts four to six hours."

"And this was Ira's idea?"

"Yes, he got it one night at my place when he was stoned and watching Adrien Arpel on QVC. The prototype works like magic, and I'm backing Ira on the original order for five thousand. They're practically free to produce. QVC is very interested, and I'm going to endorse it."

What can I say, I was beyond speechless, into thoughtless—my mind simply shut down.

"Anyway, I dropped by because I heard that you were having lunch with the Van Rensselaer sisters. I've known them since I was in the womb."

"What are they like?"

"Let's just say they prove the Paris Hilton principle: You can have money and a name and still be white trash."

Ira appeared in the doorway. "Hello, ladies."

He looked positively respectable in slacks and an oxford shirt, his hair lacquer-free, his face bronzer-free.

"Doesn't he clean up nicely?" Christina asked.

"He does," I admitted.

Ira came over, took my hand, and gave it a courtly kiss. "I love my big sister." The kid was still a ham. But he'd never looked happier.

"Let's boogie, handsome," Christina said. She slipped her arm through his, and off they went.

I arrived home to find the apartment spotless, filled with fresh flowers, tapered candles, the table set, wonderful smells filling the air. I had banished Harry to the den for the night.

"Something smells delicious," I said, walking into the kitchen. Josh was at the stove, looking adorable in a blue-and-white-striped chef's apron.

"Welcome home, honey," he said, giving me a little kiss.

The kitchen looked like a photograph in *Gourmet*: sparkling fish fillets on a cutting board, a colander filled with baby red potatoes, a salad, two crisp baguettes. Josh was gently sautéing garlic and fresh herbs.

"Wow, this all looks incredible."

"Nothing's too good for my baby," Josh said, spooning a teaspoon of mustard into the sauté.

"What can I do to help?"

"Absolutely nothing. You've been working all week. Let me take care of you tonight."

"Well, in that case I'm going to go change and freshen up. Our guests will be here in about half an hour."

Josh's outburst of neat-freakness didn't extend to the bedroom; his clothes were strewn on the bed. But he was being so helpful and was actually working. I took a quick shower. As I was lathering up, I couldn't help wondering if what happened at the party had gotten back to him, and he was making amends.

I slipped into a pair of silk chinos and a pale green blouse. I looked at myself in the full-length mirror: I thought I looked pretty good, but part of me wished I could just throw on a pair of shorts and a T-shirt and really relax.

The doorbell rang. I opened the door and found Charles Spenser, looking very attractive and un-doctory in a polo shirt, blazer, and jeans, and carrying a bouquet of lilies.

I led him into the apartment. "Charles, this is Josh Potter. Josh, this is my former professor and mentor, Dr. Charles Spenser," I said, heading into the kitchen to get a vase.

Amanda and Jerry arrived. Amanda looked beyond adorable in a little white dress covered with bright Pollacky splatters. I introduced them to Charles.

"Nice to meet you. Will you excuse me?" Jerry said. Without waiting for an answer, he took out his cell phone and headed into the study.

"They're always making money somewhere in the world," Amanda explained, an edge in her voice. Josh brought her a glass of wine. "My goodness, Shelley, you've tamed our wild beast," she said, fussing at his hair for a moment in a flirtatious, proprietary way.

"It's not me he likes, it's the apartment."

"Many a truth is spoken in jest," Amanda said, taking a little sip of her wine.

We all chatted for about five minutes. The doorbell rang, and I went to answer it. Dr. Marge stood there, wearing a pale-blue linen pantsuit with a white silk chemise cut quite low; her skin glowed with that fresh-from-the-spa look.

"I haven't dated in thirty years," she whispered.

"I think you're ready." We smiled at each other. "Just be your irresistible self."

I led her into the living room and made introductions.

Just as we all sat down, Dr. Marge's cell phone rang. "I'm sorry, I have to take this. It may be a patient," she said, taking the phone out of her purse. "Will you excuse me a moment?" She got up and walked into the kitchen.

I had just finished bringing Charles up to date on Alison Young when Dr. Marge walked back in.

"They want me to host the *Baby Talk* pilot," she announced. "And I promise I didn't arrange that call."

I jumped up and hugged her. "That is such fabulous news!"

"It calls for champagne," Josh said.

The champagne flowed and, buoyed by Marge's fantastic news, the evening took on a giddy tone. Charles was genuinely enthused, which I took to be a good sign. Josh tended to the meal, refilled people's glasses, and passed the hors d'oeuvres.

We all batted around ideas that might work for *Baby Talk*—the usual suspects like breast-feeding and developmental milestones, of course, but Charles suggested segments on how other cultures dealt with pregnancy, birth, and child-rearing issues. I thought of Arthur, Brooklyn's unofficial anthropologist. He could help Dr. Marge find families from just about every culture on the planet, right across the Brooklyn Bridge.

"All this baby talk is making my guilt meter rise. I'm going to give the kids a quick check-in call," Amanda said, and went into the kitchen.

The conversation moved back to Alison Young, and Dr. Marge, Charles, and I were quickly deep into shoptalk. I saw a distracted look cross Josh's face.

"Time for another bottle of champagne," he said, brightening. He went into the kitchen.

Charles was telling Dr. Marge and me about a challenging case he'd recently had, when a squawk of "Hey, baby, shake it, shake it," came from the direction of the den.

"Oops, I forgot to feed Harry," I said, getting up.

As I walked toward the den, I took a quick look at myself in the hall mirror. I fluffed at my hair, and then I noticed Amanda and Josh in the corner of the mirror. They were standing in the kitchen with their arms around each other, and he was nibbling at her ear as she laughed. Then they kissed, a serious kiss.

At first, I didn't quite register what I was seeing and what it meant, but when I did, a wave of nausea hit me, and I let out an involuntary gasp. That's when Amanda looked over and our eyes met in the mirror.

"Oh, shit," she said. Josh blew out air and turned away.

The worst part of the whole thing was that instead of feeling shocked or hurt or like going postal, I felt ridiculous and humiliated. Right in the middle of my dinner party, they were making out in my kitchen. Two people I had counted as friends. How about that? Josh had been playing me for a fool, which wasn't too hard. I was just a port in the storm for him, starstruck and duty-free. As for Amanda—how could she?

"How could you?" I said, watching her in the mirror as she walked toward me.

"Oh, Shelley," she said. She took my arm and led me into the bedroom while I assured myself that whatever happened, I was *not* going to cry.

Amanda closed the door behind us.

"I hope you're not going to cry," she said.

"I'm not planning on it."

"It's really not what you think," she said.

"Number one, you have no idea *what* I'm thinking, and number two, of course it is."

Amanda sat on the edge of the bed and sighed. "Oh, all right, it is. I mean sort of. We haven't actually . . . Damn it, I just want a man paying *attention* to me. I mean, you've met Jerry." She ran her fingers through her hair. "Oh Christ, I'm not going to make it worse by trying to make excuses."

"Please, I'd enjoy watching you try to excuse it."

She sat up a little straighter on the bed, as if she was the one who had a right to be angry. "There's something you don't understand about having all the money and all the time and all the crisp, capable staff you've always wanted. It's one big, fucking *bore*. I mean, when you can snap your fingers and just buy whatever you want, none of it means anything."

"Kind of like the way you bought me, you mean."

"Yes. No. All right, here comes the raw truth: I'm jealous of you. You've *got* something, Shelley. You've got a career and a calling, something you love, something you've earned. You didn't buy it or marry into it or sleep your way to it. You made it happen yourself, with your brains and your hard work and your passion. No one's going to take it away from you. That's what attracted me to you in the first place." She let out a mirthless, ironic little laugh. "It's funny. You thought I had what you wanted. The truth is, you have what I want. And believe me, Shelley, I'm not talking about Josh."

"Well, you can have Josh. And if it weren't for the little inconvenience of eleven years of schooling and residency, you could have my career, too."

Amanda looked down at her hands and said in a quiet voice, "I'm a very competitive gal, but you're right, Shelley, and I apologize."

"You're a day late and a kiss short. And if you want something to give meaning to your life, maybe you should take up needlepoint." I took a deep breath. "I have guests who I care about, and I want them to enjoy the rest of their evening."

Amanda nodded.

During the meal, I smiled at what people said, commented on this and that. Luckily, Marge and Charles were in expansive moods, and they carried the ball.

Charles left first, followed by Jerry and Amanda. Josh went into the kitchen, leaving Marge and me alone.

"Charles is fantastic!" she gushed.

"I had a feeling about you two," I said.

"You're a natural matchmaker. We're going to the theater next week."

"I'm delighted."

"And *Baby Talk*. Shelley, you've single-handedly turned my life around."

I smiled.

"Are you all right?"

"Just a little tired."

Marge nodded toward the kitchen.

"He's quite something."

"Do you think so?"

She hesitated for a moment. "He certainly has a lot of charm, so smooth, and a total hunk. Well, I better get going. I can't thank you enough for a wonderful time."

"I can't thank you enough for . . . everything."

"Are you sure you're all right?"

I nodded.

We hugged.

When Marge was gone, I went into the kitchen, where Josh was making a great show of loading the dishwasher. He looked over at me with a chastened expression that slowly dissolved into an aw-shucks-I'm-a-bad-boy grin.

"All right, Josh, it's time for you to leave."

"Oh, come on, you must be kidding."

"Why would I be kidding?"

He rubbed the back of his neck and gave an exasperated sigh.

"So you're serious? You just want me to walk out of here, like there was never anything between us?"

"Whatever it was couldn't have been much."

"Amanda and I were just flirting. It doesn't mean a thing."

"It means a thing to me."

I looked him right in the eye. He couldn't hold my gaze.

"All right then, fine, fuck it. I'll leave." He went into the bedroom and got his bag. He walked to the front door, opened it, looked at me, and smiled. "Hey, it was fun while it lasted."

I closed the door behind him and stood there in semi-shock. I could feel hot tears welling up. I sat down at the dining room table and waited for them to flow.

But they didn't.

So I went into the kitchen to finish the cleanup.

37

I OPENED AN eye and looked at my bedside clock—6:15. Early, but I figured I might as well get up—I hadn't slept for more than five consecutive minutes all night anyway. I made my way to the bathroom and splashed cold water on my face. Then I put on a robe, went into the kitchen and sat at the banquette. Heavy clouds were rolling in from the west, beginning to darken the morning sky. Cold water and heavy clouds. Perfect.

The townhouse gardens looked lonely in the gray light. I hugged my robe around me. I kept seeing that kiss between Josh and Amanda, no matter how hard I tried not to. I felt tears welling up, but this time I didn't try to stop them. The funny thing was, I wasn't crying because I was upset about losing Josh. Really, I wasn't even angry at him. But I was seriously pissed off at my own stupid self. I'd opened myself up to these people and let myself think I was going to be accepted into their world, and this was what happened. I felt sad and foolish and vulnerable, just like I had when I was little and the kids at school had teased me for studying during recess, for always raising my hand in class, for getting all those pretty, perfect As.

I'd always had a need to prove myself, to achieve and succeed. I was convinced it was the only way I'd ever be accepted, but more often than not, it just made me feel like an oddball outsider, even in my own family. And if last night was any example, I hadn't learned all that much.

I'd fallen all over myself trying to win Amanda's approval, trying to fit into her Blahnik and Balenciaga world. And I'd been so dazzled by Josh's charm and breeding, I didn't notice that he didn't have very much of either. As I sat watching the gathering clouds, my real motives became clear to me, embarrassingly clear. If those two had embraced me into their inner circle, then I really wouldn't be the schlumpy girl from Jackson Heights ever again. I'd be . . . but I guess I hadn't thought it all the way through. We all want to be somebody, but it probably helps if you have a better idea of who.

I sat there at the banquette, numb. I wanted to crawl back into bed and spend the whole day there, but I couldn't. I had a commitment to meet with the Van Rensselaer sisters. I made a pot of coffee and sliced a banana into a bowl of cereal. At least I still had my reliable old appetite.

When it was time to head over to my lunch, I got into a simple dress and put on a sensible pair of flats.

The day was warm and humid, the clouds heavy and leaden. I walked over to Madison Avenue quickly.

At La Goulue, I immediately spotted the Van Rensselaer sisters at a corner table, chatting on their cell phones. They were both thin and deeply tanned, with streaked hair, wearing tiny pink dresses and lots of "fun" gold jewelry.

I waved as I approached their table. They both ignored me. I got to the table and stood there. They both just kept chattering away and laughing on their cell phones, as if the world was one big private joke. Finally, one of them looked up at me and batted her eyelashes.

"Hi, I'm Dr. Shelley Green."

"Our baby doctor is here," she said into her phone, and then she roared with laughter at something the person on the other end of the line said. The other sister continued to ignore me.

I sat down.

They still kept chatting. Finally I said, "We have an appointment to discuss your babies. I'd really appreciate it if you'd respect my time."

The sister who had spoken looked at me in wide-eyed mock shock and actually got off her phone.

"I'm Serena," she said, in an affected voice. We shook hands across the table.

Tatiana kept chatting. I reached my hand out toward her and smiled. "You must be Tatiana," I said. "Would you please get off the phone?"

Tatiana narrowed her eyes at me, hung up, and said, "Pushy pushy."

"You called *me* about this lunch," I stated.

The sisters exchanged glances. There was a long silence. A waiter came over, and we all ordered salads.

"So, tell me how your pregnancies are going. Do you have any questions for me?" I asked with an encouraging smile, trying to get things on track.

"I have a question," Serena said. "How well do you know Amanda Walker?"

"I take care of her children."

"Amanda's darling, but so nouveau. Mummy calls her the *arriviste du jour*," Tatiana said with a dismissive little flick of her hair.

"Her money's so new it hasn't dried yet," Serena said, and they both laughed.

"The Van Rensselaers have owned big chunks of Manhattan for over two hundred years," Tatiana informed me.

"The Greens have lived in a rent-stabilized, two-bedroom apartment in Jackson Heights for over thirty years," I informed her.

The girls exchanged appalled glances.

"Not even the nicest part of Jackson Heights. But you know what, Tatiana? It was a wonderful place to grow up."

"Really?"

"It really was. My mom's a part-time guidance counselor at P.S. 149, and my dad is a mailman. They're both kind, decent, hard-working people, and I'm proud of them. You know what they taught me, Serena?"

"We're both dying to find out," Tatiana said.

"Well, lots of things, in fact. But mainly to treat everyone with respect. Interesting idea, isn't it?" I stood up. "I'm happy you own so much of Manhattan. After all, someone has to. But I'm afraid that isn't going to help you get me as your pediatrician. I work on my own terms. If you'd like to hear what those are, I'd be happy to discuss them with you. If you don't have the number for Madison Pediatrics, it's in the phone book."

Then I turned and walked out of the restaurant.

It had started to rain, fat splattering drops. I crossed Madison Avenue and started to head east. My hair and dress were getting soaked, my makeup was running. I didn't care; I wanted it all to wash away.

I reached Park Avenue and waited for the light to change. All around me people were darting under awnings, opening umbrellas, hailing cabs. I just stood there in the rain.

The light changed and I crossed the avenue. I didn't know where I was going, but I had to walk. A man ran past me holding a soggy newspaper over his head. Halfway to Lexington, without thinking, I took my cell phone out of my bag. Then I put it back. I kept walking. I took my phone out again and dialed. Then I hung up before it started ringing. I reached Lexington and crossed. I took out my phone and dialed. I took a deep breath, and when he answered the phone, I said, "Hi, Arthur. It's me."

"Well, well," he said. "So it is."

"I'm not interrupting you, am I?"

"Actually you are," he said.

I felt myself sink a little. "I'm sorry," I said. "Anything important?"

"As a matter of fact it is. Dickens. *Pickwick Papers*."

"Oh, Arthur. I don't think I ever finished that one."

"It's all right, Shelley. I didn't either. That's why I picked it up again."

"It's never too late, I guess."

"Sometimes it is," he said.

There was a long silence, and I stood on the corner watching the traffic splashing through the puddles on the street.

"Are you all right, Shelley?"

"I'm great," I said, and even I could hear the desperation in my voice.

"I'm glad to hear it."

"Yes, everything's great. It's just great."

"You don't sound so great."

"Well, maybe not *so* great. I mean, I made a mess of a couple of things."

"We all make a little mess sometimes."

"I know. But this was more like a big mess."

"The bigger the mess, the more there is to learn from it."

"You think?"

"I think the learning curve ends in the coffin."

I passed a well-dressed woman huddled in a doorway, cradling her tiny dog.

"Arthur," I said, "I enjoyed seeing you the other day."

"I enjoyed seeing you."

"I don't know why you would. You seemed so happy with . . . Jennifer. I guess it's a serious relationship. I mean, it looked like it was. The way you were. You two."

"Looks can be deceiving, Shelley."

"They can?"

"Sometimes, yes."

"What about this time?"

"I'd say they might have been a little deceiving."

"Really?"

"What about you and Josh, munchkin?"

"Oh, one big fat, foolish deception."

I started to cry. Again. But this time it was different.

"Shelley, are you out in this rain?"

"I was having lunch with these horrible women and I made a scene and I stormed out of the restaurant and I don't have an umbrella and . . ."

"Where are you?"

"I'm on the Upper East Side. It's pouring."

"It's not raining as hard out here in Brooklyn."

"No?"

"No. Maybe you should come over."

"You think? The subway's only a couple blocks away."

"Or you could take a cab."

"I'm soaking wet."

"I'll have a warm bath waiting for you. I'll make you a cup of hot chocolate."

"I'm off chocolate."

"That's all right, Shelley. I'll make you a cup of tea."